HEARTS AS BIG AS FISTS

OTHER BOOKS OF INTEREST

ILLNESS & GRACE, TERROR & TRANSFORMATION
Heather Tosteson and Charles Brockett, Editors.
Wising Up Press, 2007.

HEARTS AS BIG AS FISTS

&

OTHER STORIES

Heather Tosteson

Wising Up Press
Decatur, Georgia

Wising Up Press
P.O. Box 2122
Decatur, GA 30031-2122
www.universaltable.org

"My Counselor" was first published in *Nimrod* 2001; 45(1):97-107.

Catalogue-in-Publication data is on file with the Library of Congress.
LCCN: 2007938462

Wising Up ISBN-13: 978-0-9796552-1-0

TABLE OF CONTENTS

To Davin, Betty, Cindy, Henry, Greg, Jody, and Ruth
who teach me so much in sickness and in health about the mysterious fullness of life...

KNOW YOUR SOURCE

Every day or two, I make a new list and stare at it until all the names blur. I wish you were here and could choose for yourself. It makes such a difference what you get saddled with at birth.

"G-L-O-R-I-A," my father would always greet me as a kid. Adding, "in Excelsis Deo," when I began to pout—summing up very neatly all the reasons why I hated the names they'd imposed on me. My mother may have been responsible for Gloria, but my dad was responsible for the Excel. It looked good on his billboards. Excel Ford.

I had a friend in grade school, Rhonda, whose father built housing developments and named the streets after his three girls, his wife, and his mama. Rhonda Lane, Sharon Circle, Mabel Drive. You get the idea. But it wasn't the same. No one teased Rhonda. Maybe because she was a sweet little button of a thing. I wasn't.

"You have options," my father would console me when I complained. "You can change your name once you turn eighteen. Until then I'm claiming you, like it or not. Maybe you'll fall in love with someone named Wurm. Will Wurm. You can change your name to Glo. Or maybe Andrew Euphoria. Gloria Euphoria, that's it." There was a gleam in his eye. He refused to take my distress seriously. But he should have. I meant it. I didn't like what they had laid on me and I needed him to see it.

My father's name is Andy. Andy Excel. Better than Adonis Excess, he always told me. My mother's name was Estelle—and that was only one of the reasons she shouldn't have married my father. I may as well go into the others because sooner than later we're going to be family. You and me. I'm hoping by then I'll have found some word you won't mind answering to and I won't get tired of calling out ten, fifteen times a day.

My mother shouldn't have married my father because she never really cared for him and because she was the kind of person who used up all the air in every room she walked into. She didn't believe in sharing.

I can say these things now that she's dead because she won't take them personally. There really wasn't very much about Estelle that was personal. She was a force of nature, like a hurricane, tornado, or flood. People always remark on how accepting I sound when I talk about her. It wasn't like I had a choice. Why waste your anger on what you can't change (unlike a name)? Doesn't mean, of course, that it wasn't painful to be around her.

"She just needs lots of room to maneuver," my father would say to me. "She's a big woman, your mother. In every way."

We would stare glumly at the newspapers scattered over the floors, the clothes strewn over the banister, the breakfast dishes mounded unwashed in the sink, while my mother's deep raucous laugh cascaded down the stairs. God knows who she was talking to. One of the other drama queens from the local theater or one of her latest crushes from Pete's Taverna. (Heaven forbid she'd go to a joint with the word bar in it. Estelle had her standards. Moderation, straight shooting, and understatement weren't among them.)

My dad was right. She did need a lot of room to maneuver. If I wasn't directly in her path, I loved the largeness of everything Estelle did. It carved out some space for me too as I followed in her wake.

She'd march into the Calico Inn with her two toy poodles on leashes that matched the color of her dress and sit down in the middle of the room, pulling out a chair for each of them. I was expected to seat myself. My hair ribbon more often than not clashed with the leashes of the dogs.

You'd think the waitresses would object, but they liked my mother. The way she fixed on them like they were the most important people on earth because they could meet my mother's immediate need. And all my mother's needs were immediate. Most of the time, the women that waited on Estelle swelled right up with the attention. They didn't have any idea how contingent it was.

One time, I may have been eleven (I know I was very reluctantly wearing my first training bra), my mother and I were at the beach and went to a fancy restaurant. Estelle was on the prowl, dressed to gather attention with her electric blue voile blouse (no bra) and a red skirt cut up to her formidable thigh. She was more than a little smashed. When the waitress didn't come fast enough with our orders—or Estelle's second glass of wine—she threw rolls at the waitress each time she passed.

The waitress was an older woman. Already little wrinkles tightened up her mouth so it looked too pinched to pucker. "Grow up," is all the waitress said as picked up the roll and put it back down on the table for my mother to take aim with again. She looked at the air above my head as she spoke, but I knew she was speaking to Estelle. She didn't seem angry or insulted. Just tired. Bone tired. Estelle could make you feel that way. Prematurely aged. I wonder some days how Estelle might have aged.

That night she looked ravishing, her thick black hair tumbling over her tanned shoulders, her big smooth breasts pouting from her low neckline.

I'm not saying my father shouldn't have married her, you see.

There's no one I would rather have for a father—his name aside. And there's something to be said for Estelle's genes. She was lovely to look at. And she made an impact.

When I was growing up, my father never made me feel at war with myself the way it's possible for mismatched parents to do. My dad always claimed to like what I'd inherited from my mother. I have her black hair. I have her deep laugh. I have what my father politely calls her stature.

In other words, I am, like her, a little larger than life.

I really believed my father when I was growing up. I liked finding favor in his eyes. But whatever my dad said, whatever space he made for me, that all changed when he remarried—and put the lie to anything he'd ever said about the advantages of being statuesque.

Let me put this all in perspective so you don't go thinking I'm some kind of Southern gothic. I'm not a monster or anything. Far from it. People might even call me beautiful if I weren't so big. I am six feet one in bare feet, and I weigh less than two hundred pounds, but not by very much. It sounds enormous—but it's not. In phys ed, using the pinch test I never came out obese. But I am not, like Chase, my father's second wife, a sweet little button of a thing. Not by any means.

I don't want you to get Chase wrong either. She's not sweet. She's possibly even more unconventional than Estelle ever was, but she's concise about it. She would never throw rolls at old waitresses. Or break mirrors or build bonfires to burn up the wardrobe of her old persona. She doesn't drink. She keeps an immaculate house. She teaches yoga at the YMCA two nights a week and a course on journal writing, "Find Your Personal Voice", at the community college. She runs her own art gallery. She says her journal classes are pretty evenly split between women my age and women hers. This isn't an invitation to feel closer to her, and it isn't taken as one. It's only an observation. We're both of us big on observations. We both have found our voices—we're just careful not to use them much in each other's hearing.

My friends can't see why I've taken against her. Even when they meet her, they just can't see it. *Look* at her, I tell them. Just *look* at her. Obediently they do, then look back at me even more puzzled. They like what they see. Who wouldn't? Chase could be on the cover of *Self* magazine—if they did an issue on older women—she's that fit. I don't think there's a single muscle, even in her baby toe or pinkie finger, that she doesn't exercise regularly. I'm not suggesting she's vain. Her muscles are an object of intellectual interest to her. She calls them her keenest sense.

My dad likes his women physical. Estelle was very physical too, although it was a wilder and more voluptuous energy. My dad is no slouch. He runs and plays tennis and sails—and judging from how regularly he runs his hands down Chase's back and ass, I gather he engages in other forms of intimate exercise on a regular basis too.

Whatever age you are, I expect it's a pretty disgusting thing to think of your parents as sexual beings. Except in my case, it is kind of inevitable, however edgy it makes me. Estelle *was* sex—she smelled of it, projected it, talked about it constantly. I kind of thought it was a one way thing, especially as she got crazier and my dad got quieter and more withdrawn in response— but once I saw my dad with Chase I began to wonder. Chase obviously turns him on. Maybe Estelle did too. Once upon a time.

Until, that is, she got so big in her wildness that there wasn't any space at all for anyone else's need. Estelle needed to be needed, not for what she could do for you but just for what she was. It was almost religious, this insistence of hers on being an end in itself. Unfortunately, it didn't extend to others. They needed to work so she could just be She needed someone to tell her morning, noon and night what a delight she was. No matter what she'd done: Forgotten the birthday cupcakes or brought them to school on the wrong day. Passed out on the kitchen floor. Spent the night at the house of one of her 'girlfriends' without calling to let us know. It was kind of crazy. We went around feeling suffocated and also frantically puffing her up because somehow we knew that if we punctured that big bubble of hers there would be nothing left.

I'm not saying this to make you scared. I'm big, *really* big right now, but I'm solid. I won't need to be puffed up. I just want you to be prepared, that's all. Isn't that a mother's job? I don't want the world to take you by surprise. I want you to know what you can count on.

I don't think either my mom or my dad did a very good job preparing me for the world. It's been a big surprise to me from day one. Just like they have been. You're not meant to have to notice your parents—they should just be your backdrop. So, as they say, I have my issues. One of them is consistency. I mean, if you act one way, you set up expectations. You can't just change in the blink of an eye and have the people who built their lives on your original behaviors not feel short-changed. Not to mention unmoored. Uprooted. Choose your own metaphor, just as long as it is one of abrupt loss. That's my biggest issue with each of my parents. That's why I'm sharing it with you so soon. I don't want it to be an issue between us. With Estelle, it's a done deal. Nothing is ever going to change again. I know that deep inside me, but there are days, like this one, when I'm driving along, my mind going a mile a minute, kind of energized with anger and resolve and feeling vital when Estelle comes alive to me again. Everything that happened comes alive too, and I think, *How dare you.*

It's not only the people she took out with her—a blameless couple in their late sixties returning from their granddaughter's high school graduation. It's how she proved my worst fears—that that energy of hers was a danger to her and to everyone around her, whatever she might say. However drunk she was, she aimed into oncoming traffic. Responsible. You better believe I hold her responsible. But there was a part of me—still is, I expect, or the pain wouldn't be so alive—who still wants to feel that with a little tweaking her way could work—that one can live life as an extravagant drama, that there is no piper to pay if we hold it in just a little. Share the air.

I blame her for making me praise her, cherish that crazy energy of hers, justify that selfishness as somehow fitting, I mean, really *believe* some portion of that excess might some day come to me as an outrageous gift. I blame her for making me, her daughter, take her at her own evaluation—however much I pretended not to. Until one night when I was seventeen, making popcorn and watching a video with my dad and feeling guilty about popping up the second pan, *wham*.

Briiing, Briiiiiing, the phone rang. Neither of us rushed to get up. Finally, Andy answered it, gesturing to me to turn down the volume on the video. The two of us got quiet so fast, maybe we already knew.

"Speaking," is all he said. Then, after a long pause, "I see. Where will you be taking her?" And before he finished the question he was thumbing through the yellow pages. His gestures were so sure, it was like he had practiced this in his mind a hundred times. Maybe he had.

I *hadn't*. That's the truth. I know some of my friends wished their parents dead at times. But I never did. Perhaps because with Estelle the probability was too high. And with my dad, the implications were too big. I never imagined I could survive alone with Estelle. I was no match for her. Face it, I'm no match for itty bitty Chase.

After he heard my mother was dead, my father ran his finger down the right column and then the left on the page he'd located in the yellow pages. He closed his eyes for a second and the pain in his face made me want to reach out and slap him. He read off the name of the funeral home, gave them the phone number and address.

"How?" is all I asked him when he put the phone down and came over.

I was sitting there with the remote in my hand, the video running with the mute on. We were watching *Home for the Holidays*. I still can't watch it to see how it ended. All I can remember is that scene where the mother, played by little Holly Hunter, calls her daughter and talks to her like the daughter is the responsible party and she is the needy child. "I should have stayed home with you," she tells her daughter. Or something similar—like I said, I've never been able to watch it again. But I can't forget it either. It was such a wistful little scene. I wish, just once, either Estelle or Andy had called me sounding like that—like I was the true center of their universe and I could reassure them I was still there.

Maybe someday you will call me sounding like that. I'll be ready. That's all I'm saying. I'll be ready. I have practiced it in my mind a hundred times. The roles will be reversed. They will be right. I will be the mother. You will be the center of the universe. *My* universe.

The call I really got, two years later, my first semester in college, was Andy saying, "I've found the woman of my dreams."

"Say what?" I said. Nineteen, you can't say, "Get a hold of yourself." But my own father sounded as goopy as any of the girls on my hall. I'd never heard any guy talking like that. Still haven't, for that matter. Don't know if I could stand it.

I'll talk to you that way, don't worry. But there it's fitting. Mother's fawn on their babies. You can see it in any supermarket or down at the playground. There's this one little magic period—somewhere between a month and a year—where adults can behave like retrievers and slobber with joy.

But a father should not do that in an only daughter's late adolescence with a strange woman only half her size. That's what, in my deepest darkest moments, I want to say to my dad.

It wasn't just the eagerness in his voice that took me by surprise—it was the reality. I came back at Thanksgiving and there was this woman just his age and half his size that he couldn't take his eyes from.

"Isn't she great," he said to me. He didn't ask. He said.

"When's the wedding?" I asked. I was just teasing, trying to introduce some sense of perspective. He was beginning to sound like Estelle—no moderation, nothing left to the imagination. And then he hit me with it.

"Three weeks."

"What about Christmas break?"

"We've arranged it with your grandparents. They'll come to the wedding and then take you back with them. It will be more fun for you anyway." My dad has three sisters who all live near my grandparents in Augusta. Since Estelle died, we had spent our Christmases there. It was easier than being alone together. "We're planning to spend three weeks in Europe.

I've never seen Paris. Can you *believe* it," he said. He brushed his hands through his brown hair, making the silver threads glint in the light.

"Why didn't you warn me?"

"Warn you?" He looked totally puzzled. "I told you how great she was and how I was seeing her all the time. I thought you'd be as happy as I am. I thought you would be happy for me. I've waited so long for this, Gloria. You of all people should know."

It was then, not having to look up or down to get his attention, realizing my growth spurt had truly ended and from now on we would stand like this, shoulder to shoulder and eye to eye, that I realized that in his mind I was a completely different order of existence from Chase. She was a woman, and I was—I was—

Well, now, with you coming along, we know the answer to that. I am going to be your mother. And mothers are women. Some women are mothers first, like me. Some mothers are women first, like Estelle.

Chase is neither. I mean, she doesn't have children. She has her well-toned body and her yoga mats and blocks and belts. She has her journal writing classes. She has her gallery and all those demanding artists she mollycoddles. And now she has Andy.

And I have you—and these issues.

When I tried to talk to my friends about my feelings about Andy and Chase before the wedding or right after, they would get a funny look on their faces. They would rather hear about Sarah's experience with her new vibrator, Alison's latest bout of was-she-or-wasn't-she bisexual, Jennifer's tantric experience over the internet, even Jamie's straight, engagement-ring-sanctified missionary position. This was about sex and it wasn't and it was as distasteful to them as it was to me to think about all the feelings milling around. "You're just jealous," Jamie said. "It's like you felt he was your boyfriend or something—and he was just your dad."

"It isn't about jealousy," I said. "It's about consistency. About setting up expectations and then honoring them."

"You never expected your father to marry again?" Sarah asked.

"I never expected my mother to die." Even as I said it, I knew it was a lie.

"But given that she did," Jennifer said, "didn't you expect him to hook up again?"

"I never looked that far ahead," I said.

They all three looked at me. Sarah picked up the teddy bear in which she stored her vibrator and held it to her chest. *Why not?* their faces all said.

"Not this fast," I said.

"It's been two years," Jamie said. I began to dislike her intensely. Her fundamentalism. Her size four jeans. Her engagement ring.

"You haven't said anything bad about her yet," Alison said. "And from her picture she looks—"

"Just your type," I said.

"I'm not into older," Alison answered. "But other than that, I think I'd look twice."

What I didn't like about Chase—or my father when he was around her—was they didn't seem to need my approval. Alone with me, Andy did. But his terms were ones I couldn't meet. He wanted to talk to me about Chase as if I were one of the guys— a sensitive guy, one willing to let him get all mushy and enthused.

"The first time I saw her, I just knew. There she was, barely visible, surrounded by people—and then I heard this warm laugh, and the people somehow parted and there was this small woman, so put together, and I thought, how did that sound come out of her? She looked so cool, you see, and that laugh—I'd never heard anything so large and inviting."

"You liked Estelle's laugh too, if I remember correctly," I said. "Or at least you always claimed to." Just as he claimed to like mine, which sounded just like my mother's. But I left that unsaid.

I guess what I couldn't get over was my father choosing to love someone so *un*like me—or my mother. He was in love with those things we couldn't ever be. It was so obvious in every word he said. *He liked how small she was.* He liked being able to make a space for her in his own large arms. He liked not feeling shoved aside. He liked being in the driver's seat and not aiming blindly, suicidally at the lights. I have never accused Chase, even in my angriest thoughts, of chasing my father. It was obvious, so obvious, that she was what *he* wanted. Once he let his actions speak for themselves, you'd have to be stone deaf not to hear what they were saying.

I've spent years wishing myself stone deaf. But this wasn't, just like I kept telling my friends, about jealousy. It was far deeper than that. Far more devastating. It was about how someone like me—someone who was just as much Estelle as I was Andy—was ever going to feel at home again now that I'd seen how shallow, how contingent those encouragements of his really were. Think about it. What *should* you feel when you learn that who you are, what you are, is not of ultimate value to the very person who brought you into being? I'm talking about height, of course, but something heavier too. Rock hard and bitter. Very bitter if you're twenty and haven't once had a boyfriend who said, "I can never get enough of you." Who always seemed to be saying, instead, "Bring down the volume, pull in your stomach, stoop your head—let me feel like a man." What kind of womanhood is that you're being invited into—and all for things I never had any control over—like Andy and Estelle's libidinous impulses twenty years before. I did not ask for these damn genes.

We count on our parents to love themselves in us and to help us learn to love them in ourselves. That's how we learn to take up space. That's what my father was doing every time he praised my stature. Making me feel natural, desirable. Just like he had done with Estelle herself, until he tired of it. But, you see, when he praised me that way—even after he had stopped with Estelle—he made me feel I was in some ways my mother's best self. In her crazy way, Estelle may have been better at helping me take up space in the world than Andy. There was no end to her self-flattery—and since she always saw me as part of herself, when she praised herself, in a completely unforced, unconditional way, she praised me too. Until the day she died. She never took it back, you see. I'm smart enough to know if she'd lived long enough to feel any threat from me, everything would have been different. But she left me with that consistency. And with that very inconsistent and dangerous mix of feelings that I have toward everything she was. Everything I could be.

This wasn't, it still isn't, about jealousy. I can't emphasize this enough. It's about consistency. And having some space to grow into. However else do you become an adult?

That evening with my father when he was telling me about his rapidly approaching marriage, when he was talking to me sensitive guy to sensitive guy about Chase, I turned away from him and waved at the waiter and ordered another batch of onion rings. My father didn't join me, instead looked impatiently at his watch. He and Chase were going out to a dinner party with some old friends of hers. He'd just thought he'd give me an hour of his precious time beforehand. I extended it, by eating slowly, to an hour and forty-five minutes.

"Remember to put any dishes you use in the dishwasher," he said as they were leaving. I could see she was a little miffed at our lateness, but she just smiled sweetly and picked up her purse.

As he talked to me like a backward child of ten, he slipped Chase's coat over her narrow shoulders, opened the door, his keys in his hands. She glided under his arm—with a lot of room to spare—like they were doing a square dance. He'd never bothered to dress Estelle. He wouldn't dare.

"It's nice to wake up to a clean kitchen," he said.

I looked at him, my mouth twitching, but he was serious. How many times had this man said to me, "Let it go, honey. Just let it go." Some evenings, Estelle out at another play practice, we'd walk in and just stare at the kitchen. Finally I'd wade in and put the gloves on and start the water running and take that long handled brush and work on the crud that had hardened on the plates from dinner the night before. "Let it go until the morning," he'd say. "We'll have more energy then. Let's order in a pizza."

So, I could see, really I could, what he meant when he told me that he loved Chase because she created a tranquil environment, a place of peace and beauty. And I could understand, although maybe not so easily, why out of loyalty to everything I loved about Estelle, I had to leave the chocolate cake out on the counter, the black crumbs scattered everywhere, the dirty plate and milk glass in the sink.

"I'll do it," I heard my father say when they came in later that night and they saw the mess I'd left in the kitchen.

"She's twenty, Andy. She heard you. Make it clear you heard her too. Have her do it as soon as she wakes up."

"She just forgot."

There was a silence. Then Chase's voice, cool but very clear, "No,

Andy. She did not forget. If you show her you heard her, it won't escalate. Let her claim her issues. Just do me a big favor and don't apologize for loving me, marrying me or any of the changes it requires."

"She's doing her best," I heard my father say. "Why can't you see that?"

"You see a little girl. That's completely natural. But I don't, Andy. And that's natural too. I see a woman. A big decided woman who knows her own mind. And what I see is that she doesn't want to have anything to do with me. Or if she does, it's on terms I can't get into. I can't be cleaning up after a woman of twenty. I don't want that kind of relationship."

"Neither does she," my father said a little huffily.

I could hear everything clearly through the vent in my bedroom. This is how I'd kept track of what was happening most of my life. But now I felt, oh, little and enormous, enraged and embarrassed. I felt, no doubt about it, like a third party. A voyeur. *In my own fucking house.*

That changed quickly enough. Chase decided they needed to sell both their houses and buy a new one in the next town over. Close enough they could keep their businesses, far enough away they could begin again socially. I don't blame her. I wouldn't want to keep running into Estelle's ghost around every corner.

I'd felt it myself, but it had eased up for me once I stopped going 'home' except for brief visits. For one thing, there wasn't any home—there was just this new house where they were starting a new life. One that had nothing to do with Andy and Estelle. One that really had nothing to do with me, or the family the three of us had been. I wanted a larger horizon for myself, but not in Yanceyville, a full 5,000 higher in population than Dayton. I stopped going back because it was just too uncomfortable. Third party, fifth wheel. Gloria in excess.

They never said anything. They didn't have to. The smallest things made it clear. The way they never asked the other what they wanted for breakfast—just made sure it was there. And it wasn't anything I was used to. Soy milk. Granola. Green tea. The way they said *we* when they talked, and it was clear it referred only to them. The way they held hands over the table.

I guess I could have asked them to stop—but it would make me look as foolish as wearing sunglasses inside the house at night.

"You must be so happy for your father," Mrs. Richardson, my favorite teacher from high school, said when she ran into me at the mall the last time I went back to visit them. "After all he's been through."

"My mother's the one who's dead. In comparison, I expect he came off easy."

"She speaks highly of you," Mrs. Richardson said, putting her hand on my shoulder. She was a big woman, but she had to put her hand up to do it. It made me want to cry—the reaching, the touch, everything. I trusted her. I *had* trusted her. In her classes I had written essays about Estelle that made her cry, made her write in red on the backs of several pages what a wise and accepting young woman I was. I loved writing my essays because I could tell the truth without anyone taking it wrong because they didn't even know that I was writing them. (My parents never kept much track of my school life except to assume I'd be good at it.)

"I take Chase's journal writing class," Mrs. Richardson said. "You two have so much in common. I mentioned what a good writer you were and I had the impression she knew it first hand." Not unless she was pawing through things that didn't belong to her.

When I went home that afternoon—or to what passed for a home—I announced I thought I would be making a surprise visit to my grandmother and my aunts and my cousins (who, although not as tall as me, would never be called diminutive). That night, I packed up everything that had anything revelatory in it—all the scrapbooks from my childhood, any school work from high school, especially those incriminating essays, and even my high school yearbook with all its cloying messages about hard times and new beginnings. I said the boxes were filled with books and clothes I wanted to share with my cousins and hauled them out of town. I didn't mean not to come back for so long—but once I took those things away, there really wasn't any reason to come back. This visit will be the first time in, my goodness, five years, that I've visited them in their house.

It's not as if we haven't seen each other. It's never been anything that drastic. Sometimes my father and Chase would come and visit me at college or wherever I was working for the summer. Other times we'd meet at my grandmother's. If my father and I met alone, we'd talk some about Estelle, but usually about how wonderfully independent I was—a fellowship here, an internship there, anything to put a roof over my head. Finishing college was anticlimactic really. I felt finally I could stop pretending—just settle into the resentment that I did—and do—most truly feel. Problem was, there was no one to notice it at such a distance—and soon my life got so busy with my work and then graduate school that it all kind of faded away.

Or I thought those issues had just faded away—but I'm having second thoughts now that you've appeared on the scene, my little manikin. Given all these hot buttons, it would be poetic symmetry to be pregnant with a girl—but that's not what the doctor told me.

He can't tell me who the father is. I mean, I haven't come out directly and asked, but I've poured over the images and can see nothing one way or the other. I've brought the ultrasound pictures with me, thinking their color blindness may work in my favor. Who can't be taken by the way you fly right out of the frame. Later, when they learn, they'll be more accepting. That's my hope.

I've waited to tell them until things have gone so far it's obvious abortion isn't even an option. I've waited until I can bring my father up almost as short as he brought me when he announced he was marrying Chase. I'm giving him four months rather than three weeks notice, but the shock may be, given the different circumstances, just about equal.

It makes it sound like I am having you in some kind of reaction. Nope. It just happened. But like most everything, it has symbolic ramifications. I'd just like to have them tidied up a bit before you come.

I just want you to know that you are wanted. *Intended*. However muddled the reasons. The timing, everyone tells me, couldn't be worse. I'll receive my degree, I'm getting an MSW, two weeks before you're scheduled to arrive. How can I expect to find a job in my condition, my belly bulging so much at five months I can barely slide behind the wheel? Maternity leave will be the first thing people will think when I come in for an interview. And if I don't have a job, what will I do to support myself? *Us*. What will I do to support us?

It is true, I'm savoring the look that's going to cross Chase's face as she imagines sharing their house, their tranquil and exquisite house, with me and this puling, wailing, burping, belching, bellowing little bundle of unrefined humanity. *I* know I would never take her up on the offer, but I don't intend to let her know that until I've really seen her squirm. This too will fall under the category of relationships she wouldn't choose to have with me. I don't think Chase is ready to see herself as a grandmother, to discuss over the breakfast table the relative benefits of breast feeding and soy formula, or the color and consistency of your little stools.

I know what I'm doing is what I want to tell them. I guess when I imagine telling them, I'm really imagining telling you how you came into being. I don't see any father on the horizon. Chances are there may never be one. Men go for the little buttons. I decided to have my family first and let the man-woman love, if it comes, take a healthy second place. I guess I'm having you because I miss Estelle—all those things I was sure I never would miss—that laugh of hers, the way she would look at herself in the mirror with transfiguring relish.

"Just look at these boobs," she'd say, hefting them like honeydews. "Look at these hips. A man looks at me and he thinks, *life force*, that's what he thinks. Some day it's going to happen to you too, baby."

I would look at her, turned off and also incredulous. My stick-thin thirteen year old body already visible above her in the mirror. If I didn't breathe, I thought, if I didn't grow even a quarter of an inch more, there'd still be room for both of us in the mirror.

Now there's barely enough room for you and me there, even when I stand on the far side of my bedroom. Granted I have one of those cheap narrow mirrors, but even so. Even so, I would love to have someone call me beautiful. A life force.

I can't get over the feeling that Estelle would, although another part of me thinks that's crazy. Estelle never saw me as anything but an extension of herself. I was the ground, the negative space, that brought her into focus. Into being. She needed me. Oh, how she needed me.

You will too, for a short while. But I may need you longer. That's what's bothering me before you're even here. I want you to see me, little one, as beautiful. I want you to see me now, right now, so enormous with you, as beautiful—and you're never going to be able to. You're going to have to take my word for it. I *am* beautiful. Because of you.

Your possible fathers—one works at the clinic where I'm doing my internship and the other is in my statistics class—look the other way if they happen to see me. I know each one is praying that you aren't his. You never will be, whichever way it plays out. You will never, I promise you, ever have to beg for acceptance.

I wanted you, this is the simple truth, to myself. And I want you to feel, whichever genes you've come from, perfect in your skin, your stature. George, the psychology graduate student, is black, six-feet seven-inches. But Lee Yang is, oh, about Chase's size, five four at the most. For a man, to be that short is a big challenge. Almost as big as it is for me to be six feet one. Why did I do it? I found them both perfect in their own way. I wanted them to cancel each other out.

I want you to feel that you are, whatever your dimensions, exactly the man you should be. And, I suppose, I want you to always remember that half your genes are strangers to mine. Even if you never learn who those genes belong to, you'll always know there's more to you than can be explained away by my strengths and weaknesses.

It's strange, really. I suppose I did kind of imagine you being a girl—and may have thought that whichever way you ended up, something would get resolved—that love would pour in to replace some of that rancor that I no longer have the strength to carry. You'd be *my* daughter, whether you were Chase's size or Estelle's. I'd look at you and know I had to help you love the kind of woman you were going to be. I wouldn't pull the rug out from under you like Andy did to me.

What I never imagined was what happened when I drove up and sat in the drive of my father and Chase's house because only Chase's car was there and I had wanted to take them both by surprise. I didn't expect the feeling of relief I felt when she appeared in the kitchen doorway with a cup of tea in her hands, peering at the car, then nodding without surprise. I hadn't called to warn them, of course. Walking out on the lawn, she waited for me to extricate myself from the car and come toward her. She took it all in immediately, my difficulty getting out from behind the wheel, what part of me emerged first from around the side of the car. I never imagined feeling, when she broke into that laugh of hers, the same sweet sense of invitation my father had described.

"Welcome. Welcome both of you. Do you want to come in and tell me about it?"

"It wasn't a mistake."

"I knew it couldn't be," she said. "Congratulations."

And then I started to cry and the world opened up for me as she just stood there, not moving, just holding me with her eyes, letting me take up all the space I needed. All the space I needed to be true to you too.

"Tell me what you have planned," she said after she had settled us both out on the deck with cups of hibiscus tea.

And that's where, an hour or so later, my father found us. He took it all in with a glance, like she had, and just leaned against the wall of the house catching his breath, while Chase and I sat laughing, basking in the early spring light, planning how I was going to make it happen—this life where you know from day one that I am where you belong. There is no one else in the world who could ever be your mother.

I haven't decided if I'm going to name you Will or Edsel. Chase says there's plenty of time. Plenty of room to maneuver. I could name you Magic or Mao, she suggested. I could just drop the patronymic if it felt too overbearing or deterministic. She's offered me her own name—Prospect. But she says she has no doubt that I'll do what's right for me—and I'll know it when it comes. Just like she did. I take it like she meant it, as an observation.

And an invitation—which, now that I can really feel you in there, kicking at my heart, churning up my secret waters with the exuberant power of a natural wonder, expanding into all this space I have to give you—I am free at last to hear. For years now, your world is going to revolve around me. I will be as dependable as the sun, gravity. When I move, I will make a space for you to move into, just the way they made space, all three of them, for me. I wonder how long it will take you to see it too.

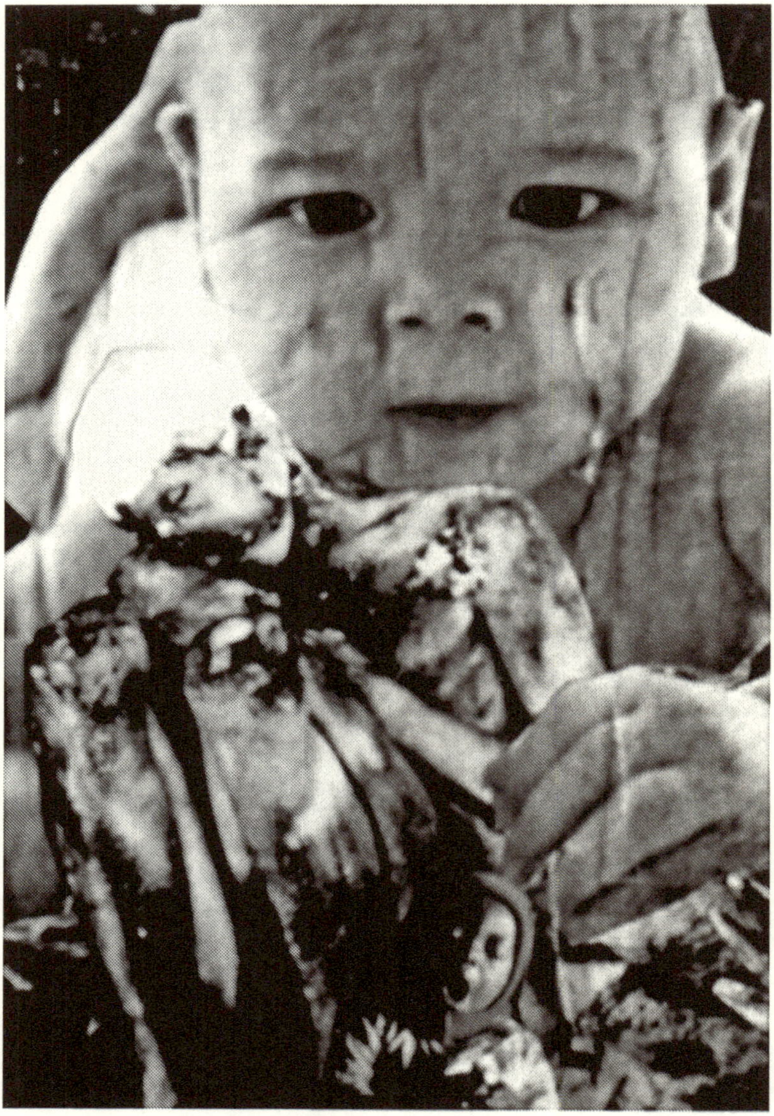

BECAUSE YOU ARE FREE

When she came in, she was taking a swig of water from a transparent gallon jug. Skin like milk. A soft voice. Educated. But she was wearing coveralls—something only a city woman would think of putting on when she was visiting the country. It was a way of accentuating her advantages, or had that effect, whatever she intended.

But I liked her right off. Something about the angle at which she tipped the jug up—something about the way she looked at me with her large black eyes, so innocent and knowing at the same time. I sent her over to admissions to sign all the forms. When she came back a half hour later, the jug was emptier but seemed to hang heavier in her hand. She wasn't trying to swallow from it anymore.

Once I had prepared her, had her pull her coveralls down until the stops and the bib were all collected between her legs like a soiled bedsheet, drawn her narrow blue cotton panties even lower than they naturally set, I took the information I needed from her. Her name. Age. That's it.

Look here, I told her soon as the signal picked it out. Oh, she said. Nothing more. Then, Oh, again as it turned its face to us and put its hand to its mouth.

Oh, she said. That's my baby there. In that hushed room, her voice spread out everywhere, bringing us all into focus.

The pictures I take, they're of all the sound our body won't absorb, that it sends back. What we're looking at are echoes. I guess that's true of light too, when you think of it, but I think of this machine, my technology, as something different. Echoes belong to our hearing life in a way that's deeper than vision. You call out in a cave, a darkened bedroom, and you listen back and you know something about yourself that's completely different from catching a glimpse of yourself in a mirror.

Oh, my husband Dwayne says when he loses himself inside me. Never anything different. Never anything more. *Oh.*

Oh, that woman said when she saw her future turn its head and look at her.

I wish my husband could see this, she said after a long pause. I wasn't sure whether she was saying that she knew this wasn't going to last long and she just wanted him to know.

Oh, that woman said, and for the first time it got to me, what I've been doing for these last six years, ever since I finished my training. I could feel that sound expanding inside me. When Dwayne makes the same sound, I feel like a stone falling through miles of water. There's no sadness in the world that's deeper, harder. But this woman's voice, it was like a bat had got loose inside me, I could hear these wings beating, see a mouth opening, crying out in a voice that was so private only a bat could receive it back. Ruth Ann, it was calling—but nothing stopped the sound. It could have called forever, just like it was in farthest outer space, a million years between itself and the next solid thing.

I busied myself catching on to the heartbeat. When I caught it just right, I could see the pulses running across the screen regular as could be, a hundred and forty beats to the minute. I turned the sound up. That's its heart, I told her. She closed her eyes, a look of contentment softening her face.

It was then I saw the other shape and cursed myself for ever saying anything. I turned the sound up even louder for a second, and switched the console around a little so she didn't have so clear a view. They tell you not to say anything at all, but that's always struck me as inhuman. You come in with all the hope and fear in the world afloat inside you and have to lie in the dark with a total stranger who sees inside you but won't say a word—just try to imagine if it was you. That's what I want to tell Dr. Mukerjee. Imagine it was you lying there.

But until today, I don't know that I ever really did imagine that sound lighting up the most hidden reaches of my own body, how that might feel.

I tell Dwayne to leave his work behind at the end of the day. Tomorrow morning is soon enough to pick it up again. He doesn't listen to me. Tonight I don't listen to myself either. All the way up the mountain, the woman stays on my mind.

Other than their heartbeats, what I do takes place in silence. That's why I started talking to the women. If I were in their place, I would find it unnerving—the darkened room, the screen, your pants pulled down right to the top of your crotch. They say this is being considerate, not asking them to disrobe completely, but to me it feels like you couldn't feel more naked, caught at that point where you don't have the protection man gave you and you can't remember either that you're a child of God and the skin you're born with is clothing enough. And then, along comes this stranger with a squeeze bottle who shakes it and pours an ice blue liquid across your swelling stomach. I always apologize beforehand, but the shock gets to them. Alone in the darkened room, the screen flickering, I can still see their eyes narrow, their muscles tense. Flight or fight. It relieves me somehow. That's the clothing they need for this procedure. I can talk soft as I want, but the truth is what we're engaged in here is a fearsome mystery.

Tonight I may be making too much of all this. I have a job to be doing, and I do it very well. I know that. The doctors always give me compliments. It doesn't help. At least today it didn't. Especially when Dr. Mukerjee came in, talking, like he always does, about how many procedures he performed a day in medical school. What kind of school is it, I want to know, has you doing one every fifteen minutes? He doesn't even know he is being offensive. The only reality for him is what's there on the screen. He never looks at the woman, never connects that milk white mound that glows there in the dark with the woman's eyes and mouth, her first day of school, her wedding night, or all the carnal acts that brought her here. I'm never sure, when he looks at the screen, his left hand doing something unaccountable with the pulsar, where he thinks all this is taking place.

Me, I get lost sometimes, if I'm not careful. Sometimes, it seems that the two of us, the woman on the table, me at the console, we're in some bigger womb together. If so, I don't know who is going to tell us what's happening. Certainly not Dr. Mukerjee. He wouldn't know if it bit him.

Sometimes it helps me to think we're all no different from what I pick up there on the screen. That maybe God is looking at a console, doing something automatically with His left hand, and then seeing these angels begin to swim across the screen. I think when He watches He feels as astonished as I do.

The truth is, all day I am looking at angels. Things not yet, or ever, of this earth.

Maybe, if I had ears to hear it, the sound I'm bathing them in sounds to them like the gravel shooting out from under my wheels hard and fast as a machine gun.

Leave it, I tell Dwayne. But I feel like, I set this aside tonight, I set aside my whole life.

We've got a capacity on our machine, it's called Doppler, lets you see the blood going in and out of the heart. It shows red and blue like the lungs were already working—but what it's really measuring is direction. Red, receding.

The heart of any woman's life is her home. For a man, I've come to believe it's his work. When I tell Dwayne to leave it there, take it up when he's out of my sight tomorrow, I'm behaving no different than the doctors do to me. They've got no interest in Dwayne. They've got no idea what happens to me when the paving ends and the gravel begins spraying out from under my wheels until, in my window screen, I see the cabin take shape down there in the woods like the image of my own heart.

Spring, like it is now, we feel blessed. Here in the hollow, there are pastures greener than dreams. The dogwood on their edges shudder like storms of moths. It was this very pasture flashed through my mind as I stepped back into that dark room the second time this morning.

I'd asked Dr. Mukerjee, please, come in and tell her. But he told me to just go on with what I was doing. Finish it all. Otherwise he'd have to charge her for two doctor's visits. His wife has had two children, but sometimes I think he must have artificially inseminated her. To save his time. I can't believe anyone who has held a woman in his arms, given and received pleasure from her, could not know the fear the woman on the examining table was feeling.

Dwayne, when I lost them back in high school, he understood. It's what holds us together even now, fifteen years later. If it had all gone as God planned, I could be a grandmother in a year or two. But I wouldn't be married to Dwayne. Wouldn't have that look of his that sustains me like the bread of life, so alive with pity that if you didn't know him like I do, you would think it was undying love. Maybe it is. Maybe it's the words that are twisted. When Dwayne enters me, he does it knowingly, I feel known. But you can't tell me to know someone isn't like dropping stone-heavy into a dark well.

Three years ago, late one Saturday, I brought my sister in with me to the hospital because she was so worried about the baby she was carrying. She was afraid he'd be like her first son, David, with the palsy. I told her it wasn't something would show up in a picture. But we went there anyway, just the two of us. We didn't take any photographs, just looked at the screen. I shifted the console as much as I could, just like I did for the woman today, and the two of us studied her baby. I showed her everything I could. Calipered his head, measured him crown to rump, estimated his age. He was so big then, it was too late to do anything about him if we had seen anything, but she went away reassured. By that age, they can seem monstrous, you can only see them in parts—the face pressed against the screen like an intruder peering into your bedroom in the middle of the night. Just the opposite of those tiny ones, who already have enough detail at ten weeks, it's like looking at the sweetest secret anyone has ever held close to herself. They are so perfect it makes you trust that there's a purpose to this universe.

Don't get me wrong, I don't think our purpose is just handed down to us from God like the promotion Dwayne dreams about. I think we play an important part in what happens to us. I just don't always know what it is, and I find it comforting to feel someone else is shouldering some of the responsibility.

And I know, just like the doctors, that this is a job I'm doing, that what I'm seeing on the screen has nothing to do with me as a person. Me, Ruth Ann, I mean. But however professional you are, you can't sit there day after day watching what I do and not be changed somehow. Anymore than Dwayne could be unchanged by all the nights he's spent in my arms, drifting off with his member still hard inside me like we are bound forever. Beast with two backs, I've heard it called. But it's sweeter than that. Like we were Siamese twins, maybe, that finally found a way to be comfortable. If that sounds kinky, I don't mean it to. I think of us as sealed, complete, like one of those dandelion globes drifting on a summer wind.

This woman's skin was the color of cream, so white there was a grayness to it. There were lines around her eyes that made me realize, even before I took her age, that she was older than I was, although you might not know it to look at the two of us. She has that softness to her face that I call opportunity. At thirty-three, I know I've lost it. From a distance, my head turned away, you might mistake me for the girl I was fifteen years ago. But you look at my face and you know life has gotten to me.

This woman was thirty-five and planning to have her first child like it was the most natural thing in the world. What, I wonder, had she been thinking all these twenty years or more since her periods started? It's like she had lost nothing, she just put part of her aside and is taking it up now when it's convenient.

It's a little strange when you think of it. I'm younger than her and I've already given up. But I liked her—right off, I felt this warmth toward her. I didn't hold her hope against her, that's what I'm trying to say. Funny, when that's what I blame myself for almost every day. How I could be so crazy grand in my ideas as a girl, I thought I could go right on with my life as if nothing had happened.

I saw that same defeated kind of thinking come to after she caught a glimpse of that second shape. Until I turned the console, she just stared at the screen, at the little white ball of dust turning there in that other chamber, wishing, like I was, that it would just dissolve. I would have done anything to stop the self-questioning she was doing. I said excuse me and went out to talk to Dr. Mukerjee once I was sure it was a second one and not a growth of some kind, but he said, just go on, it's not going to take much longer. But if you're careful, it takes at least a half hour, with the pictures and everything. That's longer than a drowning man has to run through his life.

All that time, while I was rubbing that pulsar over her stomach, setting the gages to measure its head, writing in her name and age again, she kept her arm over her eyes. Her breath was ragged, although you could see her concentrating on bringing it under control. I wanted to tell her not to worry, but Mukerjee had told me not to say anything more to her, and I thought it would make it all last longer. When I locked on to the heartbeat, I turned up the sound to reassure her, but she began to sob. She thought it was the first one, I believe, and she was listening to what she was losing.

I know exactly what you are feeling, I wanted to tell her—of course, I couldn't say anything except, Don't be upset. It's going to be all right. What you might say at your mama's deathbed. Meaningless.

I turned the sound down, but she couldn't stop gasping. I stood up and went over to her. I was so mad at Mukerjee then I wouldn't have cared if he walked in and fired me. It wasn't right to make her so frightened.

I took her hand and she held on to it hard enough to pull me under if we had been in the water, but all the rest of her body was exposed. She never pulled her arms away from her face, never tried to defend herself. Who would she be defending herself from?

I can't say more than this, I told her, but you have no need to be frightened. No more, I meant, than anyone who lives and breathes. No more, I meant, than me. But she had reason to celebrate and that I couldn't tell her. It wasn't just Mukerjee. Some part of me wanted to keep that moment from her a little longer. So, I guess the truth is I wanted her to be frightened. I wanted her to wonder, hard, what she had gotten herself into. I wanted her to grieve at the terrible choice she might be forced to make. I wanted her to think, I may have waited too long. I wanted her to think, *I too may be unloved by God.*

What she said to me was, We want this baby. My husband and I, we really want this baby.

As if wanting was all it took.

When I try to think back on it now, I can sense my own anger. But that wasn't all that was happening between us. She was suffering and I also wanted to relieve it as if it were my own pain.

Truly, I said to her, there's nothing to be worried about. I'll be finished in three more minutes and then the doctor will come in and talk with you.

That set her off again. She let go of my hand and her whole body began to shake. I stood there looking down at her, her small breasts, the nipples pressing against her red lace-trimmed undershirt, her white stomach exposed like you see in those photos of women raped by soldiers and left for dead. She could have been anyone on earth. Lying the way she was, her face hidden, no one in the world would have recognized her except maybe her own husband.

I went back to the console. Her bladder was so swelled now, it was like a huge dark semi-circle over the top of the screen. I took the last pictures as fast as I could and went out to find Dr. Mukerjee, who was flirting with May Ellen. May Ellen had that half-disgusted, half-flattered expression I expect we all put on when we have to talk to him.

When we came back in, she still had her hands over her face.

You use fertility pills? Dr. Mukerjee asked before he even said hello. He asked for more gel and squirted it from the bottle himself but used the pulsar to rub it in. She didn't even flinch this time. He ran the pulsar back and forth until he could see each of them clearly, see nothing was missing. Hands. Feet.

Congratulations, he said. You're the mother of twins.

Congratulations? she asked. And then she drew a deep breath and the tears began to come. No sobbing, just this steady fall of tears. Before this, it was like she was holding them back. It was the only thing her will could control.

Can I go to the bathroom? she asked.

Her voice was like a little girl's now. But when she sat up, she was as careful as an old woman.

No problem, Dr. Mukerjee said. No problem.

While we waited for her to come back, he told me again how many procedures he used to do. Not like here where money is scarce and people come only when they're feeling right desperate. When it costs a month's groceries, you think twice. And you expect people to take it as seriously as you do and not treat you like a part flying by on an assembly line.

Twins, she said, putting her hand out to find the examining table, blinded by the light in the bathroom and then the dark of the room.

I'll show you, he said, and he had her lie back down again and he showed her the two chambers and the two embryos, both of them floating on their backs, their little arms crossed over their chests. Two? she said—and her voice, it was like she was practicing astonishment. That was the actress in her, I guess. She was an actress, that's what she had said when she first lay down. Her husband was an actor. For awhile there it didn't matter. The only audience she had for her thoughts was herself.

But now, you could see her practicing to get the emotion just exactly right. It near broke my heart. We came so close, I thought, and then I thought, close to what. *We?* I excused myself.

After she dressed, she came out of the room and looked for Dr. Mukerjee. She wanted to be sure we'd send the pictures to her doctor in the city. And then, after she'd turned to go, she stopped and began to rummage through her knapsack. She pulled out her wallet. I watched her, amazed, not sure what it was she was intending to do. I wasn't her waitress or anything. But she pulled out this worn picture, the kind whose edges are soft as velvet.

This is my husband, she said, stepping close to me. I don't know why, but I'd like to show you.

Maybe because I'd seen what she'd only meant to have him see—or what she'd never shown him. I don't know.

I took the photograph from her. I could feel her eyes on my face. I couldn't keep myself from blinking, but after that I smiled. He's a handsome man, I said. He had a face like hers, still fat with opportunity, the only difference was the color of their skin.

Thank you, I said, looking at her again. She was several inches taller than me. The look she gave me, it almost stopped my heart, it was so knowing. You can understand why this is so important to me, she said.

I'd understand if they were both from deepest Africa.

Understand if they were from Finland too.

Understand if they were Dwayne and me.

It's not but ten miles after the paving ends till you reach our house, but it can take over a half hour, what with the inclines and the loss of traction because of the gravel if it's dry, or the mud when it rains. Sometimes there's a line up at the fords, especially times like this month when the streams are twice as wide as usual. It doesn't help to stop and think about it, you've got to just gun your motor and concentrate on the far side, but I think it is an instinct to slow down and people would just as soon give in to it as fight it. If there were another road I could take, I would be just like them, idling my motor, going into reverse.

I have driven this road all my life. When I was a girl, I lived five miles farther back on it than I do now. Dwayne laughs about it sometimes and says, Can't say I didn't raise you up a notch. It all depends on where you're standing, I guess. What you define as forward. Reverse. The colors on the Doppler, you could interchange them. They have nothing to do with oxygen, just a fixed point of reference. That's the person with the pulsar, the fixed point.

So what does that mean? When I moved to Dwayne's cabin, was I moving forward or back? Forward, I expect, if my intention was to get closer to the pavement, to the highway signs, to the hospital where I work now.

You could also say it was exhaustion. Finally, I couldn't fight my way any further back than his cabin. I couldn't bear to cross that third ford every day of my life.

I would have moved somewhere. Moving to Dwayne's began to seem inevitable, after what happened. But it took us another five years. Three for him to finish high school, and two more for him to get to earning regular with his construction job. All that time, I was driving the school bus. Just like I had before the accident. Odd how it's only after the fact you build a resistance. Now I feel sick to my stomach whenever I see one of those buses.

To this hour, we've never spoken of what happened, how, just after the second ford, when there was no one left on the bus except him, the cramping got so bad I had to pull the bus to a stop and ask him to excuse me. I wasn't thinking too clearly. I just knew I had best be off by myself. I headed right out into that pasture I love so much to look at now when I drive by. There was a tree in the middle, a dogwood in bloom, and I thought, if I can get under that tree no one will see me. I was near crazy—but my sister's described it too, so I don't think it's particular, it just has to do with delivery.

I was lying on my side at first, just because the grass felt cool on my cheek. You couldn't call it pain, exactly. Not then. It was more like an enormous pressure. At that moment, I didn't have a thought left inside me. It was a relief almost. For more than three months every minute I was thinking and thinking on it, trying to get straight in my mind what it was I should do. Now it was being decided for me and all I could feel was relief—and then this terrible fear that it wasn't just the babies being forced out of me, my own life was going to slip away too.

I started rubbing my cheek against the tree bark. It hurt, it was so rough, but I was crazy to wake up. Dear God in Heaven I was saying. Dear

God in Heaven. Over and over, rubbing my cheek against the bark. I didn't even have my hand against the bark. I didn't even have my hands against my belly. I'd lost all my instincts except this crazy scraping.

And then Dwayne was there. He wasn't but a boy back then. Fourteen. But when he put his hand on my shoulder, I turned to him like he could do something for me.

You want me to get someone?, he asked.

Don't leave me, I said. I turned over as I spoke. I can't describe how green the grass was that day. Or how blue the sky. You could see it between each blossom on the dogwood, sharp as if it had been cut out of tin.

Then I had to close my eyes.

Look at me, he said. Whatever you do, don't stop looking at me.

Then he straddled my legs with both his knees and put his hands up my skirt as easy as if he had done this a hundred times already. My panties were wet. So was my skirt. That had happened while I was driving. I knew, soon as it happened, that this was the end of it. There wasn't enough there for a doctor to fight for.

The panties he drew off me, they weren't just wet. They were red with blood. He pulled my skirt up around my waist to try to keep it clean. I told you, he said, keep your eyes on my face. Don't you look away from me, not for a minute. So that's how I seen my babies born, in Dwayne's face. And he, he saw them with his hands. They weren't much bigger than my thumb. I know that now, looking at the screen. Twelve weeks. 45 millimeters. Then, they were just a flickering of his eyelids.

What would I have done with the two of them, I sometimes ask myself. It doesn't help. Looking into Dwayne's face now, so many years later, seeing his eyes go blank like they do just before he comes, I am reminded. I am always reminded. It's just a second, but long enough for him to notice, so when he comes there's a desperation to it. Oh, he cries out. *Oh.*

Tonight, with the moon full, I am tempted to drive the road with my lights out. I feel, tonight, like nothing bad in the world ever could happen to me. That big moon glows so bright it turns the sky blue again. That's what it feels like inside my mind. Mysterious and near clear as day.

This evening, after everyone had gone home, I went back into the examining room. I could still smell traces of her perfume in the air. It had a floral scent on the surface but underneath there was something musky and persistent. I couldn't tell if I liked it or not. I don't know why I was so sure it was her perfume and hers alone. She wasn't the only person we looked at today. But she's the only one ever got through to me. Ever got me to do what I did tonight.

When I closed the door to the examining room and made my way back, blinded by the dark, I moved cautiously as she did at the end. I pulled my panties right off and brought my skirt up around my waist, and then decided to remove it entirely. I removed my bra too. I rubbed the jelly all over my stomach. I felt my eyes narrow, just like all those other women, at the cold. As I began to rub the pulsar over my skin, I saw my own body on that screen. I saw what a small place it was where all my hopes were buried. Smaller than a fist. Even this time of the month when it's as fat as it can be with unshed blood.

I turned the knobs—moving back and forth—to my bladder, over my kidneys, my liver. I went so high as the edge of my heart. I kept trying to put it into proportion, that organ, that one hour of my life.

Don't take your eyes off me, Dwayne said and I obeyed him. He wasn't nothing but a boy and he spoke out of his truest instinct. I do believe this. But I'm not sure it was the right thing to do. If I'd kept my eyes shut, maybe I would have left my body along with the babies, just like he was afraid of. But maybe I wouldn't have. Maybe I would have gone into myself and found what I found tonight.

Tonight I found a rage past bearing. I found there was no place left to put it. No place but behind me. Beside me. All around me, rage was like the ultrasound that would bring me into focus. All those years, I thought I was mad at myself. Mad at myself for getting into the mess in the first place. Mad at the way it turned out. Mad at all the years that came after. All those months, swelling, collapsing. For nothing.

There was no reason. That's what I thought tonight, my body reflecting its earthly shape in the glass, my organs taking strange unearthly shapes on the screen. My body is no different from any other woman's. There's no reason I have been singled out. I thought that was what I was after. Some proof that what had hurt me had hurt me for all time, that I carried it deep inside me like a real scar.

But there was nothing out of the ordinary there. I sat staring at myself, afloat on the surface of the screen, the light from the hallway outlining the door just a crack, like a knife had pried away the edges of a lid. I was centered inside that doorway, inside the screen.

Standing there, still as I could be, the pulsar pressed to my belly with both my hands, I felt the pressure begin and then the pain, so sharp it made me curve over. Made me take my eyes off myself. And then, in the dark, alone with the pressure and the pain thrusting itself straight up through me like a dagger, I heard this voice speaking out for all the world to hear. *This is my daughter, with whom I am well pleased.* I knew I had been waiting all my life to hear these words. They echoed through my whole body.

Why, was all I could think to ask: Why did you make me wait so long?

Because you are free.

Free.

Like Dwayne, waiting, his fourth beer of the evening warming in his hand.

Like the woman this morning.

Free and enslaved every day of our lives.

Look at me, Dwayne said. Don't take your eyes off my face.

If I had dared ask the same of God, what would have happened. Would God have seen in my face what I saw in Dwayne's? It wasn't the death of the babies got to me, it was looking into this boy's face, so earnest, pure as an animal's, and understanding that this was innocence, this was grace, and as soon as I knew it sure enough to call it by its name, it was lost to me entirely.

Oh, Dwayne says when he enters me. Oh.

I have never said anything back to him.

Why should I? He wants to know the dimensions of the dark. Only the echo of his own voice can teach him that.

Tonight, the moon holding us in its gaze, I will close my arms around him. Oh, I will cry out as we tumble in the dark. The sound will press back around me closer than his arms. *Oh!* God's skin thrums like a drum at the edges of the universe, sending it all back to us if we will only listen. Cry out. Listen again.

Tonight, alone in that examining room, I understood that this moment I'd always thought back to as the loss of everything was really the seed of my salvation. But to find my salvation, I will have to accept everything, Dwayne's white hands streaked with blood twisting in the rain drenched grass, the clay streaking the backs of my legs, accept that the expressions on his face were a mirror of my own, that we were neither of us lost, but found as completely as the babies we buried with their afterbirth beneath the dogwood.

It's not just me I've got to free. It's Dwayne too.

He never did touch me until our wedding night. He wanted to make my life over just as bad as I did. He's never once asked me who their father was. We've never talked back to that afternoon, so how could he? Which is not to say I'd tell him now. It's nothing dark or startling, that's not why I keep it back. I just don't want it to distract us.

When Dwayne knelt over me in the field, he knew even less than me about sex. (I knew one night in the back of a pickup when I thought I was going to be suffocated by all that white, the moonlight and the clouds of frost escaping from my own lungs, the smell of whiskey, a pain so sharp it was the last thing expected, then a dark so bitter and deep it was like a grave. I knew I had made a complete fool of myself.)

The boy who knelt over me in the field wanted what he still wants. As I sit here, the motor still running, the headlights fixed on the back of our little house, the light fading away in darker and darker circles, I feel so sad I want to sleep just at the idea: *He wants to make her safe.*

I must say this once because I do not know if I will ever dare to say it again. My husband Dwayne loves me with his whole being. I have never doubted this. Never doubted he would die for me if I needed it.

But he does not love the body I inhabit.

When Dwayne knelt over me in the tall green grass, he loved me just the way I believed God should. At the point in time when the world hasn't been split in half by desire.

That's what we've been trying all this time to do. To return to the world before we assumed the power of life and death.

Oh, Dwayne cries out. It is a cry of relief, and of grief that knows no comforting.

There have been years I have wondered, if I were the men I believe he dreams about, would this make it easier for him. But I think, if I went in there and asked him, if he could answer me the way he might answer God, he'd tell me no, that what breaks his heart is that union is impossible. Male or female. He doesn't know he's learned that from me. He thinks it is a fact of life.

I'm afraid all he's ever wanted is to make me safe and to deny himself.

I don't want this to be the truth. It feels too hard. I'm no different from him. I want to look into his face and feel my whole body open out like it did tonight when I heard God talking to me. I want him to look in my face and feel his own face glow, feel when he's entering me that this was what God intended for the two of us because we *are* loved.

When Dwayne knelt over me, before he even touched me, there in my private parts, his hands were covered with blood. There's no way either of us is ever going to be able to go back before that point. It is the heart of everything that has come after. What I am trying to say is that what we made of it, taking it for a sign that we might be unloved by God, that was where the tragedy lay, not in those small angels. Where we buried those children, we buried all our hopes for our future.

Maybe that's why, in spite of what I imagine I should feel, that pasture always calls to me in the deepest and most promising way, why, even now, I have never dared set foot in it again but I have never stopped desiring it with all my heart.

And then it comes to me what I need to do, what we should have done years ago, but we knew no better. We have to go down there together, Dwayne and me. You see, we were each of us trying to protect the other. From what? From the only thing might set it right. The voice I heard tonight. Why did you take so long? I asked and I heard the answer. *Because you are free.*

I want to use that freedom. I want to go ask God what has been haunting us all this time: *What exactly is this gift you've given us?*

I want to see my whole life as one piece. Dwayne's bloodied hands turning in the grass, the dogwood blossoms shivering so sharp and white against the blue sky, the pain that divides my life like a hatchet divides wood;

the woman I am now standing anchored inside the knife edge of light, strange shapes forming and dissolving inside the screen; the man Dwayne is now, moving restlessly inside our house like an idea inside my mind, the idea I can't get rid no matter how hard I try, that he dreams of men, that I am his only protection from what he truly loves and what he can't bear to know about himself. Just like he's been for me.

If God were a headlight, we would each be the figure standing there, hands out, protecting the other figure lying helpless on the ground.

We have deprived each other—out of love—of the love that reveals us to ourselves. The love that heals.

I do not want to find out that my husband does not love me—but even less do I want to think we will live together forever unable to change our natures or to accept them—unable to accept how much I desire the promise of life locked off inside my body, how much he does. I want to believe that I will go in to Dwayne and we will come with me down to the field and that we will lie down under the full moon in the tall grass and that all the love he has thrown out into the world, all those cries, will come to rest in me now. *Because we are free.* I want to believe that I will grow fat with opportunity.

I believe and I do not believe.

Look at me, Dwayne says, terrified, don't ever take your eyes off me. I don't know how to say, as God has said to me, healing with the same stroke that severs bone from marrow: *no.*

HEARTS AS BIG AS FISTS

There is something implicitly sexual in the metaphor that persuades her, but she doesn't realize this until days later, after the decision has already been made. When she understands, for a second she is stricken by the guilt that occasionally assails her when she remembers the sequence of affairs she had early in her marriage, how her daughter, who is now as closely connected to her as her right hand, then seemed something completely alien, devouring, and she turned to her young lovers as if their mouths could draw something more from her breasts than the thin blue milk that spilled into her daughter's mouth before her lips and bald gums could even close around the nipple.

It all seems so trivial now, even the guilt. What binds them together is beyond speech but not beyond bearing. Sometimes she imagines they are, the four of them—mother, father, daughter, son—the chambers of a heart. The image sustains her, some days, as if there is another will that surrounds their lives, transparent, resilient as a muscle.

Something happened to all us, she told the doctor, when they severed the sinus node. She sees him shift forward in his seat as if to answer. Something, she goes on quickly, that the pacemaker doesn't solve. This, she believes, was their true loss of innocence. Her son's heart will never beat on its own anymore. I don't think you can imagine what that means to us, she tells him. It was at that moment they understood they would all be changed beyond belief. Birth, she thought, was the closest you could come to the sensation—and, like birth, it took place without words, every nerve and muscle bundle registering that there was no retreat.

Now, when she remembers the peccadillos of her youth, what

astonishes her is the faith they implied. A life where personal satisfaction was the one true religion. Beautiful, the lover sighed, touching the contours of her breast, her lips, and what she felt was something close to spiritual transformation, some assurance she needed with all her being that she was among the saved. She tells herself that it was the way she was raised, it reflects as much about her culture as it does about herself, but it still astonishes her. Now. Where she's come to.

The difference, he tells her, between what I do and what a surgeon does is that although I can't see the heart with my own eyes, I can go as slowly as I need to. I run a catheter in and make one incision in the septum—

Two, she interrupts him.

One, he repeats. We enter through the pulmonary artery.

I take a balloon, a small one, and expand it. Then I stop. We measure everything. I expand the balloon a little more. Then I withdraw it and use one a little larger. We cut the gradient in half, we stop. We're not looking for perfection here.

I would like to pray for a miracle, she says as she kneels before the altar rail. She happened upon the church as she was returning to the hotel where her daughter and son are waiting for her. She has never been to a healing ceremony, has never been back to the denomination since she was a child. She remembers it as a temple to rationality.

The priest is a woman her own age. The priest listens intently as she describes the choices, the operations. She closes her eyes when the priest places her hands on her hair. The priest prays that she and her husband will be embraced by God as they make these difficult decisions, that the image of her son secure in Jesus' arms will imprint itself on her heart. The image that comes to her instead is the four of them at the lake before the last operation, the one that silenced the heart of the family. She sees her son swimming from one of them to the other. Four and buoyed by trust. She watches him strike out toward her. She sees the water spread out behind him like a train of light. She pulls him close to her, turning him around and letting him paddle on to his sister, who releases him in turn to his father. What more, she wondered, could you give your children? It wasn't enough. She was the first person to agree with that. Just imagining birth, the infant's confusion before the blare of voices and vertiginous flurry of color and light, that cry that sounded so small and inconsequential in the hubbub—it all made her want to choke. What reparation could any of them ever make?

I don't know how many articles you would have to read to match the expert knowledge of the people involved in this case, he says.

We have been told we will have to trust someone, she agrees.

I want to pray for a miracle, she tells the priest. I don't want to come to peace with this, any of it, ever.

You must remember, he told her, our hearts are no bigger than our fists. Late that evening, showering, he stares at his own pressed against the damp tile of the shower stall. He has a desire to turn, drive it, once and without hope of return, into the frosted glass door. He feels trapped beyond belief. Where did they come from?

If it were my son, he told her, I would do this. And I believe I still love my sons.

He just couldn't stand the sight or sound of them. A brutal age. Literally. They are all flesh and friction, these boys swaggering around in the bodies of men as they once did in his operating greens or his white lab coat. He is just saying this. They are perfectly at one with themselves. He is the one who looks at them and can't imagine where their souls are hiding. He can't believe they are reduced to this. Flesh. Friction.

Do no harm.

He doesn't know a doctor anymore whose phone is listed. The boys complain about it all the time. What are you afraid of? they ask him. One of those kids is going to come back from the grave? He has set himself up for this. Those are the ones he counts too.

He counts two. Seventeen and fifteen years in the losing.

Don't blame me, his wife says. Don't you dare blame me. And what, she asks him, are you complaining about? Captain of the football team. A freshman starter in lacrosse. You act as if they're losers.

The den is filled with their gauntlets and pads. Exercise bike. Bar bells. The wide screen television they bought at Christmas. Sunday afternoons, the place smells like a locker room. He's suggested they plant Ban and Rightguard around the room the way at Easter they used to plant eggs so even a moron couldn't have missed them. The boys were so busy competing, half the time they still didn't see. Just ripped off each other's basket.

What's your issue? his wife asks. Think you have a lock on testosterone in this house? It's not just the smells that are getting gamey. It's their psyches. All of them. Some days he can't believe what he and his wife say to each other. The laughter loud as the slaps his sons exchange disentangling themselves from mounds of writhing flesh on the mud-scarred playing fields.

Three—four years ago, he would have said, if someone thought to ask him about his marriage, that it was a good one. Whatever that means. What he meant was that it was a done deal. Wife. Two kids. You were in it for life so the best thing was to stop thinking. Live.

All you know, she said, looking off through the window into the air well that barely alleviated the dimness of the office, is the medicine. You make a decision. Intervene. Evaluate the difference. You have to understand, we live every day of our lives with the consequences of your actions. Good or bad. Right or wrong. These make no difference. I live, she said—and the very simplicity had something melodramatic about it—for my son's next breath. His father does. His sister. You have to understand, we're not complaining. Nobody is asking you to go back in. No one. We do not want to jeopardize what we have. You paint these dire scenarios and every time we let you go in something happens that makes things better, you bring a gradient down in one chamber, and something happens that makes things worse. Another valve is weakened. You cut the node. I can't help thinking that if I'd never let anyone operate, he would be better off than he is now.

Without us, who's to say he would be here at all, he thinks and he feels he is back in his own house matching his wife's volley. This is the playing field, he tells her. These sutured leaflets, this plastic ventricular wall. This severed node. You can't go back. We're here to decide what is the next best step.

When he comes out of the shower, his wife is already in bed and asleep.

He thinks he will give her pleasure without waking her. He kisses the back of her neck, cups her breasts, then runs his hand slowly over her belly. He imagines her dreams suffused with the same light he saw on the horizon as he drove home along the river. He brushes his palm gently back and forth over her pubis until her breath begins to quicken, then he inserts his finger between the labial folds. So like a valve, he thinks before he can stop himself. He is about to leave it at that but she is awake now and presses back against him. He had meant to set the head of his penis softly against the mouth of her vagina, gently enter her, but she firmly grips his penis and inserts it, then drives her hips down, enveloping him quickly, completely. She draws away, rolls over on her stomach and he enters her again, pushes deeper into her, rising up into the darkened room, his two hands balanced flat on her shoulder blades. He spreads his own arms out. Hold me, she says. She means, hold her back. He spreads his own arms, pinions her wrists to the bed. Anatomically, he finds it difficult to see how she gets much pleasure from this position. Neither of them speak. The force with which their bodies meet takes their breath away. For a second he imagines he is on the bottom of the pile-up on his son's playing field, listening as the bodies build above him.

When she comes, he pulls out immediately. From now on, he thinks, I want to wear condoms. He has no plans, just a desire to constrain himself.

What's the matter?

Nothing.

No, tell me.

It just wasn't what I imagined.

What was that? she asks. A corpse?

He imagines running his fist through the fogged glass wall of the shower stall, but now instead of the force and release of his muscles, he imagines the jagged blades of glass, his unprotected wrist, the concentration he must use to extricate himself.

In the presence of strangers—all doctors fall into this category—her son never raises his head. Instead he absorbs every word. His posture, then, is an advantage. They discount him and speak as freely as if he weren't there.

It's a question of lifestyle, the first specialist tells her. I believe it is good for every child to take gym.

She feels a wave of sorrow, then one of rage. She looks at her son's small chest, the pectoral muscle on his left side distorted by the large, visible rectangle of the pacemaker.

Her son breathes rapidly through his mouth, the breaths a shallow and noisy compensation for the congestion in his lungs.

They want to put a balloon in there, he tells his father, so I can run like other boys.

She takes the receiver from him.

Honest to God, she tells her husband. That's what he said. I can't believe he could be so stupid. She turns her face to the wall as she talks. What does normal have to do with us?

Her daughter takes her son and seats him on the floor in front of the television. They are watching Lethal Weapon III and playing Clue. Her husband waits a moment, then begins to speak. She listens, getting her breath back. This feels normal. His measured tone. Her daughter's caretaking. Her outbreak. Her son's laugh, no less labored than his breathing, but pure as a bird's first flight.

How long am I going to have to put up with this? she once cried out to a therapist. As long as you have to, he said quietly. If she could, she would preserve this moment forever. The children in front of the television, arguing over Colonel Mustard, the rope, the conservatory. She and her husband consulting over the telephone, engaging for a second, a week, a year, in the luxury of choice.

The truth is they have no choice and they know it. At some point, they are going to have to trust someone. This doctor. Another one.

I went today and prayed for a miracle, she tells her husband in a lowered voice. She moves over to the window as she speaks. She can feel that stillness that overtakes her daughter when she is listening, more intense even than that of her son. It doesn't matter. They have no secrets from each other, any of them. They do, however, have the forms of normality, separation, and believe, all four of them, in preserving them. Arbitrary and beautiful as the chambers in the heart. Child. Adult. Life. Death. Blue blood. Red.

She pulls the white gauze curtain away from the window and stares out at the city. The horizon turns a salmon color and then a pale, heart-piercing yellow. If she turns in the opposite direction, the sky over the city is a deep translucent blue, coherent as the emotion in this room, ineradicably romantic.

It was chance, she tells her husband. The service. The woman priest so like her in appearance they could be mistaken for sisters. The prayer.

When I come next week, I'll go with you, he says. They talk about second opinions, which they will rigorously gather over the next five days, but they both know the decision has been made. They say if they don't do this, in two years they will need to replace the mitral valve. The building pressure could damage the pulmonary and tricuspid valves and these they may not be able to replace. They say. As if establishing a speaker could strip away the authority, the terror. They were—all of them—forever telling stories. No one more binding than the rest.

This is the playing field. What did he know? What could he possibly know?

Four years ago, when they had the last operation, there was a family in the hospital they became close friends with. The couple had a daughter her daughter's age. An infant son. He was five months old and had had as many operations. The last time, just after she and her family had left the hospital, the surgeons went in and put in a new aortic valve and the pressure blew out all the other valves. At the memorial service, it was all she could do to go up to the mother. Her daughter and theirs shook hands awkwardly. Their grief, she insists even now, has nothing to teach her.

There is no point, she and her husband decide, in their returning home before the procedure. Tomorrow she will schedule it; he will schedule his flight. For the next five days, she and the children will masquerade as tourists. In preparation, she pulls out of her bag the caps she has bought for each of them. She distributes them to the children as she says good-bye to her husband. She doesn't bother to tell him she misses him. He doesn't bother to tell her they are all he thinks about. These words, too, are part of the silenced heart of the family.

The silence, a voice speaks to her in her dreams, is alive. She holds her son's shivering heart in her hands and she feels a sound rising inside her so large and so fast it might flood the world. Already her whole head is ringing with the reverberation of these waves that are coming faster than anything the brain can assimilate.

She wakes, her heart pounding, her breath coming in short almost erotic bursts. She goes into the bathroom and locks the door and fumbles for the faucet in the dark. She runs cold water over her face, as if this would simulate tears. She puts her fists to her eyes. Her body convulses. Silently.

He is careful to explain every step of the procedure again to the father the day before he goes in. This time, the wife spends all her time looking out the window, blinking back tears. He feels exasperated with her. If only she would listen, he would be able to relieve her anxiety.

Who is he kidding?

The father listens attentively. He takes notes. He has clearly read up on the procedure. All the questions sound coached. He begins to feel like he is in Grand Rounds. I'd like to go back over that 49% that were not successful, the husband says, baring a fresh page in his notebook.

The wife's face is completely wet. She doesn't fumble for a handkerchief. She doesn't hide her head. He wishes she could control herself. What does she think, they don't care? A teaching hospital, his own wife always says to him, is not where the money is. It is where the bucks stop.

If it were my son, he says.

At this she turns and looks at him. He stops. There is no need to complete the thought. Something also makes him slightly uneasy. What was it he had said when the two of them met alone together? What has come over him that he has begun to repeat himself.

But he's not, the father says calmly. He is our child. He recaps his pen and flips his notebook closed. He slips it into the pocket of his jacket. He stands up, signaling the end of the interview. He goes over and puts his hands on his wife's shoulders. She smiles, shakes her head, and rises to her feet. The father extends his hand, and he reciprocates, taking it in his own firm grip. The father matches his pressure exactly. Halfway across the waiting room, the wife realizes she has forgotten and returns to shake his hand.

Until tomorrow, he says.

The pressure of her grip exceeds his own. She closes her eyes, rocks a little on her heels. He puts out his other hand to steady her but withdraws it quickly when she reopens her eyes. She has enormous green eyes. Faint streaks of mascara run down each cheek symmetric as tribal markings.

Tomorrow, she repeats. And the day after, and the day after that.

Their daughter and son rise from the couch in the waiting room. The boy shakes the etch a sketch globe until all the markings he has made disappear. The father waits patiently as the boy shakes then inspects the silvery sphere, then shakes again.

He waits patiently at the waiting room door for all of them to leave. The mother embraces the son, the father rests his hand on his daughter's shoulder as they walk down the hall. The boy says something and they all break out laughing. He walks back into his office and closes the door. In the summer, the leaves crowding at the windows tint the air in the office a pale, claustral green so he feels he is living under water.

He sees the police car as he turns the corner into his own street. His foot instinctively goes to the brake, then just as instinctively returns to the clutch when he realizes it is parked in front of his neighbor's house. He gears up once, twice, as he drives toward it. He pulls the car up to the garage door, but doesn't push the garage door opener. When he gets out of the car, he hears his sons out in the backyard. Laughing. Something hits the ground. His older son swears. He leans into he car and gathers his papers. Something hits the water. More laughter. Lighten up, he thinks. His wife is waiting for him in the doorway. She is wearing one of his t-shirts over her bathing suit. Her legs are as long and slim as when he first met her.

Just tell me it isn't us this time, he says as he leans to kiss her on the cheek. Count your blessings, she says. She walks back into the kitchen. Twice in the last six months they have had to collect their younger son at the police station. Graffiti on the high school walls. Drinking under age. One more time, he has warned him.

And then what, his wife asked. You're going to send him off to military school?

She has gone herself to talk to the coach. Asked him if he could take a greater interest in the boy. More laps. More push ups. More damage.

I'm going to shower, he calls to her. He could be washing away the traces of another woman's sweat and scent the way he goes at his skin. This fucking frosted cubicle is what his home life has come down to. The only place he can feel at rest.

What's eating him? his older son asks his wife as they sit down to dinner.

He's thinking of all the lives that depend on him, his wife says. She passes him the salad.

Never in a million years would I do what you do, his younger son says. He looks up, surprised that the boy can stitch so many words together without profanity or guttural ejaculations.

Huh? he says. He hands the boy the salad.

No way, the boy says. He is two inches taller than his father already. Forty pounds heavier.

Too constructive for you? he asks.

No, the boy says. He gulps a forkful of pasta, a single frond flicks at his lower lip, then disappears. Brutal, he says.

Smiling, his wife looks down at her plate.

I do not have to put up with this, he thinks as he sets his knife neatly on his plate and reaches for his glass of water.

It's worse, his wife insists when he tries to call her on the behavior later. If you really imagine what you're doing to them. These boys are playing. What you do is for real.

Her husband has taken the children out for a walk. She sits at the window of the hotel room watching for their return. Her thoughts whirl. She recalls vividly a black and white snapshot of herself in her playpen as an infant, staring out somberly between the bars. Had she felt safe in there? Now the images gets to her as if someone had ripped off a half-formed scab. She sees her son the last time he was in the hospital, his body subdivided by the restraining bars drawn up on either side of his hospital bed. She was sitting in the chair beside the bed, so she sees him at an angle, subtly enlarged, his pale skin, his brightly figured pajamas. His small hand resting flat against the wrinkled white sheet is perfectly framed between two of the bars.

I just want to keep them out of jail, the doctor said to her. He latched his hands together behind his head. She was standing and he looked up at her and she realized how the armchair and the desk had never been on the level, she had had to look up. It gets better, she had said.

All they like are these brutal contact sports, football, lacrosse. All they like, he repeats as he gets to his feet, is to do damage.

And you raised them, she says. She is joking, chiding. The image that comes to her is her own daughter bending over to straighten her son's shirt and tuck the tails in. The thoughtless grace of the gesture.

The doctor smiles at her, intimately. No, he says. It's my wife's fault. She raised them. I was never home. He throws back his head and roars with laughter.

For some reason, she can tell no one about this. Not her husband, her daughter. She can't describe the leaves broad as hands spreading out on the grimy window panes. The element of seduction. Vulnerability. She feels the pressure of his hand in hers. Two blocks away, walking toward her, their figures often indistinguishable from the trunks of the trees flanking the sidewalk, she makes out the three familiar figures. The sky is a pearly gray as it has been all day, because of the heat and humidity, so the image of her family seems like an old black and white photograph. She can still feel the pressure of the doctors' handshake. She watches her husband pause, bend over their son, then, kneeling down, offer his back to ride on.

She has the door to their room open when they exit from the elevator, singing. She helps her son dismount then shoos him into the shower. Do you want to go with us tomorrow? she asks her daughter. Why do you ask? she says crossly. She takes the girl in her arms. Her daughter's long hair brushes across her shoulders and some primordial memory surfaces and dissolves before she can put a word to it. She presses her hand flat on her daughter's head. They are of a height now so at times it feels as if they have shifted places in a mirror. But her daughter's skull is so firm, so perfectly shaped, she knows she has had as little hand in molding it as she has in molding her daughter's admirable character. There is nothing to be afraid of, she tells her. Her daughter pulls away, laughing.

You should hear yourself, she says. She imitates the break in her mother's voice perfectly. Do me a favor, her daughter tells her. Leave him to us tonight. You've got a bad case of the tragedies.

It's not true, she thinks. Before all this, she always saw her life in black and white. In two dimensions. Now she sees it in kodachrome, is constantly amazed by the mysterious densities and levities of the flesh.

That's what gets to her tonight. How young they all seem. Her son's skin is unmarked by anything but the doctor's scalpel. Her daughter, at fifteen, is eros incarnate. Even her husband and she, when they undress for bed, see bodies that appear a decade younger than their faces.

Her son comes out of the shower releasing a cloud of steam into the air. Her daughter goes in. She helps him dress for bed then gives him over to his father. The two of them sit together with their heads braced against the headboard of the other double bed. Her daughter has, in an unaccustomed fit of selfishness, claimed the second bed and put her brother in the fold-up cot. The claim is so unusual, she hasn't objected and neither has her son. Even her husband has let it pass without comment. She hopes that her daughter will do the same with this reversal when she comes out of the shower.

She busies herself unlocking and lowering the cot, double checking that the sheets have been changed so that her daughter will have no basis for complaint. She lies down on the other double bed and listens with her eyes closed to the harmonies of her husband and her son's voices. This strange rhythm they always make together. Her husband's voice, low, mellifluous, rapid. Her son's voice interrupts occasionally, each word turned over in his mind, polished by consciousness, before it is shared.

Are you scared? her daughter asks her in a whisper as she sits down on the edge of the bed and unwraps her wet hair from a white towel.

What a question, she says, taking the brush from her daughter's hand. She holds a fistful of hair close to the scalp, stroking gently from the roots out.

What's wrong with it? her daughter asks. She can see the muscles in her daughter's shoulders relax with each brush stroke.

What's in a name? Scared? Alive? We are all alive.

Her daughter smiles slightly and closes her eyes.

This, her husband says in his low, steady voice, is the aorta. This is the pulmonary vein. This is where the wire, they call it a catheter, will enter your heart.

What color, the boy asks, is the balloon?

When their son is no longer conscious, the nurse ushers them out of the room. She kisses the boy's forehead. His father squeezes his hand.

They both nod at the doctor, who smiles automatically then turns back to the screen.

In the waiting room, her husband pulls out some papers he has left to grade. Her daughter opens up a beauty magazine. She tells them she is going to buy some coffee. Neither of them offer to accompany her. As she leaves the waiting room, she almost stumbles, as if a wire is attached to her navel, driving right back through her spine.

This is not a mystery, her husband said to her son the night before. A man, a wire, a balloon

Remember, he said. Our hearts are no bigger than our fists. Many of these procedures were done on infants. Imagine the size of their fists. Their valves. It shouldn't surprise you that some of them died.

I don't know for sure what we'll find, he said. Every valve is different. Every heart.

The chambers of the heart aren't hollow, they are filled with cords. This is what she found almost shocking when she first looked at anatomical photographs.

She has imagined the stitches in the leaflets of her son's mitral valve. Imagined that the patch that divides the walls of the ventricles is clear enough to see through, clear enough to throw your reflection back at you. She imagines herself on either side of the patch, red blood, blue, and knows that wherever she stands what rushes against the far side of the window is black as the future.

As she descends alone in the elevator, she can feel the exact pressure of the doctor's hand in hers. No different in texture from those half-forgotten lovers. From her husband. Are you scared? her daughter whispers. There is no mystery here, her husband tells her son. She thinks sometimes she married him for his voice, for its sweet promise of reason. It has never betrayed them.

On the ground floor she searches out the chapel. She has never entered it before. She kneels at the back of the room away from the altar, as far as possible from the cross that she is relieved to see bears no crucifix. This morning, she would tear it off if she saw it. She does not believe in suffering. She closes her eyes. She feels a stabbing pain in her groin where the catheter enters her son's vein. In the empty chapel she hears her son's labored, beloved breathing, she feels her daughter's hair fanning out over her shoulder and her breast, she feels the moist direct pressure of the doctor's fallible hand, she hears her husband's slow, low reasonable voice. This is the blood, the vessel, the violent heart of her faith. She has never known such desire.

The relief of work, he thinks, the incision made, the catheter in place, the first balloon inflating, is that you can think of nothing else. Before he clears his mind completely, he imagines his son sitting on the opposite side of the gurney listening to him as attentively as the young resident.

I do love him, he hears himself tell her. His mind empties. He is the screen. The wire. The clear mask over the boy's mouth. The valve giving, slightly, ever so slightly, as the balloon fills. He stops. Calculates. Begins again. He will do this as many times as he needs to.

Remember, he says to the resident, we are not looking for perfection here. Only some measurable gain.

The boy dreams he is swimming toward the bottom of the sea. The light spreads out like a thousand beckoning arms. He retreats, skimming along the surface of the water, looking with one stroke up at the blazing sun, with the next into the dark heart at the center of light that unfolds petal by petal below him. He laughs as he hears his hands slap against the water furious and strong as a racer's. He doesn't want to stop, even if he wins. He wants to keep going, and going, and going.

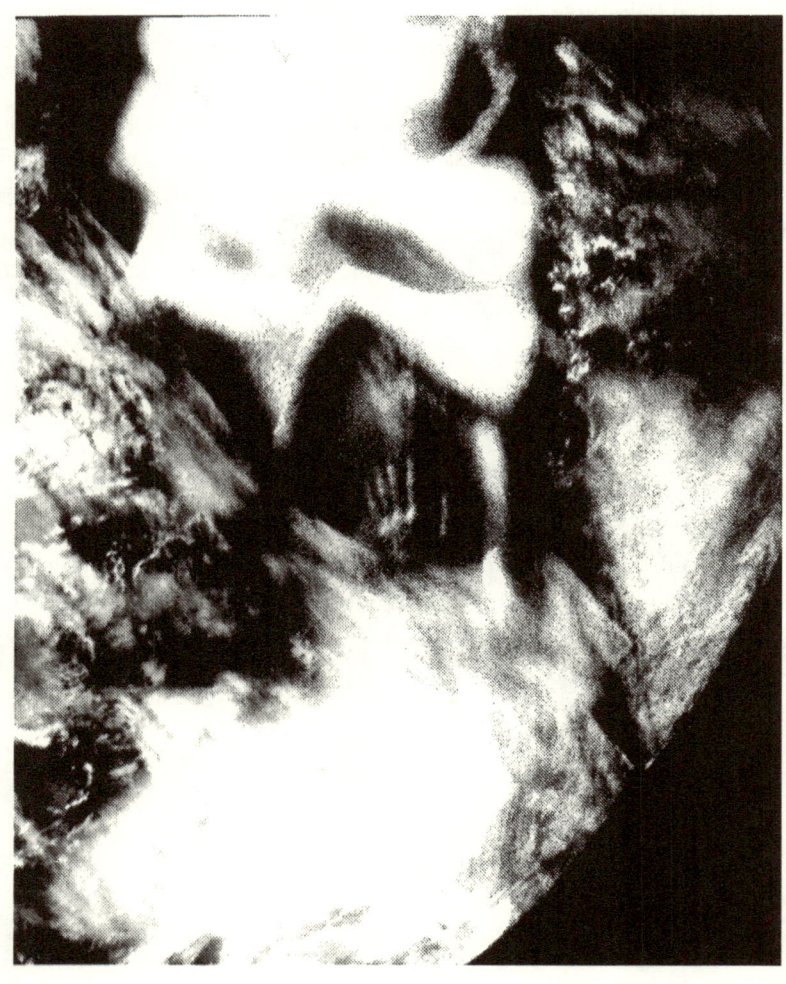

HANG GLIDING

They say I am lucky that I discovered it so early, that it hadn't spread. A little operation, a little excision from the muscle on my left calf. I can see it spinning in the little jar of alcohol my surgeon held up to me in the recovery room.

"Six weeks radiation for insurance and you'll be right as rain," he said. At least he didn't say little again.

What I want to talk about is something big. Permanent.

What they can't change is that at the age of nineteen years and thirty-two days a veil was ripped away from the world and nothing can replace it. I'm not of a mind to, although people find that hard to believe, but some days I can't stop blinking my eyes, the colors are so sharp, the odors so astringent. Maybe a veil is a bad metaphor. It is isn't out there, after all, that the change has taken place. I remember my baby sister Cindy after she was given glasses exclaiming about how bright the world was. She discovered edges, categories. But I don't find this process reassuring at all. Maybe it is like, too late in life to assimilate it, having light hit the retina for the first time. I bet those late seers feel like me, betrayed, amazed, invaded by something so pervasive there is no relief. They too feel they'll never be able to relate any of the categories they've learned to this sensory bludgeoning the world calls sight.

I wonder what I will be able to say in the dorm when I return next month.

In my dreams, tumors orbit like planets.
There is a space that seems to last for a century between every word I hear.
I am cured.

My mother and my sister Cindy and my brother Will look at me when I come down for breakfast with the same expression of eagerness on each of their faces. They want me to tell them that everything is back to normal. It troubles me that I refuse them this little gift. They have been so loyal to me, why can't I reciprocate?

After my father died ten years ago, my mother did everything possible to make us feel that we were normal, that this shouldn't make us suspicious of the world, or our own genes, or God. My father didn't die of cancer, or someone else's drunken turn of a steering wheel. He died absurdly young of heart disease. A congenital valve defect that went undetected. I forget which valve it was now, although time and again Mom showed us the pictures in the medical textbook she studied constantly for the month following his diagnosis and the months following his death. Now, she keeps assuring us, the surgical techniques are better. We would none of us die on the operating table like my father did. If we had a similar defect. Which we definitely don't. She has taken us all to the cardiologist for ultrasounds and keeps the photos in a large brown envelope in his desk in the study, ready to pull them out to show us at a minute's notice that we are all fine. We went along then. I even went over their images with Will and Cindy to show Mom how well I understood those mysterious shadows, to show she could always count on me. I would keep up the refrain when she was at work or out shopping. Normal. We were all normal. Normally sad. Normally hopeful.

When I looked at that little glass jar with the tumor floating in it, I thought at first I was seeing a little embryo. It might be the after image from my first semester biology lab, all those embryos floating in the cabinet to the left of my desk. Sharks. Cats. Fetal pigs. Humans. All with a blur of red around the edges. Something to do with the preserving fluids. I had to blink and call myself back. Tumor. This is a tumor. But I wasn't really sure. The surgeon took the jar away too quickly. I couldn't bring it up clearly in my mind to double check. I had just the vague impression of something turning, whitely veiled, in a thick liquid. Focusing in, the edges of the jar dissolve and the image of that turning globe is everything. We could have been in outer space seeing the insubstantial moon of another planet mindlessly gyrating. Or inside a womb watching the future form. Outer space. Cancer. Fetus.

Crazy life. Nothing was in its established place anymore. Fetus encysted in a muscle, making it impossible to walk. Or in the lung, making it impossible to breath.

To understand how crazy this all felt, you have to know I'm a virgin and have never had a steady boyfriend. Here I was in the recovery room seeing a fetus floating before my eyes when I've only had one kiss touching tongues in my whole life.

I'm not deformed or anything, if that's what you're thinking. My mother calls my face studious. My brother Will calls it handsome. They mean I don't smile a lot, I have a steady gaze, and my cheekbones are sharp as a pirate's. I've always known what I wanted and a teenage lover was never on the list. It might be, as my mom hints, due to my having lost my father when I was so young, but I think it may have more to do with pimples and familiarity. It's hard to imagine sharing any kind of bodily fluid with boys I've known since I was five. You could call my focus on my studies a kind of sublimation, or a very conscious eye on the main chance. College, for me, was going to be the beginning of my life, my real life. It was when I was going to blossom, and I wanted to find the best place in the world to do that. For me, this meant staying close enough to home to keep an eye on Mom and Will and Cindy, but far enough away that I could do some straying from the straight and narrow if I felt so inclined.

I didn't, actually. I was so astonished by what was permissible at my college, it was hard for me to see what more could be included. We had, from our first week there, seminars in gay consciousness, racial consciousness, gender consciousness, new male consciousness, pacifism, class consciousness, eco-sensitivity. Some friends on the hall I lived on had one on silly jokes that respect the sensitivities of every living thing. All they did was smoke grass, look at each other meaningfully, and keen like hyenas. The floor below us specialized in crudities that would make corpses cringe if they were listening.

It was a happening place, my little liberal college 150 miles from home. I went home twice a month for the first semester. At Christmas, Mom let me know she was nearly weaned and could bear up if I just came back during regular vacations. The person who seemed most disappointed by this turn of events was my roommate Melissa. She liked coming home with me. She thought my family was so wonderfully normal, mainly because my father was dead and duly beatified, while her parents, recently divorced and scandalously rapidly remarried, were turning to salt before her eyes. "You always have a home with us," my mother would tell her when we were leaving, and Melissa's eyes would mist with gratitude.

Normal. We were all so wonderfully normal.

Until that night, nicking my leg when I was shaving, I felt the lump. I had turned nineteen two days before. I was feeling less than desirable, which was why I was shaving my legs in the showers at midnight. I had just dyed my hair bright green. I was shaving my legs in order to build up the courage to shave my head. I couldn't wait two weeks for the dye to wash out. I thought.

And then I stopped thinking. My fingers went back to the spot on the back of my calf where the blood was running in a thin, blushing stream. Testing. Testing. For two weeks I kept testing, when I was sitting cross-legged on my bed reading *Frankenstein* for our world culture class, when I leaned down to slip *The Epic of Gilgamesh* into my knapsack at the end of my Introduction to Religion class. I just kept seeing a stone in my mind. Something dark but beautifully marbled, like the gallstones my grandmother used to keep in her jewelry box. I don't know how long I would have gone on doing this if Melissa hadn't found out.

I had been talking to Mom on the phone, and all the time, my hand kept going to my leg, just rubbing it automatically. "Everything's fine here," I told her. "Great."

I could tell she wanted more, so I started telling her about the reading for each of my classes. Boredom is a kind of weaning process, I think. But gentle. Normal. We were separating out painlessly, Mom and me. So I was smiling as I was droning on, feeling her attention, finally, turn away, just as it would if I were still living at home and she knew there was always tomorrow. Tomorrow. Time to pick up a conversation, drop one, start a new one.

And all the time the inside of my palm was memorizing the shape and hardness of that nugget in my calf. My skin felt so soft, and the tumor felt so definite. And this huge dark river inside me was washing away the foundations of my life while I was quietly, steadily talking to my mother. It wasn't until after I hung up that I broke down. If Melissa had been in there, I would have been able to hide it. It was just being alone, undefended before those two realities that I couldn't in any way connect that did me in. Talking with Mom, just like usual. And my hand stroking my leg. Like usual. And then there was this dark river of sound just roaring out of me. That's what it felt like, but it was just in my head, that dark roaring sound. I never let it out, just began to shake with the force of it.

Melissa walked in talking to me before she even saw me. "You wouldn't believe—," she was saying, and then she stopped. She came over and sat on the bed. I had my eyes closed but I could feel her settle down on the far end of the bed and lean forward and touch my hand.

"Tell me," she said. Her voice was so gentle, I thought, this can't be Melissa. Melissa is a great roommate, but she isn't subtle. She isn't quiet. I find this relaxing. I don't need to be listening so closely for my cues. I forget sometimes that subtlety isn't the same as intelligence. It isn't the same as kindness either.

What I couldn't handle was the kindness. The way there wasn't any undercurrent at that moment of look at me, watch out for me. That's how I was protecting myself, you see. I was saying, I won't worry Mom with this. What I meant was I couldn't worry myself. It was Mom who took us for those ultrasounds. Mom who kept the pictures in the desk in the study. I never believed anything would happen to me. Cindy maybe. Will. Mom. But never me. My job, my destiny was to be there for them. Be there for me.

"Tell me," Melissa said.

"Something's wrong. I can feel it. Something's really wrong." I took her hand and put it on my leg. "Just press down lightly. You can't miss it."

I opened my eyes then and I could see the expression on her face as she felt it and then I closed my eyes again and just went riding down that dark, roaring river for as long as I could, feeling it push me over rocks, roll me over and over like an old log. I felt so easy, not fighting off the current, the noise, the momentum.

And then Melissa was shaking my shoulders in her strong small hands. "Cry," she said. "Would you please just start crying."

The request was so impossible, it pulled me out of that place that only has sound and sensation, no language. Crying, I've learned since then, is something I only do in front of Mom and, at some level, only at her instigation. I cry to assure her that I am, that we, the Turners, are normal. We grieve. We go on.

"Will you just start crying, Claire," Melissa said and I opened my eyes, whoosh.

"Why?" I asked. My tone was so normally quizzical, it shocked both of us, and then we both started laughing. It really is dreadful being nineteen.

Tragedy. Comedy. Farce. There isn't a category that can hold for more than an hour.

"What are you going to do?" Melissa asked. "Revise that," she said immediately. She could see the river beginning to rise somewhere inside me, I suppose. "We're going to the clinic first thing tomorrow morning."

"Mom can't know," I said.

"Until there's something definite, you're right. Then she'll need to know for insurance purposes. The only thing they never learn about are abortions."

Melissa had had one four months ago. We'd made up a pool on our floor to pay for it. But we insisted she follow it up with Norplant—and better taste in men (although in our freshman dorm, men is a euphemism).

It felt so safe having Melissa there with me at the infirmary, and then at the local hospital when I went in for an MRI scan. It wasn't that she knew any more than I did about what was happening. It was just that I didn't have to reassure her.

"This is the pits," I could say. "This is a real bitch." She would nod and we would both pick up our textbooks and start studying. Anything to keep our minds off of what this all might mean.

"Don't you want your parents here?" the surgeon asked me when I went in for a consult.

"Not yet," I said. "Not until I know something definite."

"We have to operate. Isn't that definite enough?" On his desk, he had a photo of his family. He had three daughters, two of whom could have been around my age. You never know, of course. People keep pictures around that give the impression that time stopped a decade ago. Our house is filled with pictures of the five of us, but there are no pictures of us as a family of four. Only school portraits of Will, Cindy and me individually.

"My mother will take this hard. I've been trying to buy us some time. Buy myself some time."

I could see by his expression that he admired me. He had the idea I was strong and generous. I didn't see it that way. I still don't. I was being self-preserving. I still am.

That's why I can't give them that one little gift they wish for so strongly every morning. I can't, I just can't, sit down at the table and act as if everything is back to normal. I am tired to death of pretending I ever knew what that term meant. I didn't. I don't. I won't ever.

It isn't normal two days after your nineteenth birthday to discover a cancerous tumor in the calf of your left leg. It isn't normal to see your father in a coffin when you're ten. But it is life. It is *my* life. It is normal for me. Just like my love for Mom and Cindy and Will and my disgust of pimply boys. I am tired of pretending, just to please Mom or my friends in the dorm, that my own experience isn't real, definitive. Because it is. These are the experiences that have made and are making me. I don't have energy left to act as if they shouldn't be happening. What earthly use is it to me to think like that?

I understand why Mom and Melissa get on so well. They both have such clear and similar notions of the way life should be. We should all die quietly in our beds at the age of eighty. There should be no congenital defects, no childhood cancers. No meaningless accidents. Marriages should never fail.

It makes me ache to see how much energy they use persuading themselves, and, in Mom's case, those around her, that such important events as sickness, death, divorce, and remarriage are meaningless. When we can't control them, the best we can do is pretend they haven't happened, or that they haven't changed us irreversibly. What matters most to them is the way the world is supposed to be. They pride themselves on how much they can make the world conform to their preconceptions. It makes me ache because I love them both so much and I can't protect either of them from what is coming. *I* am part of what's coming.

Whatever my mother says, she hasn't gotten over my father's death. What she can't accept is that she never saw it coming. The last month, she was so busy calling doctors, checking references, getting consults, she never just sat quietly beside him crying. She never said good-bye. That is why it was so important to her that Will and Cindy and I could cry. She had so much grief she couldn't let go of except through us. We grieved for her so she could comfort herself through comforting us. I think all families have these transmutations of feelings. Maybe that is the working definition of family, those people you're unclear where they end and you begin. Or maybe that is the definition of childhood. Maybe adulthood is putting those feelings back where they belong and just aching with empathy at the insufficiency of all our categories. Me. You. The future.

Whatever. It feels to me that Melissa and Mom and I are all involved in similar processes, but they may come out feeling closer to each other than either of them does to me. It hurts me, this prediction, the same way I am hurt every morning by my inability to meet the need in the eyes of my brother and sister and mother. Tell us, they keep asking me, silently, so silently, please tell us nothing has changed. I feel so thick, so opaque. Like I am a concrete wall blocking off their view of a happy, hopeful future. I feel guilty and also enraged. I feel they don't want to see me, even though they think they do. They want to see *through* me. They want to see the way things are supposed to be. I just want them to see me. I hate feeling that maybe they never did. All they saw was an idea, a template. Like one of those silly ads in the paper: Wanted for long term committed relationship, woman who likes to take long walks at sunset, listen to classical jazz, dance salsa and browse used bookstores; 38-26-36, blue eyes. There aren't, ever, enough items you can put on that list to make a person. How would they describe me, I keep wondering as I sip my coffee and guiltily look off into space. *How would they describe me if I died today?*

As vaguely as we describe our father, Jerry Turner? As vaguely as Melissa describes the family she is wild about losing? I can't see them in the people I've met with her this week. To be honest, I don't recognize my friend Melissa in this context. I don't think she does either, or does and wants to change skins with someone, anyone, just to win a little breathing room. Melissa is the youngest child in her family, by almost a decade, so she's a bit like an only child and a lot like the youngest. In that way, our characters are very different. But we share a strong sense of what we need to do to hold our families together. Until the last two months, what I needed to do and what I wanted to do were identical. Now its as if there are two images and they're sliding off each other like a poorly printed photograph in a newspaper. There's no sense of depth, just these slipsliding cyan and magenta images. For Melissa, I'm not sure it's exactly the same.

I think she must have known for some time that she was what held her parents together. She did it by refusing to recognize that this was her job. *She* needed them. *She* was the child. If she didn't see the signs, acknowledge them, they had no significance. I ask her sometimes what hurts her most. "They didn't waste any time about it. I hadn't even left the house before they were shacking up with other people." But another time she'll say, "I can't believe this is happening to me." Like she really hadn't seen this coming.

"What do you want them to do?" I ask her. "Stay together for four more whole years just so you can see them sulking together at vacations?" It feels selfish to me, her attitude. I would give anything to see Mom go out, get on with her life. Melissa just gets pissed off at me and says I don't get it. Maybe this is the difference between being the oldest and the youngest. I really don't get it. Mom always wanted me to grow up. That was my job. I was her understudy. She was the one who chose the play, the role. I just went along. But I never confused the role with me or the play with life, even when I chose to act it for my mother's sake.

Maybe that's what Mom and Melissa have in common. They believe in the lines themselves. They believe in the plays. Another is that they don't feel they did any choosing of the scripts. My mother, for example, doesn't feel she had any choice about how to respond to my father's death. She had to carry on bravely. And that meant we, who loved her and her desperate grip on life, had to follow her lead. From what I can piece together, Melissa developed her own script about the way things were supposed to be in her family, and her parents willingly played their bit parts. But their most important role was as audience, applauding the innocent inventiveness of their daughter. Only Melissa believed it was the whole world, those dinners where she regaled them with detailed descriptions of everything that went on at school or in the mall, chattering away so that no one would notice the silence and unease between her parents. Who was she fooling? Who were they?

As a by-stander, what impresses me is how long they continued the masquerade just for Melissa. Not long enough, that's what she's wild about, to preserve her assumptions about what marriages should be, but a long time. Longer than she'll admit. We've visited both her parents and their new spouses this week and if you listen to them talk to each other, the couples have been together a pretty long time. Two years in the case of Melissa's mom. Longer for her father. Although Melissa feels far more betrayed by her dad than her mom. I'm not sure exactly why. Maybe it's because his new wife doesn't fall so easily into the old pattern. She doesn't want Melissa to spend the whole evening talking about herself, about college. She wants to talk about herself. Her own children. She wants to talk about Melissa's father as if she has some personal knowledge of him. Knowledge Melissa may not share.

"How *dare* she?" Melissa says to me as soon as we are upstairs. "*We* this and *we* that! Who is she to talk like that about my Daddy."

I look at my best friend completely amazed. This isn't the young woman who took me under her wing the first week at school, who talks so wisely to my mother about what may be going on inside me, why I am withdrawn, brooding. It's true, I stand outside the living room in our house listening to Mom and Melissa talking, and I feel such gratitude toward Melissa for taking my place. Shoring up Mom. But I can't seem to do the same for her here, and I don't know why. It's so uncomfortable here, all I want to do is leave. Take Melissa with me. Not this Melissa, the Melissa I know from school and her visits to my own home. So I'm doing to her what I feel is happening to me, letting these images slip off each other, losing depth and complexity. Even if I don't want to admit it, Melissa is both these people.

I don't want to admit it. You see, in these last few months, I've come to depend on my understanding of Melissa. My understanding of our friendship. I've been able to hang on to that longer than I have anything else. I'm reluctant to give it up—especially right now before we both go back to school. But I can't be the audience she needs me to be. I need to have her be my own understudy. The play Melissa is starring in here in her father's home has no room for dying at nineteen. And if it doesn't have any room for dying, I'm not sure it has any room for me.

I feel so disloyal to Melissa at these uncomfortable dinners because I feel more like her new stepmother than I do her dad. While Melissa is chattering on so brightly, her dad looks at her with this expression of amused tolerance. Indulgent. As if Melissa is ten years old. And Melissa just goes faster and faster, hanging on to that attention the only way she knows how. But I can see someone else looking out of her eyes every now and then when she stops to take a breath and turns and sees me there, watching. Her face flushes and she bends down toward her plate. I wonder if my expression is anything like her stepmother Sophie's.

Tonight Sophie's son, Johnson, came over for dinner. Melissa acted as if he wasn't there. It was rather shocking. At my house, she's so careful to include Will and Cindy in conversations, to ask them what's going on at school or on the hockey team and to pick up the conversation the next time she comes. They can't get enough of her. Johnson is about twenty-six, so it's different. But not completely. I think Melissa's dad noticed what was happening, but he pretended not to, even when Melissa said, for the fourth time, "Daddy, do you remember when you and Mom and I—"

At other dinners, every now and then Melissa's dad would look over at Sophie and give a little shrug and a small smile, as if to say, isn't she sweet, or give her a little slack please, and Sophie would just look off into space and let her go on. But tonight, with Johnson there, Sophie did more than that. She said, "Ok, Melissa. Now it's time to hear about what Johnson has been doing. And Claire. And Walter. And me."

Melissa looked at her with the whitest rage. Then she looked at her father. "Daddy?"

Her father just smiled in this small, embarrassed way. Like he knew all the rules had been turned topsy turvy but there was nothing he could do. Melissa closed her eyes and the tears just ran down her face until it shone all over. She looked so grown up just sitting there, frozen like that. Nothing like the little girl expressions she uses when she's talking to her parents. None of us said anything for the longest time.

Finally Sophie said, "And what have you been doing this summer, Claire? Are you as eager as Melissa to return to school?"

At this Melissa opened her eyes and said, "You don't understand. None of you understand." She stood up so quickly her chair tipped over behind her, crashing on the floor. She looked at her father and said, "I'll never forgive you for this you know."

"Oh sweetie," he said as she marched out of the room. He started to get up to follow her.

"Don't," Sophie said. So he didn't. He picked up her chair instead.

I didn't follow her either and I'm still trying to understand why. I'm not sure Melissa will ever forgive me. I can understand that. What I'm still trying to understand is why I didn't do what I could feel she wanted me to, why I needed, in fact, to do the opposite. It doesn't feel right after all she's done for me. And it can't be as simple as my wanting to talk a little more with Johnson, can it?

"And you," Sophie asked again after we heard Melissa mount the last step and slam the door to the guestroom. "Are you looking forward to going back to college?"

"I don't know if Melissa mentioned it, but I took most of the last semester off."

Johnson leaned forward attentively, flashing a quick smile at both his mother and Melissa's dad.

"I dropped out the second semester of my sophomore year," Johnson said. "Best thing I ever did although it sent my parents around the bend. It was better than flunking out, which I would have done. I just couldn't make myself study. It all felt so silly, so irrelevant. How was one more course on existentialism going to change the course of history?"

"I didn't drop out to find myself," I said. "I discovered a tumor in my leg in February. With the operation and the radiation, it just felt easier to stay at home until the treatment was over."

I had two more bites of chicken on my plate. I moved them around with my fork and knife. When I talk now, it feels like each word just orbits out there in the darkness in a pattern I can't fathom. I never expect an answer, just rest in the absence of gravity, how easy it is for the world to drift apart, particle by particle. Longing is a weak kind of gravity. Loving is the kind that makes you know the universe, ultimately, turns back toward its own source. My mother loves like that. Melissa does too. I'm not sure about me anymore.

"One reason I dropped out my sophomore year was I learned that my best friend from high school had just tested positive for HIV. It knocked me silly. And it wasn't even my life. Just the idea that this guy I knew so well, who I'd told just about everything I had inside me, wasn't what I'd imagined him to be was a shock. But to think that he was going to die—that turned the other shock all around as well. I couldn't get my balance. I'd broken up with my first serious girlfriend and so I'd called him to bitch and moan about it, and he wasn't interested. He was always interested. I just didn't get it. And then all this stuff poured out. I didn't know what to say. I thought I was the dimmest guy on earth not to have picked up that he was gay. I couldn't figure out where the fraud was—the friendship itself or backing off from it. For a time there, I thought I was gay too, that maybe I'd always been in love with him and just didn't know it. I dropped out and went to Chicago where he was in school.

"I guess I thought I was going to nurse him on his death bed. Only problem was, he was having a great time. It was like finding out about this made something reorganize inside him, and for the first time he was totally sure about what he was going to do with his life. And falling in love with me wasn't where it was for him. He was into chaos theory, the new physics. 'Not every man is a turn on,' he told me. 'You were always just my friend.' I was so relieved and so offended by that 'just', I can't tell you. So there I was, alone with my own muddle. I certainly wasn't going to be able to resolve it by projecting it all on him. I was nothing to him compared to the equations he played with night and day."

"So what did you do?"

"Got a job working at a halfway house for the mentally ill. I figured I was halfway there and they were halfway back, so the understanding should be near perfect." Johnson laughed and stretched back in his chair.

"Did it help?" I leaned forward as I spoke as if there were only the two of us at the table. I could feel how his mother and Melissa's dad were feeling he was a little out of line turning the attention toward himself, but I felt tears beginning to burn on the inside of my eyes, I was so grateful.

"It got me out of my head," he said. "It gave me some perspective."

"I've thought of volunteering in a hospice when I go back to school."

"You might prefer hang-gliding. It's my latest passion. I find it a wonderful antidote to every clingy, security-oriented preoccupation I may have."

"Like living," I said. I looked at Melissa's dad and Johnson's mother, the shocked looks on their faces and suddenly I started to laugh. It was like I was just riding out there on an invisible wind.

"Hang-gliding. Now why didn't I think of that?"

"You want, I can take you sometime."

I nodded, hitting the ground with a crash. I'd never be coming back. I wasn't even sure Melissa would let me back in the bedroom we were sharing. ("My mother has a bedroom especially for me," Melissa had hissed after Sophie showed us up to the guestroom our first night. "It's always ready. But she uses this one for everyone, her children as well as me. It's like we're all just passing through. You too.")

"I had a lump removed from my breast five years ago," Sophie said. "They told me I was lucky. It hadn't spread. I had radiation just to be sure. But I'm always checking, even now. It rearranged things for me, let me make some difficult choices."

"All of which she kept from me until it was too late for me to project my own chaos on her. Talk about self-interest," Johnson said.

"It was harder to tell Johnson than anyone else. As long as I didn't say anything to him, I could pretend that it was just a bad dream, something I could wake up from someday." Sophie looked at Melissa's father as she was talking. I wondered if she'd ever told him, or if there was something, even now, she wasn't saying. Melissa's father is a physician, so maybe that was the way they met. Maybe he was one of her difficult choices.

"For me, telling my mother was the worst part. It still is." I looked first at Sophie, then at Melissa's dad. "Melissa helped me so much. I would never have gotten through it without her. She went with me to the doctors. She came home with me when I had to tell Mom. She kept on visiting me all through the radiation. She's the daughter my mother has dreamed of having, I sometimes think. They're so alike it's amazing."

Suddenly, in my mind's eye, I could see Melissa and Mom sitting at the table in our kitchen. Those tired white curtains, printed with different fruits and vegetables, which my mother put up a month before my father died, fluttering in the summer night. They are filled with such a fierce, protective rage at life. For me. They are filled with such a fierce, protective rage for me. They want me to live forever. They want me never to change, to move away, to make gentle, tremulous love to the death flowering inside me. They don't want my hand slipsliding across my shin, double checking. They don't want me hang-gliding. They want what I can never give them. Permanence.

I sit there with these three total strangers crying for everything I can't change: the look on my mother's face when she looks up from my father's open coffin; the look in her eyes when, Melissa holding my hand, I tell her about the tumor and then she comes over to hug me and begins to cry, for the first time, for herself, or is she crying for me because I can't cry for myself? Here, among strangers, I'm crying for the girl with green hair and her gentle, resigned distaste for her own body, shaving her legs at midnight. I'm grieving for the girl who read all those ultrasounds to her brother and sister. I'm grieving for the girl who can't go back in time with her best friend. I'm grieving for the young woman who will walk into her dorm room in a few weeks time using a cane and will see all those young men and women looking at her as if she were deformed, truly ugly, and who will be filled with this wild remorse and desire to go back to her home, to descend the stairs and walk into the kitchen and hold the eyes of her beloved mother and brother and sister and spread her arms like wings and say, "I just want you to know how blessed I feel to be here today."

And suddenly I feel free, anchored in my own body, my own

experience, crying at my own instigation before three total strangers who cannot protect me from who I was, am, or will be. I can feel the fierce force of my own gravitational field. I don't want to die. I want to enjoy the puzzled gaze of these three strangers who mirror my own confusion back to me so clearly and without entreaty. I want to talk with Melissa and invite her home with me. Immediately. I want to hug my mom when I get there in a way that is so absent-minded and natural it makes her believe that nothing has or ever will change between us. I want to take a photo of the five of us—Mom, Melissa, Cindy, Will and me—and hang it in a prominent place. I want to slip my own MRI scans into the envelope with the ultrasounds and lock the drawer they're kept in and lose the key. And I want to dream night after night of hang gliding with Johnson.

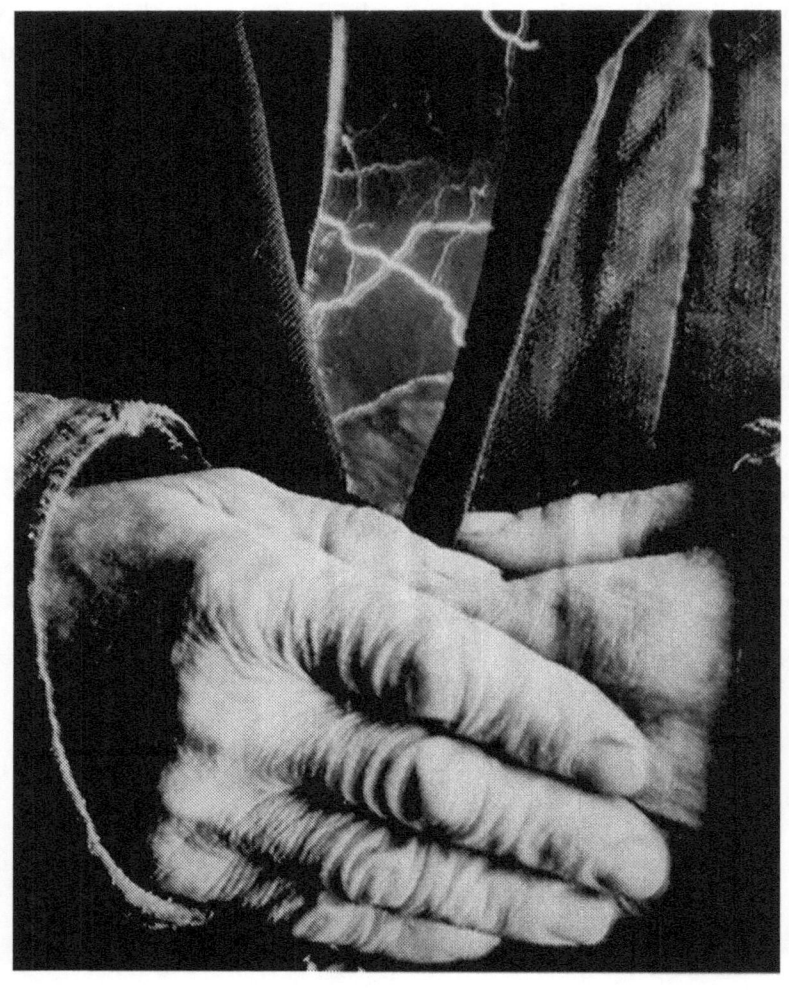

MI VOZ

Many people imagine I cannot speak at all. When I do answer, they look startled, as if the sound itself were an indictment. My voice is so low and rough it sounds as if I have yelled myself hoarse at a cock fight or in a bar. When they hear me, I see their pity harden into contempt. I don't mind. There are all types of deception. The prince wears the skin of the frog, the wolf wears the fleece of the lamb.

Today, when my *patrón* asks me to scrub the tiles above the waterline, I only nod and do his bidding. But I wonder why he must have this *piscina* with the ocean stretching out forever just behind the next row of houses. I believe it is because the pale green glow of the water at night makes him feel like a rich man. He stands up there on the balcony and looks down on the bodies of his children diving and surfacing like dolphins, and he believes that no one will imagine that he works like a slave day and night.

But I have passed by the window to his office and have seen him staring blankly across the lawn. I don't know what he sees. Now that it is the dry season, the grass is the same color as the dusty road outside the wall. His face is the color of the dust, the grass, the empty road. He sits with his fingers balanced on his forehead, holding his head up as if it did not belong to him anymore.

I cannot imagine desiring anything so much that the thought of losing it would make me long for death as he does at those moments when he imagines no one can see him. I understand then that what people might call my cross has been my gift. I have never hoped as he has.

I move quietly away from the window. I know my shadow has, for a second, covered the nape of his neck like the cool touch of a hand when you are burning with fever. By the time he looks up, I am busy elsewhere.

You have the step of a thief, my brother Luis often accuses me when I appear at his elbow without warning as he marches up and down the beach. My brother is a student of tourism. He is, like my father, a scholar of women. He works at a grand hotel on the next beach down the coast. He is twenty. At night, when he stands on the sand, the water rushing in white over his dark feet, he looks out over the water onto which the sun has bled its last light and he knows there is more in life than he can even imagine. He knows all he has to do is dive in. If he trusts himself to it, it will carry him safely beyond all our reach.

I am nineteen. I have this pool that I seine daily and scrub four times a week. Where Luis sees the horizon, I see the vivid green mold growing on the white tile. I feel the incessant pulse of my own brush.

The difference between me and my brother is invisible from a distance. When we stand with our backs to the shore, staring out over the water, I dare anyone to tell us apart. But my brother still acts as if there were some perfect connection between his will and his actions. So there is something about him pure as a child—or a jaguar. I cannot say the same for myself.

When he is not working at the hotel, my brother strides the *playa* as if it belonged to him. If a woman catches his eye, he follows along beside her, talking. He nets her with his words. He tells her how many beds there are in the hotel, tells her about the rich man, Mr. Strachey, who anchors his boat out in the harbor and comes ashore to carry on his affairs at the hotel. Affairs of the fax and the computer. He shows her the disco with its newly thatched roof. My brother can speak English well enough to move to Los Angeles or Texas. That is what they tell him at the hotel. That is what Mr. Feldman tells him. Mr. Feldman is the owner of the Los Angeles Cafe here in our town. He is Mr. Strachey's partner. He would like my brother to leave our town. He does not like the way his own woman follows my brother with her cold blue eyes as he walks the beaches.

My brother is like a tightrope walker. He believes it is his own will that keeps him from faltering. Truly, it is indecision that saves him. The desire he feels for Mr. Feldman's woman is no greater than the desire he feels for the promises of Mr. Feldman and his partner, Mr. Strachey. Indecision is not indifference. The desires my brother feels are strong as lightning. Every time he feels the eyes of Mr. Feldman's woman on his shoulders or the backs of his thighs, his whole body grows alive with the charge. It comes alive with the same charge every time he sees Mr. Strachey reading the faxes that have collected in his absence and leaning back in his chair and whispering orders to his secretary. True power, my brother tells me, never raises its voice. *Buy,* it whispers. *Sell.*

"Build," my *patrón* Jacques tells me. "I will have to build a new generator. Can you help me?" Like Mr. Strachey, Jacques comes from Canada. But he does not speak in a whisper. He talks to me as if he were talking to a friend.

Jacques speaks a language found in no dictionary. A little Spanish. A little English. French. When he falters, I smile and he begins again. For my brother, these languages are like fingers; they are designed to probe the world. They are designed to grasp. For Jacques, words are like a surf. Beneath them there is the fact. It is there, where the silence gathers, that we direct our attention. To understand him, I match the focus of my eyes to his. I see the ant trails of the numbers in his account books. I attack the vivid green bloom of life on the white tiles. I ignore the sea spreading out forever just behind the next row of houses. Instead, I participate in the mysteries of the red hibiscus, of the *piscina* glowing so green and so bright in the starry, tarry night.

My brother is right. I am a *ladrón.* A thief. Without his knowing it, Jacques' dreams become mine. In them, the *piscina* glows and inside the light I see us all gliding effortlessly as angels. We dive and we fly in the one shining eye of God. We are all at home, there, in the silence of water, there where to speak is to drown.

Finally, Jacques has snared a guest for his pension. She came to see us yesterday, but she went away. She returned without warning this morning. Jacques is beside himself with pride. "You have your choice," he tells her. "Any room in my house." She smiles and considers seriously, although it is not such a choice as Jacques would have you imagine.

His pension has only five bedrooms. He has filled each of them with many beds, but he still has only five rooms for guests. He and his family live in the guard house, which sits on the far end of the lawn, behind a grove of citrus trees. In the guard house, there are two rooms and many beds. Enough for Jacques and his wife and their three children. They come to the large house to eat every morning. They pretend that is where they really live. But the truth is in the children's' eyes. There is no home anymore. There will never be a place where they fit the way a skeleton fits into its muscles, the way muscles fit into the skin, the way my brother Luis fits into his life.

I see Jacques's daughter watching me sometimes. My silence frightens her, but less than my voice. At first, she would come up to me, straightening her little horn-rimmed glasses, and ask me questions in the Spanish she was learning from the priest's brother, a lay about from the capitol who studied at university for a year before he got bored. Now he hires himself out as a *maestro* to the foreigners who know no better.

Cómo se llama? she would ask me. *Buenas tardes! Buen día! Qué haces?*

Cómo se dice? She would ask, pointing at the hammock, the white plastic chairs around the pool, the orange tree spreading its dusty leaves out over the lawn. *Cómo se dice?* she would ask, letting her hands kite up in the air like a great sea bird.

Ave?

No! No oiseau. She would spin across the dusty lawn with her arms outstretched.

Avión?

No avión. She would stop, pulling her long limbs back close to her body, all the light pouring out of her skin, dissolving into the dust. She would look around her, her glasses slipping down her nose, her cheeks swelling with despair, which she released with an angry shake of her head.

Viento?

NO! No á bientôt, c'est français. Estás loco! Her voice was cruel as a sea bird. She pointed to the trees, the way they bent over themselves, almost human, in the endless wind.

But by then, I was as tired as she, and I turned back to my duties.

It is painful to see someone so trapped. The air in her lungs speaks a language no one on earth understands. She holds me responsible, I think. Not for the situation, but for what it has taught her about herself. That is why she has decided to pity me, young Jeanette. Why her eyes follow me so closely, then, exhausted by the ferocity of her own attention, she gives me up. When she does this, even when my back is turned, I can feel it. It is as if she has given me a small shove with her hand. It is like an assault, this hope she has for me, this outrage she feels when, daily, I betray her.

Today, after settling into her room, our new guest dove into the piscina in her bikini and the water stripped away her top. For a second, her breasts were visible and then the water fractured them like the facets of diamonds. She drew the red strip of cloth back over them and began to swim with long smooth strokes to the end of the pool. At first she kept losing her rhythm as she would hesitate to adjust her suit each time she turned at the end of the pool, and then the pause itself became part of the rhythm, a small hesitation before she kicked off from the tiles.

When she climbed out of the pool at last, she met my eyes with an easy gaze. She knew I had seen her, she wasn't pretending otherwise, but she knew that what she had revealed, what I had seen, did not have a name. Grace, the priests say, is an accident. When she rose out of the water, she was almost black against the morning sun, but then she turned to me and the color came back into my eyes. She gave me something in that moment; with the steadiness of her eyes, she gave me something.

Jacques found her at the bus station in Liberia yesterday. She was going to stay in a hotel on the beach where my brother works. Not the big hotel where he works, but a more modest hotel at the far end of the beach. She said she would consider staying here at the pension later in the week, so Jacques brought her back to the coast with him and his children. She looked at the pension, walking upstairs and coming out on the balcony to stare down at the piscina. Jacques and his wife Monique stood in the house behind the screen talking with her. Even from a distance, I could see how yearning bowed their shoulders. She turned after a moment and went back in. Then Jacques drove her back to the square of our town where she took a taxi to her hotel. When Jacques came back to us, you could see the despair coating his skin like dust.

"She did not like us?" Jeanette asked.

He did not look at her and she asked again "She did not like us, Papa? She did not like our house?"

Finally, he collected himself. "How could she not like our beautiful house?" he asked her. The laugh he forced out of himself was a gift and Jeanette had no choice but to accept it. You could see the weight of it settle on her shoulders, how she swayed slightly to be able to balance it.

He waved her off and she walked slowly, her head perfectly straight as if she were an African woman carrying a large basket on her head. A basket filled with stones and eggs.

He waved at the lawn, so pale in the midday sun it could be mistaken for snow. "Today we must irrigate." And we went, the two of us, into the cool dark of the shed to study the generator. For without electricity, there is no pump; without a pump, there is no water; without water, our world is as white as the one he just escaped from.

When she came back the next morning, was it to return to Jacques his future? Had she felt, like Jeanette, like me, breathless under the weight of it?

Business, my brother says to me of the women he meets on the *playa*, of Mr. Feldman's woman, of the man on the big yacht. It is all business.

To me, here at this pension, it is a question of weight and balance, love and silence. Dreams. It is all a question of dreams.

Last night, I dreamed that we were on a bus, all of us, Jacques and Jeanette and my mother and father and my brother and my three small sisters and my friend Hugo, who drove the taxi that took the woman away to her hotel. The bus was driven by Mr. Feldman. Mr. Strachey took our tickets. We were driving to the border. We were escaping something terrible, like the famines in Africa. Our mouths were filled with dust. Our ears were filled with the sound of the bus as it strained to cross the mountains. The sky was the color of blood. My brother stood up and began to recite all the facts he knew about the region. The heights of the mountains, the average rainfall. I turned and looked back at us and we were all skeletons. There was a chattering like a flock of birds, the sound of our bones dancing against each other, the sound of my brother's voice reciting facts as if they were the rosary. Such smiles we wore. Such unearthly smiles. And the bus stopped and she climbed on, this woman, and her skin was gold and flesh covered her bones and she looked at all of us with a look so quiet and content I understood that after the border there would be only the color found at the heart of the sun. There would be no wind, no dust, there would only be space and a quiet so deep it is like the embrace of water.

She will come back, I told Jacques last night before I left. He looked at me with an expression of anguish that hardened quickly into contempt. "What makes you say that?"

I see what I see.

She tells Jacques she does not know why she has come here. An impulse, she says. Her laughter is so low it is hard to distinguish it from the wind. An impulse, she says. But she does not appear to be running away from anything. She is too curious for that. I imagine her saying to me, *I came because I wanted to see what comes next.*

She has no fear. When she listens to Jacques or his wife or Jeanette, or watches Jeanette's two brothers fishing from the pier on the beach, she leans forward intently as if what the world promised, promised to delight. If Jacques turned to her and said, "Some days the weight of my head is unbearable," she would not draw away but would lean closer. "I agree," she might say. "But we would look so strange without them." And after the laughter, she would ask him, "How long can you live here if no one comes?" And he would talk to her as he would to a friend from whom he did not have to hide his heart.

Jeanette, when she comes down to the pavilion now, has a little haughtiness in her gait. It is because she feels so light now that she no longer has to carry her father's despair. "The lawn," she says grandly. "My father says you are to tend the lawn."

At the disdain in the child's voice, our visitor shifts uneasily in her chair. She has pulled it deep into the shadow of the hibiscus. Behind her book, I can feel her attention.

Without saying anything, I leave the pavilion and go over to the irrigation pipes Jacques has set in the middle of the dusty field he insists on calling a lawn. He does not accept our seasons because in his dreams our country was always green. In Canada, he would lie in the dark imagining the white fields of snow spreading out so far on every side a man would die before he could walk to the end of them. He would imagine he was not sick with worry, that Monique had not turned her back to him unable to stare, as he did, straight into their dissolving future. He would imagine that he was lying in a hammock surrounded by palm trees and the smell of oranges and the sweet tumult of the sea. And when everything around him dissolved into a blur of loss, he leaped boldly into his hidden green heart and he brought Monique and Jeanette and her two brothers with him.

He is a good man, my *patrón*. He is a man with strong hope.

But hope is not faith.

When Jacques rests his head in his hands, what weights him almost beyond bearing is the weight of what he is missing.

He came to escape the snow and the loss of his job and that swirl of hopelessness that is black as snow and sharp as wind—and he has found in its stead our dust and wind and the huge charred clouds that rise over the fields as the flames run, as they do every dry season, through all the old grasses, leaving only soot and ashes.

He will match dust with water.

He will match his despair with his activity.

He will match his volubility with my silence.

He will match all his dreams of success with the presence of this one guest.

I want to take a match and light the dirty grass and save him from himself. Whatever doesn't burn is what is hardy enough to live another year—the hibiscus, the orange and the malinche trees, the house and the *piscina* and the wall that surrounds us. We too would survive because, like monkeys and dogs, we know how to retreat. We know how to preserve ourselves.

I would teach Jacques how to preserve himself. I would teach him so his daughter and his wife and I would not have to watch him so closely. For we watch him as closely as this woman now watches me. What does she see?

Today she came up and began to speak to me. She spoke slowly, with the same hesitation in her rhythm that she has swimming in the pool. She told me she had once lived for a year in Columbia. "So, why don't you speak our language better?" I asked her.

"*No sé.*" Her voice was like feather drifting over my left shoulder.

"Why don't you speak better?" I asked her. I just barked this at her and she smiled. There was only the slightest flicker of surprise in her eyes when she heard my voice and then she opened herself to it. She took my voice inside her and I knew then that she would also receive my body and I was determined that I would never be received that way, like a diver sinking into an endless sea of pity.

I want her to need me.

After work, I go to the plaza to see if I can find my brother. My friend Hugo tells me he is five miles away at the hotel but another man tells me he saw him with Mr. Feldman. The sugar man, that is what we call Mr. Feldman. But not because his restaurant sells rich desserts.

I go to Mr. Feldman's restaurant to see if I can find my brother. Mr. Feldman is sitting with some of his customers. His woman is talking with the cook. Mr. Feldman's woman is tall, taller than Mr. Feldman, taller than my brother. She has white skin and hair the color of the sunrise. She has hard eyes. They are very pale blue and when she looks at you, you feel she sees every pore in your skin. She can't see anything that lies beneath it. That is the difference between her and the woman who has come to our pension.

I do not enter the restaurant, just look inside to see if I can see Luis anywhere. Mr. Feldman's restaurant is only for the foreigners who have escaped here. It is not just the prices he charges that tell us we are not welcome, but the way all conversation stops whenever one of us pauses, as I have, on the road outside.

Mr. Feldman looks up and sees me. I can see his face harden. He stands between me and his woman. "Hey Luis," he calls out. "What's happening?" I do not turn around. He comes down the stairs of his restaurant. "I have a deal you may be interested in. All you have to do is fly to LA and back. There are papers I need to have signed right away. It will only take two days. You'll be my courier. These damn mails here—you can never trust them."

I shield my eyes from the dust as I stare down the road at the approaching bus.

"Interested?"

I turn then, just as the bus comes up beside me. I shake my head. I stare boldly back at him just the way my brother would. Then I climb up into the bus.

Through the windows, I can see him turn back to the restaurant. His woman asks him something, but her eyes are on the bus. She is searching for my brother's face. I turn to look forward. I can feel her eyes, how they follow the line of my nose, my chin. Like Mr. Feldman, she cannot tell the difference. It grieves me to think my brother would be satisfied with so little.

This morning she finds me swimming. It is not something Jacques has forbidden me to do, but I know it would trouble him if he found out. She does too. That is why she smiles at me when I rise from the water with the same smile she wore when she knew I had seen her without her clothes.

"There are so many things I would like to ask you," she says to me, "but I don't have the words and you—" she pauses, a slow smile softening her face, "don't have the patience." Her voice is cool as the touch of the water in the pool.

When she speaks, I feel her eyes touch my throat. I can feel the weight of every inch of air that separates us. She slips into the pool. For the next hour, as the family rises, Jacques sets himself about the business of the day. He pulls out the ladder and begins to replace the spotlights. Monique prepares the morning meal of fresh fruit and bread. And our guest swims without stopping. She swims with the unbroken rhythm of a sleeper's breath.

I want to startle her awake. I want to wander in her dreams. Instead I walk as far from the pavilion as I can go and still stay inside these walls

My brother has no doubt that he has something that Mr. Feldman's woman needs. He has something Mr. Feldman and Mr. Strachey need too. It is my brother's particular gift that he never questions this.

I don't know what it is that makes this woman follow me with her eyes.

I believe she is equally confused. But she knows I too am alert to her presence like an animal is alert to the dark. If she asked me why, I would tell her, *because everything hides there.*

"Why didn't you tell me?" my brother whispers to me in the dark. I can hear his anger. I can smell his fear. "Why didn't you tell me that you talked with him?"

He shakes me to be sure I am awake.

"What are you trying to do to me?"

He thinks I hate him. My brother thinks I hate him.

He stares at me in the dark. He can't raise his voice because it will wake our mother and sisters.

Fear covers him. He is afraid he will suffocate under the weight of it.

I have no idea what they said to him, Mr. Feldman and Mr. Strachey. Perhaps they did not need to say anything. Just as he does not need to say anything to me for me to understand that something between us has changed forever.

My brother no longer can take me for granted the way he does my mother and sisters and the *playa* and his own beauty and the restless, pulsing continuity of the sea.

Here the difference between us becomes evident. My brother is terrified by the contempt he sees in Mr. Feldman and Mr. Strachey's eyes. How annihilating it is—and how impersonal at the same time. It is one thing if people wish us to die because our presence in their world is overwhelming, our importance to them unbearable. Another entirely to wish us dead because we are a momentary inconvenience. Nothing more than a dog. An insect. A pitcher that won't pour.

What my brother sees in their eyes does not terrify me. Haven't I seen it all my life? All those years at the school as the teacher forced herself to listen to me. At the church, in the impatient silence of the confessional. In my brother's face when I appear without warning at his elbow as he stares out at the sea.

What terrifies my brother is the idea that I would knowingly put him in this situation.

He will never forgive me for this.

So I plead ignorance.

"Nothing," I tell him now. "I said nothing to him." My voice is like a wild animal let loose in our house. "How was I to know he couldn't tell us apart?"

"You must come with me and show them their mistake. Like a play with mistaken identities." He laughs, but his voice is desperate. The way it used to be when he asked me to help him with his schoolwork. Appearances matter to my brother. The pleasure he took at school when the teacher complimented him on the essays I had written for him was sincere. He is what people believe him to be. That is why the indifference in the eyes of Mr. Feldman and Mr. Strachey is so terrifying to Luis.

Who are we when the world does not see us? What do our words mean if no one can hear them?

Little Jeanette in her horn-rimmed glasses spreads her arms and tries to fly on the wind of anguish that swells her lungs.

"You must come with me," my brother says. He thinks that if I go with him, they will see that everything that has happened is an accident. He will be able to forget his fear.

The true loss of innocence is to reach the limit of our will.

"You must come with me," my brother hisses in the dark.

The true loss of innocence is to doubt ourselves.

"Is something wrong?" my mother asks us. "Your father? Has he come back?"

"Nothing," we tell her. "No."

It has been a year now that our father began living in another house but she never stops hoping, my mother. Every time we return in his place, she hates herself a little more.

"You must," my brother says again. He has his hand on my shoulder. He is sliding it toward my throat.

In the dark, in his fear, his voice sounds exactly like mine.

"Tomorrow then," he announces. "After work. I will meet you at Mr. Feldman's restaurant."

I sigh deeply and pretend to sleep. He takes this, as I know he will, as a sign of agreement.

I must not lose courage. I know, for my brother's sake, I must see this through.

In my dreams, I am swimming in the ocean. All around me there is light the color of honey. When I break the water, the light turns the color of blood. When I put my face in the water, another face rises to meet mine. It closes over mine in a kiss. When I lift my face to breathe again, the world is completely dark. There is no difference between the weight of the night air, the sea, the air in my lungs, and the air I release into the mouth of this woman who matches her every stroke to mine, so the sweep of our arms through the water and air is one unbroken circle.

When I wake at dawn, I feel deeply at peace, but when I remember my dream I am puzzled. What is the name for this feeling? In desperation, Jeanette straightens her glasses and spreads her arms straight from her sides like wings. She is drowning. In the rhythm of my dream I could live forever, flying in the embrace of the sea.

"Tonight then," my brother says as I am leaving the room. I nod my head and move into the pale light, into the sounds of the birds and the wind.

As I walk down the road toward the pension, I see Jacques' guest far off in the distance where the road disappears into the forest. She holds her hands up near her breasts. They are closed around something. She is surrounded by a pack of small dogs. They are all barking. Every time she tries to move, the dogs lunge at her.

I begin to hurry toward her but a herd of white cows starts across the road. In this thin light, the leaves of the trees are almost black. The trash fires set during the night still smolder. The dust on the shoulders and back of the cows is the color of ash. As they cross the road, the cloud of dust they create is so thick I can see nothing beyond it. All I can hear are their hoofs and the surf and the high quick barks of the dogs that surround her.

My heart beats as if I were running but I am standing still. And then the cows have moved across the road and I am walking along the road again, slowly, as if I have not yet seen her. She tries to move again, and again the dogs crouch, snarling, in a perfect circle around her. She looks back toward the forest. She looks, without hope, in my direction. Is there any distance at which she would recognize me?

She tries to move again. The movement is slight. It begins only in her hip. Her hands are still held high and close to her chest. But the dogs bark loudly and then edge, teeth bared, bellies dragging along the dust, closer toward her.

I call out then. It is a sound without human shape to it. It is one they recognize. I make it again. And then a third time, and they begin to slink away from her. She looks in my direction, confused, a little afraid. I cry out again and wave my arms the dogs retreat back into the yard of one of the large houses.

Suddenly ashamed, this hideous inhuman cry of mine still echoing around us, I turn and go through the small back door into the pension. I walk through an arch of red hibiscus. In the garage, where I am gathering my work tools, I hear her unlocking the padlock to the large gate.

When I come out with the net to seine the pool, I cannot see her. I don't know what I was expecting, but suddenly the weight of the long pole feels unwieldy, uncontrollable, and I pause for a moment, staring down into the pale green water. And then I can feel her somewhere behind me. I can hear her breathing, the way she must breathe deeply to try to settle the fear. I don't dare turn. I begin to wave the net through the water in the same rhythm as her breathing and then I make it move more slowly, more slowly still, and I can hear her, somewhere behind me, begin to match this new rhythm and again I have no word for what is passing between us. It is then I realize that, for the first time in months, the wind has stopped.

When I turn, she is seated in a chair in the shade of the pavilion. She clasps a camera bag in her hands. She is watching me intently.

"Those dogs—"

"What?"

She does not recognize me as the one who saved her.

I shrug and turn back to the pool.

She rises from her chair and comes over to me. We can hear Monique in the kitchen beginning to prepare coffee. Over the clatter of dishes, Monique says something and I hear Jacques laugh.

The woman at my shoulder speaks in a voice so low only I can hear it. She is not hiding anything. She sounds this way because she is speaking to me, only to me, and she knows I am listening.

"Do you have a brother? On the beach where I spent my first night, I met a man who looks very like you."

"Luis. His name is Luis."

"And will you tell me yours?"

I turn to her.

"It's no use to talk to him," Jeanette says from the top of the stairs. "He can't answer."

We both turn to the small girl. She straightens her glasses.

"My father asked me to tell you that breakfast is ready."

The woman smiles and moves away toward the child.

Red leaves swim in the water like small fish. I surround them with my net. It moves in the same rhythm as her footsteps.

"There is something wrong with his throat," Jeanette tells her as they climb the stairs.

"But not his ears," the woman says. She puts her arm around the girl's frail shoulders and you can see Jeanette's step grow lighter with the touch.

For a second my anger is so great I imagine there is a wall before me, that I am breaking it down into dust and rubble just with the force of my arms. And then the pressure of the water recalls me, steadies me. The red leaves turn inside the white net, so free, so free.

She knows me.

When I leave the pension after work to meet Luis, she has not yet returned from the beach. She left immediately after breakfast with her camera and her bag.

Later, Jacques drove Jeanette and her brothers to the town forty miles away where they began school today. Then he went to the bus station. He went to look for more people to bring here. He does not know that it is not what he says that will bring them here but the look in his eyes, the way it belies that brave laugh of his. He will bring people who know what it is like to reach the limits of their will. He will bring people who can see themselves in us—and still want to live.

But this afternoon, Jacques returned only with the children. His sons were as quiet as he, but Jeanette could not stop her tongue. "No one? No one, Papa?" she kept asking. "How many buses?"

"Enough."

"And this woman? How long will she stay?"

"Until you bore her to death with your questions," he said, then stopped himself with a shake of his head.

Words are so much heartbreak.

He ordered the children to go play. Jeanette insisted they all play school. Her brothers looked desperate, so I threw a blue ball into the pool and the youngest boy, Daniel, stripped off his shirt and dove for it. So they played all afternoon in the water. Catch. Tag. My sisters are seven and four. I wonder some days if I should bring them to play but I understand that although Jacques speaks to me like a friend he would not want to know them. All that holds him up now is his foreignness. There is no wealth without poverty. No rebellion if where you run to you are taken in like a brother.

As I walk from the pension into town after work, I know my brother waits for me at the end of the road but I do not hurry to meet him. Each time I pass one of the beach paths between the houses, I look down toward the glassy sea and my heart quickens then slows again as if someone were choking off its movement with her bare hand.

As I walk, I prepare myself for this meeting with Mr. Feldman. I turn over the words I might say, trying to make them fewer and fewer. For every word I speak robs more of my voice from me. The doctors have told me soon I will be silent as the moon. I think and I think and still I do not know what it is I can say that will bring my brother to his senses.

"At last," he says angrily as he comes to meet me at the corner. He is not long suffering, Luis.

"Come," he orders. And he starts walking up the street away from the beach toward the restaurant. Tonight, the Los Angeles Cafe is filled with Americans and Canadians. They have come to dive. They glance at us as we stand at the top of the stairs, then look away. We mean nothing to them. We are the people who bring them their drinks in the hotel, who make their beds and drive their cars. When their appetites are satisfied, we no longer exist in their eyes.

A couple come up behind us. Her shoulders are so red it is painful to look at them, but her companion puts his arm around her and she leans against his chest without protest. Both their gaits are unsteady. For them, life here is a party, an endless party.

My brother smiles and looks around the restaurant. I can hear him calculating in his mind who is staying at his hotel, who may be staying at his competitors. He does not count the number who may be staying at the pension.

The smile he flashes at Mr. Feldman is absolutely sincere.

"I hear you got me confused with my brother." Luis slaps me on the shoulder.

Mr. Feldman is short for an American, but he has a big chest covered with gray hair. He says in the United State he was a lawyer but here he dresses in ragged shorts and t-shirts. He wears sandals. But there is something not right about his eyes. They are too judging to be those of a man who has given up all serious business, as he claims to.

"So you'll go?"

His woman stands by the door to the kitchen with her hands folded over her chest. Luis never glances at her, but you know he is aware of her attention.

"How much?"

"It isn't every day you get a free trip to LA."

Although a look of annoyance crosses Luis' face, I can see he is going to agree. Mr. Feldman can see this too, and I can feel how something in him exults because he knows now it is only a matter of time before my brother is completely expendable. As soon as Luis is in Mr. Feldman's employment, he will be of no use to Mr. Feldman's woman. Mr. Feldman knows this.

There, in the restaurant, Luis can feel something is slipping from his grasp, but he doesn't know what it is. As I stand beside him, I find myself adopting his posture, the way he throws his head back slightly. The way he spreads his legs a little wider than necessary. His smile is so big and beautiful I can see a woman here and there turn to look at him. I can see a thought cross their minds, then disappear as quickly as it arose. My brother has no meaning here.

"Where?" I ask Mr. Feldman. "Where is my brother going and what have you asked him to take?"

Mr. Feldman can't understand me because I don't speak English and after five years here, he still can't speak our language. He looks at my brother for an explanation. I can see other people have turned at the sound of my voice.

Luis shrugs and translates.

Mr. Feldman laughs. "You share everything with your family?"

I want to tell him Luis and I are Siamese twins. That when they separated us, they gave Luis the voice and me the brain, Luis the lungs and me the heart.

He tells Luis he will send papers with him. Luis is to take them to a lawyer's office and hand them personally to the lawyer. When he comes back, he will bring walnuts for Mr. Feldman's restaurant. A hundred pounds of them. They will be waiting for him at his hotel. All he has to do is put them in his suitcases.

Mr. Feldman talks loudly. He stares over our shoulders. He doesn't care if his story convinces us. Mr. Feldman thinks we can all be bought. You can see that in his posture, his expression. He has no fear of exposure. He believes he is free of all law. In his heart of hearts, Mr. Feldman believes he is God. If so, God has no imagination.

So I try to save my brother in another way.

"She has kissed you and still she cannot tell the difference between us."

"Enough," Luis says to me. He is furious but for a minute he also believes what I am saying. Then he closes the truth of what I say into some deep, unrecoverable place in his heart.

"How much?" he asks Mr. Feldman again.

"How much do you want?" Mr. Feldman looks at him now, an odd smile touching the corners of his mouth. He is enjoying himself.

"A thousand," my brother says.

"Only one?"

"Ten, then." My brother laughs. He thinks he has won.

A customer comes up to Mr. Feldman and slaps him on the arm. They are all friends here. They are all thieves. Mr. Feldman puts his arm around the man's shoulders and walks him out of the restaurant. We wait, the two of us, there in the center of the restaurant. We can hear Mr. Feldman out near the road talking and laughing. My brother throws his head back. The waiters move around us. Mr. Feldman's woman still stands over by the kitchen, her arms crossed over her chest. She is concerned at first, and then she understands what has happened and you can feel the anger run through her body and for a moment I feel sympathy for her but the look on her face is pure calculation and I imagine my brother with all his beauty and his bravado is just a mouse batted between these two, that it is what happens between the two of them that matters—my brother will either be devoured or let go. It is all the same to them.

My brother continues to stand there, in the center of the restaurant. He understands what has happened only when the customers begin to cast embarrassed glances at us and quickly glance away again. I touch his arm, but he steps away from me angrily.

When Mr. Feldman finally comes back up the stairs into the restaurant a half hour later, Luis walks over to him.

He knows the answer but he cannot stop himself from asking the question. "So when do you want me to leave?"

"What?" Mr. Feldman pantomimes bewilderment. "Oh, that, forget it. It's taken care of. No big deal." And then he looks away, bored. His woman smiles at him as if nothing has happened, and he smiles back.

My brother walks out of the restaurant with his head high, but his movements are slow, forced, as if the air had suddenly thickened and resists him like water. He does not wait for me but I know he feels my presence behind him like an enormous weight on his back. I can see the effort it takes for him to resist me, to keep his back upright.

I would not lift the weight from him, even if I could. It is the weight of manhood he carries. It is what it means to be truly free. Who are we when no one sees us? Who are we when we no longer know ourselves?

I do not go home. As I walk, the dark closes around me. We are not so different, my brother and I. As I walk in the dark, I feel a weight behind me that forces my body forward as if I were being blown by a wind. Nothing holds me up anymore except my bones. But I cannot stop myself. Like Luis, I know the answer but I cannot stop myself from asking the question.

When I return to the pension, the doors are all locked. The rock I left wedged in the back gate has been kicked aside and the bolt set. Jacques is a good *patrón*, careful of his property. From across the street, over the wall, I can see the lights still glowing in the big house. I stand there waiting, but I don't know what I wait for. Words fill my throat like stones. I know I am going to drown from the weight of them, but I have no idea whose life will pass before my eyes.

And then I hear a movement by the back door. A thief, I think. I will discover a thief and Jacques and Jeanette and the woman who has stolen my heart will know I watch over them always, like a good angel. But it is only a cat walking across the top of the wall. It leaps from the wall into the garden and lands with a low moan.

I hear Jacques call to Monique and then I see the lights go out in the big house, all except the one on the balcony. When I step back into the grove of trees on the far side of the road, I believe I can see her sitting alone there on the balcony. She is reading.

I stand there staring up into the shadows, shaking with rage. What is love if we can never touch it? I have no voice. I am no woman's choice for a lover. I have no key to this house. How could I have deceived myself so?

I will never be able to shape what fills my lungs. I will always be alone. I understand for the first time that what has happened to me is terrible. Terrible. And I understand God has consciousness and no pity. For me. Luis. Jacques. Jeanette. Or this woman who will remain forever out of reach. To hope without faith is terrible. But faith without hope is more terrible still.

In the grove behind me the cattle sleep still as stones. Who can plunder the dreams of animals? Who can plunder the dreams of the dead? Who can bear to hear the sea forever throwing itself against the insensible sand?

I am what I am.

On the balcony, the woman raises her head and looks out into the dark toward the sound of the sea. She rests her head on her hand. She is content there behind the screen of palm and hibiscus. There in the unearthly glow of the *piscina*.

She smells of the sea, of salt and oil and brine.

I was alone. I was alone on a road in a foreign country. Wild dogs surrounded me. I was alone and afraid. They bared their small white teeth. Their black lips glowed with spit. Everywhere I moved, they closed me in.

And then I heard your voice.

I close my eyes. The shame is unbearable.

I heard your voice, she whispers. *And what I heard was love.*

And this time I turn and she opens her mouth to me and I let everything that I have stored up all these years free and she accepts it and then returns it to me changed by the shape of her own lungs. I release the cool night wind and the tumult of the sea and the bitterness of oranges and she returns to me the vivid hibiscus and the pale green water and the dust and the wildfire. This, I think, is how I will know myself from now on. *Loved.*

I sleep there, with the cattle, beneath the malinche trees. When I come to work, I shower behind the garage. She is sitting already in the chair she has pulled deep under the hibiscus. She is waiting for me and when I come out from the shower she rises in her chair.

"I am leaving this morning. I wanted you to have this." She gives me a book covered with black leather. "Don't open it until I leave," she tells me. She smiles at the look of disappointment I can't hide.

And then my friend Hugo is at the gate with his taxi and I help her carry her bags out to him. When I return to the house, already Jeanette is wheeling around her father asking, "Why did she go, Papa? Didn't she like us? Didn't she like our house?"

"She will come back," I tell Jacques. When he looks at me, I see how strongly his despair competes with his desire.

I have so few words left, but I know I must use them. Here. With him. I can't wait for her return.

So I repeat myself.

"She will come back. And there will be others. It is a beautiful house. A beautiful house."

I exhaust my voice. For him, I exhaust my voice. And still he doubts me, my brother, my *patrón*.

So I show him the first page in the book.

The paper gleams, clean and bright as the *piscina*. Completely empty. All around us is the weeping of the wind and the pounding of the sea.

He matches his gaze to mine.

I begin to read what was never written: *In the beginning was the word. And the word was desire. Without voice, without ear, it was nothing. Without us, nothing.*

Jacques sets his hand on my shoulder. Silence devours me. Desire devours me. Jeanette leaps into the light. Her arms beat against the wind. The water shatters into a thousand pieces. A seabird screams.

Just so, God suffers to reach us.

And then Hugo is driving his taxi back through the gates to the pension and a cloud of dust swallows his car and swirls toward us.

She comes out of the cloud of dust. She sees us at the end of the pool and smiles and walks quickly over to us.

She comes straight up to me.

Jacques looks puzzled, but he says nothing. Perhaps he thinks I am a thief.

"I want to thank you. For yesterday. I was afraid. I couldn't get them to leave me alone and I didn't know what to do. I couldn't move. And then you frightened them away."

I frightened them away with my voice.

"What I want to say is that I know what it cost you." She touches her throat and my own skin catches fire.

"In my country, there are operations that can give you back your voice. We could arrange it." Her voice is barely audible. And then she calls me by my name and the sound of it in her mouth is more painful than the silence because all I can think about is never hearing that sound again, never feeling what runs now through my entire body.

She reaches out and takes my hand.

"What I am trying to tell you is there is a possibility."

The pain I feel is nearly unbearable, but I do not bend, I do not change the expression on my face.

"I know what this may mean for you." She touches my hand but turns her face away from me.

In my mind, we stand, the two of us, staring out over the sea. It is the color of blood and honey. I stare out at the horizon and know there is nothing holding me here but the weight of her hand, the pressure of her shoulder. If I throw myself in, soon I will be out of everyone's reach.

"I know you have never imagined—but that is what you must do. You must begin to imagine what it might mean for you. For your life."

It is true. I have built my whole world around this idea. *Ladrón* of dreams. Refugee from pain.

She turns to Jacques and talks to him more quickly, in English. He looks over at me, surprise and compassion and then shame crossing his face. He has never imagined making his way through my life. What has he thought? That the wind does not beat on me with the same force it beats on him? The dust does not coat the inside of my mouth as it does his, with filth that feels like velvet?

She comes back to me. She pulls a pen out of her pocket. She smiles and takes the book from me. She writes her name on the first page. "So you will know how to find me."

She looks up at me as she closes the book. I can see now the fine lines around her eyes and mouth. Her eyes are a cool green, the color of the sea at midday.

"Please think about what I have said. It is true. In my country, there is hope for you."

I close my eyes with the pain of what she is saying. I expect to find dark but what I find is light. Her hand steadies me. Jacques' does too.

Jeanette's voice carries even here, where I am. "Of course," she says. "Of course he will do it. Juan is nobody's fool."

Which is worse, I wonder. Not to be able to reach the world or to be able and refuse?

For a second I hate her for what she has exposed me to.

I hold the book close to my chest. I imagine the blank pages, so bright and so unmarked gleaming inside the heavy covers, brighter even than the *piscina* in the noon sun. The glare is enough to make you go blind. But the pages are hidden. I open them and read the words that are not yet written.

What is love if it can never touch us?

What is faith if it cannot save us?

What is the word without the voice, the voice without the ear?

"Imagine," she says. "Just imagine."

So I do. I imagine my voice, my own voice, raised in a song of such rage and truth and beauty that it brings God, weeping, to her knees.

SACRIFICE

It was in all the papers five years ago when my husband Benny gave my brother Dennis one of his kidneys. They wrote how we all saw Benny as a savior. I wonder, if a reporter could be bothered to come and visit us now, what he'd want to report. We wouldn't, my sister-in-law Janet and me, have any time to talk—we're too busy ferrying the two of them to the dialysis center twenty-five miles away. What could we say that wouldn't make things worse? I don't know how Janet feels, but I'm blisteringly angry at everyone except my own daughter Annie.

"It was one of the risks. I knew that when I offered," Benny tells me. His face is all puffed today because he's waited too long to go back to the center. He doesn't really care, or so it seems to me, whether he lives or dies. He says it's all in the Lord's hands. I think that is a terrible thing to teach his daughter—that you give and you die and God just beams down on you indifferently, whether you're a saint or a sinner. Like you have no right to any feelings in the matter—even when it's your own life that's at stake.

"You didn't ask me if it was a risk Annie and I wanted to take."

"He's your own brother, Carla," Benny says, his eyes widening.

"You didn't *ask* us," I say again, grinding the gears of the truck as I force it into reverse.

"Are you telling me you would have forbidden me?" Benny asks. He closes his eyes and leans back in the seat, which we have set reclined. His skin looks gray, his eyes look gray—just like the day, just like the future. He's so many down on the waiting list for a transplant that there's really no chance. At least Dennis is further down on the list.

Yes, I really said that. And I mean it. If Dennis lives and Benny dies, I'll never forgive him. But then, I'm not a saint. I'm a twenty-six year old mother who is trying to accept the fact that, the way things are playing out, she will be going it solo in less than a year. Will it be any worse than what's happening to us now? I never knew I could feel this alone totally surrounded by people. Now that Benny is on disability, we've moved back in with my folks. Dennis and Janet and their son Ben are living there as well. I'm lonely and, at the same time, don't have a minute to hear myself think.

People say suffering brings you closer—but that's crap. My mom and dad look at us at the table and you can see their eyes lock and then they both get busy studying their knife and fork like they were hypnotized by the light flickering off them. They don't know what to do, who to console, or how. The only ones that seem to be immune to the tension are my daughter Annie and my nephew Ben, but that's because they're forever excusing themselves to go off and play in the yard. Ben is four and a half, born six months after Benny gave Dennis his kidney. That's why they named him Ben. Annie is six. They're more like brother and sister than cousins, the time they've spent together this past year. Which means they kind of ignore each other out there in the yard. Ben has his sand pile and his trucks. Annie has her treehouse, which is filled with dolls her grandma buys for her. I don't have the time or the money.

One time I went up there and she was playing dialysis clinic. All the dolls were on little squares of white sheet. They had straws taped to their arms. Annie was humming happily as she moved from one to the next. "Your turn," she said. "Your turn." I think that was the moment I realized I was never going to forgive Benny for what he's done to us. I married him to get away from sickness, to get away from my family and have a chance for a normal life.

I'm four years older than my brother, but it seems I've always been in his shadow. At first, it wasn't because he was sick—just that he was a boy and both my parents favored him on that account. My mom was forever buying me dolls, even when I asked for a catcher's mitt or a bicycle. She has her beliefs—and lives them out admirably. Women are made to serve joyfully. And this she does. Her house is tip top clean—no grease on the stove, no grass stains on my dad's work clothes. Even in this day and age, she makes her own clothes—and Janet's and Annie's. She'd make mine except I have no interest and have told her so. It's cheaper to buy coveralls, which is what I favor, at the Wal-Mart.

"You're such a pretty girl," she used to tell me. "Why won't you let the world know."

I didn't need to have the world know. Only Benny. And he did by the time my breasts began to grow. What I have loved about Benny is how he made me feel like a woman and also free. He's never objected to my being a mechanic, coming into the house with the creases in my knuckles still gray with goop. He doesn't go in for things like that himself. He is—or was—an accountant. The most he's ever spilled on his hands is a little ink from his ball point pen. But he understands I like getting my hands dirty. I like working up a sweat. I like fixing things. Not only cars but roofs and washing machines and fences.

It hurt me more than him to leave our house. It was only half done, if that. Ramshackle, my mom said—but I could see already what it was going to look like when I was done with it. I still visit it in my head every night before I go to sleep. I set off in my car and drive the forty miles to Clarenceville and head south to the river. And then I'm there, unlocking the door, calling out to Benny and Annie, who Benny's been minding. I pour myself a glass of ice tea and take it down to the dock and sit on the end of it, where I've started to restore the rotten boards. Benny comes out with a chair and the baby. I take Annie and pull up my t-shirt and she attaches herself to my breast.

Every night I go back to that summer evening five years ago when my life felt just right. I was filled with plans for the future—how I was going to start my own business. How I was going to finish the dock—and then the floors and the kitchen. I looked up at Benny and just laughed with the pleasure of the warm evening air, Annie's little mouth tugging at my nipple, the sweet constancy of Benny's smile. "I am a happy woman," I told him.

"Nothing's sure," Benny tells me, when we're talking these days, which isn't all that regular. "I could have died in a car crash. That would be even more unexpected. You'd have had no time at all to prepare yourself."

But I'd have known his last thoughts were about us, about how much he didn't want to leave us alone. The more time passes with Benny in this condition, the more I see his death as intentional—and cruel.

I can't say that to anyone. I'm sure they'll all say there's something twisted in my thinking. But maybe there's something just as warped in theirs.

Why am I supposed to be resigned to Benny dying? Why am I

supposed to act as if this is God's will? It's Benny that did it. And everyone else may think he's a saint, and some days I do, but that doesn't make him God.

"You didn't *ask* us," I say to him again today. I can't get over that.

What drives me wild is Benny doesn't seem to have any sense of what he gives me here and now.

"You'll have Annie," he says to me. "She's part of both of us—so when you look at her, you'll remember what we were together."

I don't *want* to remember. I want to *be* what we are—for a long long time. I want Benny to want that more than anything in this world, just like me.

Benny doesn't see any difference, really, between this world and the next. "I'll be with you in spirit, Carla," he tells me. I want him to be with me in the flesh—even this gray, dry, itchy flesh that closes around him these days tough as an elephant's skin.

Janet knows I hold what's happened to Benny against Dennis—and against her too. I'm not sure Benny would have done what he did if he hadn't known she was expecting. He wanted to give Dennis the pleasure of being with his own child for a year or two. But Janet and Dennis knew the risks they were taking when they made Ben. Dennis was already on dialysis. He'd already been given his death sentence. Janet and he just couldn't accept it—and that's why they made Ben. And then Benny couldn't accept it either, so he did what he did. Did they know all along that was the pressure Benny couldn't resist, given what being a father meant to him?

I'm being unfair, I know that. As soon as I learned about Dennis, I'd gone ahead and had myself tested, just like Mom and Dad, to see if I could be a donor. Janet would have except she was carrying Ben. But Benny was *my* family, not theirs. He had no business stepping up that way.

It's a terrible cost to pay to belong. I didn't even know he had those kinds of longings in him. Benny has no family of his own. He grew up in foster homes and I guess I just loved how much he wanted to start a family with me, like we were Adam and Eve, the first two people on all the earth. We used to plan so hard when we were young, saving ourselves for marriage, but giving ourselves over every day to the elaborate dream life we were building.

A life where we were the center—just the two of us—and all kinds of good things came from that—like Annie, Benny's business, the house by the river.

I guess I wouldn't have thrown myself, by the time I was thirteen, into all that dreaming if I hadn't found my family so unsatisfying. There's nothing wrong with my Mom and Dad. There's nothing wrong with my brother Dennis. It's just that I always felt like an outcast around them. When Dennis began to get sick, when he was about twelve, everything that didn't work just got worse. My mom expected me to spend all my time entertaining him—or helping her. "Quiet now," she'd say if I played my radio. "Your brother's resting."

They'd never say, my parents wouldn't, that they favored Dennis—just that he had more needs.

They'd probably say the same today—or maybe they wouldn't. Maybe that's why they inspect their knives and forks with such attention.

I think everyone is afraid, if I open my mouth, I'll say what can never be unsaid.

I've been afraid of that too, ever since Benny got the infection that ruined his other kidney and put him on dialysis. Dennis' body rejected Benny's kidney just a few months later, like it couldn't bear the guilt—even though both Dennis and Benny tell everyone there's nothing to feel sorry for. But I feel as sorry as can be that Benny's death is for nothing. Not a plumb thing.

I'm furious with my brother over all this—but I understand him better than I do Benny. My brother has fought—and is still fighting—to stay in the here and now. He wants one more day—and then one more—with Janet and Ben. He knows the pleasures of the spirit can't compete with the pleasures of the flesh. Why should they. They are one and the same.

When I say that, I'm not talking sacrilege—whatever the expression on Benny's face might imply. I believe God gave us life for a reason, a good reason, and that to turn your back on that as easily as Benny seems to be doing is a sin.

"I love you, Carla," Benny cries out in his dream. There's a crust on his lips, and his eyes are moving back and forth under the lids.

"I know," I whisper as I turn the blinker on and turn into the clinic parking lot. "God help me, I know."

After I've stopped the truck, I wait for a minute to see if he'll register the stillness, but he doesn't, so I undo my seatbelt and lean over and put my hand on his cheek. He turns his face into my palm, his mouth making little movements just like a little baby seeking a breast. I think my heart will explode, my rage and craving are both so intense. I reach out with my other hand and undo the lock.

"Wake up," I tell him. "Wake up."

And Benny does wake up, long enough to walk into the center and lie down on one of the beds and have the nursing aide hook him up. He tries to hide it, but I see the look of anguish on his face as he pulls himself up onto the bed.

I ask the aide to jack the bed up. It's his heart that's paining Benny. Pericarditis. It's not enough that he's not got a kidney, or that his feet have gone numb, or there's an itching worse than bathing in straight poison ivy that's with him day and night. It's his heart that's getting troubled too. Not the heart exactly, but the envelope that's meant to make it safe. It's inflamed, they tell us, and I can see one of those Catholic pictures with Jesus' chest laid bare and his heart on fire. Mario, who works with me over at Basic Auto Repair, has a little plastic coated card like that he keeps tacked up over the tool bench. After I learned what was troubling Benny, I asked Mario to take the card down. Mario doesn't speak much English, so it took some time to make my meaning clear.

"It hurts me to look at it," I kept saying to him.

"No believe God?" he asked me.

"I just can't be looking at it, ok?" The only time I have to work now are Benny's hours at the dialysis clinic—fifteen hours a week. I spend another ten hours working out of my parents' garage on cars people in the neighborhood bring by. And another fifteen keeping an eye on Ben while Janet and Dennis take their turn at the center.

"You don't have to work," my mom said.

"It helps my temper," I told her. It was too much trouble to ask her didn't she see the writing on the wall, didn't she know, come next year, I'd need to be pulling in a steady income. But I bit my tongue.

None of us is blind.

Not even Mario.

After our boss, Arthur, took him aside and explained about Benny (I found the diagrams, one kidney erased, the other blackened out, the red circle around the heart), Mario replaced his Jesus card with a Virgin of Guadalupe one, which I found easier to take.

"I pray," he told me, tapping at his own heart and then pressing his palms together. "Each day I pray for you husband."

I thanked him. I truly am glad he's doing that. Personally, I'm so ticked at God I can't pray two words before I start raving. For all our sakes, I've stopped trying. I need to conserve my energy for what really matters. But I find it relieves me to imagine Mario praying for Benny—holding in his mind that picture I can't stand of Jesus with his heart on fire. I can't look at it—but that's because it feels too accurate, and I need someplace to escape, even if only for an hour or two at a time.

Benny's got his own places to escape to—but I'm always calling him back. The doctors don't know why he isn't responding to dialysis. Theoretically, he should be able to live this way for years. A half life, maybe, since so much of it is spent hooked to this purifying pump. But it would be enough for me and Annie. Just like it is for Dennis and Janet.

But it's not working out that way. Every day, Benny seems to get a little slower, more confused. They say it is the by-products of the uremia backing up into his brain. And the pain that's pinching his heart so tight it can hardly beat, they can't seem to do anything about that either.

I do wish Benny and I could have one real talk before it's too late. One where he could ask—and I could give—forgiveness for everything he's so carelessly robbed Annie and me of. But Benny, unfortunately, feels he's not done anything that needs forgiveness. It makes me feel right crazy not to be able to get through to him. As if he's left us already.

As I'm getting ready to leave the center to go work over at the auto shop, the nurse calls me over and tells me Doctor Long wants to talk with me. It usually takes a couple of weeks to get an appointment to see him, but they already have me down for this afternoon without even asking.

"Don't you think I might have other things to do?"

"This is important, Carla." The nurse is a soft-spoken man named Ralph.

"I'm not sure I'm up to it," I say, suddenly just sick with what I know is coming.

"You want to call someone to come in with you?"

"Who?"

Ralph looks at me and presses his lips together. He doesn't know the answer either. My family can't take this anymore than I can. "Mrs. Putney maybe?" Mrs. Putney is the social worker—and a terrible gossip. Everyone in town will know our business soon as she does.

"Thanks but no thanks."

"I'd do it if I weren't so swamped today," Ralph says.

I wouldn't mind his being there. Ralph doesn't feel we all have to do nice nice all the time.

"It's the hardest thing in the world to let go of the person you've built your life around," he says. "I *do* know that, Carla." That's as far as he can go. Around here, we don't ask, we don't tell. But I know he means what he's saying and that helps. But not much. Not enough.

There is this sick feeling, like a dark hole just sucking me in. "I'm not ready," I say.

"But maybe Benny is," Doctor Long says when I say the same thing to him an hour later. "None of us has any idea about the pain he is in."

"How long a wait does he have for a transplant?"

"You know the answer Carla."

None of us, you see, can do anything to help Benny. We've all gotten ourselves tested again, even Janet. But there is something unusual about Benny—his blood or his tissue—and we don't match. Doesn't seem like anyone does. It isn't fair, here he's being shuffled aside like some no account, just like he was all his childhood.

"He dies, I die too," I tell Dr. Long. "Why would I agree to that? I *want* to live. You don't understand, he's everything to me. He's not just the father of my child or my best friend. He's my hope for the future. He's what makes life worthwhile, workable."

"We can't help him, Carla. He's in so much pain, he can't stand the idea of waking up every day. He's not talking suicide here, he wants that real clear. He's talking about letting nature take its course, about giving himself up to God's will."

"Crap," I scream. "That's so much crap. That's just Benny coming to believe all those worthless, shiftless people who passed him around all his life. That wasn't nature. That wasn't God's will. That was people. Careless people. And you're no different. You just want to pass him off too—can't stand to see his suffering. Well me, I *can* stand it.''

When I first started keeping company with Benny, he was thirteen like me. Small for his age, but tough looking. He had to be or he'd never be left in peace in the group home they'd put him in as soon as he became a teenager. So it was a surprise to me when I started talking to him that what I was flooded by was his sweetness. Benny didn't have an ounce of blame in him. For the mother who had left him in a cold apartment without food when he was two, the foster homes that shuffled him off whenever he was the least bit of trouble. I'm not saying Benny was blameless, mind you. He loved fire, for one thing—so there had been some bonfires in wastebaskets and out on front lawns when his words failed him as a little kid. And even though he loves putting numbers in tidy boxes, I've never seen him return a plate or a piece of clothing to its natural resting place. And he had—still has—a way of tuning you out when he wants to that is completely unnerving.

But Benny—until he made that decision about giving Dennis his kidney—never ever tuned me out. I was his sweet place from the very first. He could let me fold him in my arms and something in him came to rest. He didn't need to tell me this. I could feel it. And it made me feel so good and powerful. Me, Carla, the clumsy, the misfit. Here I was, everything Benny had ever dreamed about—and more. It's how I came to understand myself over all the years we've had together. Who wouldn't hold on to that?

But the truth is, I no longer feel like home to Benny. Even when I hold him now, he can't get comfortable. His skin itches with a pain he likens to touching an electric fence. And now there is this worse pain closing in around his heart, oh, it's like a perversion of everything we ever were to each other.

I can't live knowing I'll never again find the peace I have felt inside his hands, like I finally fit sweetly into this life of mine.

But it's gone already, that's what Dr. Long is telling me. I can't get near Benny without feeling my own heart start burning with a pain that it takes all my energy to contain.

I fold my hands over my chest and stare at Dr. Long. I can see the diplomas and books on the wall behind me reflected in his glasses. His eyes flick back and forth behind the reflections, then hold.

"I don't know what I would do in your position, Carla. If Benny were a little clearer in his thinking, I'd leave the decision up to him alone."

"How long were you married?"

"Forty-five years. Not long enough. I'm sorry, Carla. So sorry. But he's like my wife, Benny is. He believes he's going to a more restful place."

"And you? Is that what you believe?"

"It was a great solace to me to know my wife *did* believe that. It still is."

"Think on it," Dr. Long says when I don't say anything.

"I can't."

"Here are the answers to some questions you can't ask. It would take about two weeks. We'd need a written directive, signed by both you and Benny, that it was his choice not to keep coming back to the center. Much of that time, he'd be in a coma. We would arrange to manage the pain."

"No."

"Think on it, Carla. I'll understand either way. But Benny was clear when he asked me to bring it up with you. He knows what he is asking of you."

"Why couldn't he say it to me in person?"

"He said it would be ten times more painful than the pain his heart is in right now—and that is already past bearing."

I can feel it, you know, those fires of hell rising up around his poor swollen legs, closing in around his heart, turning his gray skin black, then red as the flames themselves as the skin splits and pulls away.

"I have to get out of here." I grab my bag.

When Dr. Long stands up from his desk, I put my hand up as if he is about to attack me.

"You leave me be," I tell him. "You goddamn leave me be."

It takes me about ten minutes to realize where I am heading. I just know I need to get away. But my hands have a mind of their own and once my thoughts begin to form again, I understand what my hands are doing. They are taking me home.

This year, I haven't even noticed spring coming, but on my ride out to our house by the river, I see the redbud and the dogwoods, their blossoms small and green yet, and here and there, tall purple swags of wisteria. I keep thinking, if we could hold out until summer, if I could have another baby, maybe Benny might change his mind. I keep thinking of all I'd need to do to move us back into the house—how I'd have to clean it and get a hospital bed in and maybe see if we could get our own home dialysis machine. Maybe that minister that Benny had come visit him, Rev. Larson, could get some kind of drive going like they did before with Dennis.

As soon as the road snakes down over the crest of the hill and I can see the river down below me, I come to my senses. The house isn't ours anymore to move into. We signed the papers on it three months ago. I was the one who insisted. Said we needed ready cash for all the medical bills. We needed to be able to buy time.

But my hands won't let go of the wheel, my foot won't lift from the gas pedal. Home, the word just sits in my mind like a plane has written it in the sky. That is where I am heading. *Home.*

I must have registered the smoke somewhere in my brain because I find myself driving faster and faster, too fast for the curves, and the truck begins to complain. Its balance shifts wildly as I spin the wheel; the tires squeal.

When I pull around the curve, I see all the fire engines. There are no sirens, just lights flashing on the engines and the flames leaping along the roof. I pull up onto the neighbor's lawn and jump out. A fireman in his heavy coat and pants and boots comes over to stop me.

"We're having a practice burning. It's all under control."

"You set it on purpose?" I ask him. "You burned up my home *on purpose?*"

"What's your name, miss?"

"*Mrs.*," I scream. "I am still *Mrs.*"

"I think there's been a misunderstanding, ma'am. This house was donated for the training exercise. Hold on a second and I'll have the chief talk to you."

But I am not real open to talking.

"What right do you have to destroy someone's home?" I scream at the chief. "That was my history."

"There must be some mistake. The house was given to us by a Mr. James Pendergrass. He said he needed to level it anyway. Said the house wasn't worth the cost of repairs. He's going to put up a new prefab. His brother's a firefighter—that's why he's letting us use it for our exercises."

"He never told me that when he bought it. He never said my home was worthless. Would I have sold it to someone I thought would destroy it?"

I try to step around the chief and go down to the dock. He puts out a big sunburned hand to stop me. "It's not safe to get any closer. No one meant any harm, ma'am. No one thought you'd have an opinion one way or the other."

The smoke pours black as pitch out from under the eaves. Little flames weave like snakes over the roof shingles. There was so much I could have done to make our home good and strong. I would have loved every minute of it.

The firemen yell at each other, grab the hose from one truck, pull it closer to the house, and shoot water in the front door, while the ladder on the other truck lowers toward the flaming roof. The air is so still the smoke rises straight up in the sky like a dark tower.

But even here at the edge of the yard, the heat burns my skin and sets my eyes to tearing. Over the chief's shoulder, I see Mr. Pendergrass. I step to the left to get around the chief. The chief is a big man with real red skin—like he spent most of his time fishing or drinking. But he has a kindness to his eyes.

"I'm sorry no one told you. Sorry you had to happen on it this way."

"I see the owner over there." I step a little farther over to the left. "I need to have a word with him."

"You'll need to walk on the roadway. No one but the fire department is allowed on the property."

"What's he doing standing on it?" The chief turns around and waves Mr. Pendergrass back, who nods and steps back onto the asphalt.

It is my fault. Benny told me to wait on selling the house, told me I might regret it. He hadn't liked Pendergrass, I could tell by how he looked at him, but he never said why. When I asked him, Benny just shrugged and said, "It's bad luck to benefit from someone else's misfortunes."

I wouldn't hear a word of it. "He met our asking price," I said. But really, I thought it meant Mr. Pendergrass valued what we'd done to the house. I thought I'd drive by now and then and see the house getting better each time and feel something in me that would ease the fierce grief I felt at giving it up. A grief I didn't share with Benny because it felt like a betrayal, since what was happening to him was obviously so much more important.

For however fierce the grief I felt at giving up the house, my determination to do it was even fiercer. Benny was everything to me—I wanted to buy more time. I wanted to buy us eternity.

By the time I cross behind the sheriff's deputy's car and the fire chief's car, I have a hold on myself. Mr. Pendergrass turns to me with his silvered sunglasses, where all I see is my own face, my hair hanging in oily strands across my sagging cheeks. I don't look twenty-six, I look fifty. He has a bored look to his mouth. He turns back toward the burning house.

"I should have asked your plans. Before I sold, I should have asked your plans."

"No secret," he said. "I'm building a bar-restaurant and marina. Thought I'd put the house to some good use before I got started. Civic duty, you know."

"It had promise. Our house had promise."

Mr. Pendergrass looks at his watch. "Sorry to cut this short," he says. "I have an appointment in Clarenceville. Just thought I needed to put in a presence here."

"Civic duty."

"Sorry about your husband's illness." He turns so I can look at myself again in his silvered lenses. "Know this all must be hard on you. That's why I didn't dicker about the price. Gave you everything you asked for."

He puts his hand on my shoulder and squeezes. I have this terrible impulse to bite it. It makes me pull in my breath so hard I almost gag. He flinches.

"Sorry for your misfortune, Mrs. Dove."

"*It isn't enough*," I scream in the truck once I start back up the mountain. "*Sorry isn't enough*."

But that is all there is. My mom and dad looking at their knife and fork. *Sorry*. Dennis coming and sitting down in the other lounge chair in the living room, looking just about as gray as Benny. *Sorry*. Janet holding Ben to her chest over there by the sand pile when I sent all Annie's little dolls flying out of the tree house. *Sorry*. Dr. Long's eyes beginning to tear when I put out my hand as if he were attacking me. Benny crying out in his dream.

"I *will not* survive this," I whisper. I hiss the words, putting the whole world, God too, on notice. "I *will not*."

When I walk back into the center, my mind is made up. Ralph is over by the desk writing something on a chart, but he puts his hand out to stop me as I walk past.

"Carla, what happened to you?"

I stop, my hands on my hips. "What do you think?"

"I'm talking about your face, honey. It's a mess. Go into the ladies' room and clean yourself up."

For some reason, I don't fight off his voice, the order in it. I turn and go into the ladies' room to see what he's talking about. My face is black with soot. My eyes looked wild, what with the smears where I brushed the tears away so I could keep driving. But it gives me a sense of reassurance, this mess I'm in. I look like I feel—like I've been to hell and there is no hiding it. Part of me doesn't want to do anything to change it—and another part of me looks at me through Benny's eyes and I can feel how it would hurt him to see me like this. So I bend my face toward the sink and set to scrubbing my cheeks with the harsh antibacterial soap they have in the dispenser. I even comb my hair back behind my ears with my fingers.

"A little better," Ralph says when I come out. "He's sleeping. You want to have a cup of coffee with me in the lounge?" It isn't really a question.

"They burned my house," I say right off. "For an exercise. They burned my house like it didn't have a bit of value in this world."

"Who did?" Ralph asks. "Your mom and dad are all right? Dennis and Janet? The kids?"

"Not their house. *Mine*. Benny's and mine."

"The one you just sold?"

"They *destroyed* it. I didn't sell it so they could *destroy* it."

"No," Ralph said. "You sold it to help Benny."

"I can't."

"Can't help him—or can't keep him alive?"

"Why can't he take my kidney? He's got my heart. My mind. Why can't he take my fucking kidney?"

"I had a friend I lived with for ten years. He died four years ago. There isn't a day I don't wake up and expect to hear his voice." Ralph pushes a styrofoam cup over to me. "It's vile but stabilizing."

"I want to kill somebody."

"Who?"

I shrug.

"I'm serious. Who? Benny? Dennis? Your mom and dad? Janet? Annie? Yourself?" Ralph sips his coffee, grimaces.

"Not you. Sorry."

"Don't waste a split second on sorry, Carla. I wouldn't be here if I couldn't take it."

"Is that what this is? Some punishment you give yourself every day?"

Ralph leans over and spreads his hand flat on the table in front of me. He looks at it like it belongs to someone else. We both glance up as an older woman, Mrs. Landsman, knocks against the open door.

"I'll come back later." She blinks, put her hand to her cheek. She pulls the door closed behind her. Her husband is on one of the machines. He is older than my father.

"I've had a full life," he says every time they hook him up. He seems a little off in his head. Maybe he has always been like that. But she always pats his hand and answers, "We *both* have, Ed."

Some days that conversation breaks my heart. Some days it makes me want to barf. But it is regular as the sunrise. That's all that really matters.

"It's not a punishment," Ralph continues. "I feel real here like I don't other places. I feel like I haven't lost the part of me that loved my friend. I don't think I could live thinking that part of me was gone. Some people might call it a punishment. I had a therapist who tried to get me to believe that. But I told her it was a gift—this being recalled again and again into the thick of things."

"We started so young. I do not know myself without him. My *real* self. He's what let that happen."

"And he's still doing that, Carla."

"No. He's taking everything away from me. What does he think? Annie and I can go on living with my family like nothing *happened*? Like *he* didn't happen to *me*?"

"Oh sweetheart, you don't think that's really the case, do you? That people don't see what he's done for them?"

"For *me*," I said. "I want him to see what he's done for me. I want them to."

"You think they don't?"

"Our life wasn't meant to go this way. Benny wanted me to be my own self."

"What is it truly that you want for yourself?" Ralph asked. "Not what you think people would say you should want. What you really want."

"I want him to love me as much as I do him. I want him to fight for me just as hard as I'm fighting for him. I have so much more I want to give him." I put my hand down on the table. I need to feel something definite under my skin. Something that won't give way.

"He wants you," Ralph says. "He'll never stop wanting you. You need to believe that, Carla."

"Praise be, you're back," Benny says when I come over to him. He looks dazed, sicker. They say it's because his body doesn't like all the rapid changes the dialysis makes—even if they're cleansing.

"I'm sorry," he says once I've gotten him back to the house and into our bed. "I know what I'm asking of you, Carla, and I'm sorry."

He looks at me then and for a second everything clears out within him and between us.

"I'll hang on as long as you need me to."

"I wanted such a good life for you, Benny. I wanted to make up for so much. It made me feel strong to think I could do that for you—for the two of us."

He smiles that soft, sweet smile of his. "It couldn't be much bigger than it is right now, Carla. God whispering in one ear, you and Annie in the other. Problem is, I'm just not strong enough to hold it all. Can you do that for me?"

I just sit there with his hand between mine. I can see how he flinches a little because his skin is unbearably alive now. I can see his eyes begin to cloud over, the way he breathes so shallowly so the fire won't start up around his heart.

"I do know exactly what I'm asking of you, Carla. I'm sorry I didn't ask before—but I'm not sorry for what I did. But I'm as sorry as can be for what it's costing you."

"And Annie," I say before I can stop myself.

And then I can see the fire start up around his heart. I can see the little flames snaking around it, just like in Mario's picture.

I put my face in the sheet then, and it is like I'm a child saying my nightly prayers, except the grief I feel is bigger than the universe. It just keeps expanding and expanding, putting all the fire, all the light out, pushing and pushing until there isn't even a millimeter there left for God. The strange thing is that I can keep it to myself, all that wild howling. When I stop shaking and look up, it is dark outside. Benny is sleeping, his breath just this shallow coming and going.

I go next door and look in on Annie, who my mother or Janet must have put to bed. I stand over her bed, listening to her breathing too. It is sturdier, coarser than her father's.

I go down the backstairs and out into the yard. I climb up into Annie's treehouse. My mom and Annie have set all the dolls back on their little white sheets. I try to move them to one side as neatly as I can.

I hear this voice, so clear. It isn't mine. Or Benny's. *"Your heart is larger."*

"Than what?"

And then it is as if something opens up inside me now that all the fire is out and with each breath, I take in another memory. They are all so alive. The first day I saw Benny in seventh grade. The white t-shirt he wore with the sleeves rolled up like the high school boys. The first time he walked me home from school. All those afternoons riding our bikes out to the park or the new development and talking about what we were going to do when we grew up. Benny talking about all the children he wanted to have—as he walked through one of those big unfinished houses. Our dreams were so simple and so big. So mass produced.

I see him on our wedding night, so shy as he took off the only nightgown I ever owned. I see the strength flashing through his body as he entered me that first time—taking in that his time had come, this *was* his future. I see him taking Annie in his hands, how his face, so tight and thin, relaxed with tipsy glee. *"Our* baby," he whooped. *"Our* baby."

And I see him coming into my parents' living room with Dennis after the news had come back about their tissues being a good match. I see how he didn't look at me once while he was talking. No one had any idea he hadn't told me what he was up to. I see how I sat there in the lounge chair, gripping Annie so tightly by the shoulders that finally she cried out and everyone turned to look at us. Everyone but Benny, who looked over my head out the window at the autumn leaves. I see how I let go of Annie then, and she slipped out of my lap and ran over to him. He knelt down and pulled her up to him and buried his face in her hair. *As if I weren't there.*

Janet was holding Dennis and crying with happiness. My parents were standing on either side of Benny and Annie, smiling. Up there in Annie's treehouse, in the dead of night, I take it all into my heart. How I sat there in the lounge chair, just watching—so in love with Benny and enraged with him I couldn't think a straight thought.

I take in the operation, all of us sitting in the waiting room while they did the surgery on Benny first and then on Dennis. The shamed look on my parents' faces when they took Dennis home first and Annie and I kept visiting the hospital for three more weeks until Benny was released.

I take in those summer nights in our house by the river before all this happened, just the pleasure of my whole body aching from whatever work I'd done on the house that day, and the sweet comfort of watching the way Benny played with Annie like now, for the first time in his life, his heart was truly light.

I take in the flu that kept Annie in bed for a week, then me, then Benny. How I didn't have any idea the danger we were in—until Benny didn't bounce back, started sleeping in late, going to bed early, taking naps. Once his skin began to go gray—it all clicked. I'd lived it all out before with Dennis— but this time there was no escape, no Benny to create a whole new life with. I take in the look on Dr. Long's face when we went in and he ran the first tests. I take in the look on Dennis' face, on my parents', when I told them. I take in the look on Benny's face when he learned that Dennis was rejecting his kidney.

"Can't we put it back in Benny?" I asked Dr. Long. But the rejection destroyed the kidney, Dr. Long said. After that it was worthless. My Benny's sweet sweet flesh, worthless.

I take in how we all stopped looking at each other, Benny and me first, then everyone, as the news got worse and worse. I take in the light in everyone's eyes when Ben or Annie come running in, flush with the surprise of an ant's nest, or the first bird song in spring. I take in Benny lying with his mouth open, his cheek pressed against the truck door this very morning. I take in all the smoke billowing from our lost home.

All around me the night air is thick as muscle, but still, like a heart that has stopped. There is no pain anymore. Just this thick, comforting dark. I feel a sweetness seeping through all these memories. Something so purely Benny I would know it anywhere. That's when I choose. I choose to hold on. That's what I choose to hold on to.

In my heart and mind, I keep returning again and again to that new place in myself I found that night. It has kept me safe through everything that followed. Safe as I watched Benny slip into a coma, die. Safe as I saw Dennis get his second transplant and Janet's body thicken with her second child. Safe as Annie and I filled up our u-haul and set out to make a new life. I call the sweetness and power that comes to me when I remember that night in the treehouse *Benny*. I'm not being sacrilegious. I don't know how any of us can expect to know God except through those who touch us in our flesh, open our hearts to the utmost, and change our lives forever for the better. I hope Benny, where he is now, feels me in the air he breathes and knows I never, ever, let him go—and rejoices in my stubbornness. And yearns. I hope he yearns every second of every year for what he has missed down here with me.

MY COUNSELOR

My children tell me I talk too much, but that is because they don't listen. The ones that are left to me: my son Darrell and my daughter Josephina.

Darrell asks me, just like his twin Louis used to, "Can't you hold it in, Mama? Just this once, can't you get a hold of yourself?"

"Why?" I ask him. "Is that going to bring back Maurice? Is it going to bring back Louis?"

Darrell, he just shrugs and walks off. Louis and Maurice, they were my strength and my light, I tell my counselor.

Darrell's son, he's called Darrell too, or Rell for short, he's got his uncle Maurice's ring, the one I gave Maurice for graduating from school. Ten years, Maurice nagged me about it, telling me I'd promised it to him, telling me it showed I didn't care. When I finally bought it for him—it's got a little diamond in the middle—he lifted me right off the ground. But I never saw it on his hand.

Now Rell wears it around his neck where he thinks I can't see it. Or maybe he's hiding it from his cousins. But they didn't want nothing from their uncle Maurice—except Pryor wanted the snakeskin boots—until he saw how Maurice had cut them off in the back so they was like mules.

Pryor is Josephina's son. He can afford to keep his distance. He can't remember how Maurice watched over him before he could walk or speak. Maurice only fourteen and Josephina not ever a full year older. Rell now, he remembers what he owes Maurice. He's lived most his life under the same roof with him. Mine. Darell, Rell and Maurice, they were my home boys. I miss Maurice something fierce, but it doesn't seem the same for Darell and Rell. Rell's got his own father to worry about now—that's what Josephina said. But she only said it once and it might have been spite. She did it just before she left for work this afternoon, slamming the door behind her. No need for her to come over. She send me Pryor or Juju, her daughter, and I can do just fine. No need for her to keep checking on me like I am up to something.

"Can't you hold it back?" she asked me. "Don't you think Rell has enough to worry about now, what with his father."

"What you mean?" I asked her. "You trying to tell me something?"

But she was gone by then, marching down the steps with her shoulders pressed back like a soldier. She knows what I think about her work, but she just tells me a man that's put off by a woman's strength ain't got no business with her.

She got no business with men period. I don't know how she got that way, seeing how good her brothers were to her.

My counselor, he tells me, never mind what they say.

My children love me. But that don't mean they won't pick up and go without notice.

"He told you," Josephina says to me. "Louis told you over and over again."

"Told me what?" I asked her. " Not that he had something like that. You think if I'd knowed I wouldn't have given all my blood, think I wouldn't have given it to the two of them? " You tell me what else mothers are for? They give kidneys. I just read about a man got his own daughter's heart. So couldn't a man take his mama's blood? They say they can't put a stop to it, this disease, but they're wrong. They took my blood, they'd still be here, my boys.

My counselor tells me to put my mind at rest. My boys never did drugs. Louis, he was a supervisor at the telephone company. Louis, he was my staff. Maurice, he was my light.

"Makes three in a year," my sister Rose told me when I called her today with the news about Darrell. "I don't know how you hold up."

"I have my counselor," I tell her. There's nothing I can't tell him, nothing I have to keep hid. Some days I think, I can't go to work today, so I don't and I sit and talk with my counselor instead.

I'll never leave you, he tells me. Set your mind to rest, Marvella. I will be by your side whatever happens.

"I don't know how you stand up to it," my sister Rose tells me. I know, soon as we hang up, she'll call all my brothers and sisters. "Three," she says, like I can't see the fingers on my own hand.

"You don't have to protect me," I remember telling Louis as we sat downstairs waiting on Josephina and Darrell. They'd gone upstairs to pack up Maurice's things. That's when Rell found his uncle's ring. In a glass cookie jar filled with cat's eye marbles.

"I'm strong," I told Louis. "I can go up there and see where my baby lived. I can take it." But he told me to sit where I was.

"There's no need to put yourself through that," he said. His lips were in a fine tight line. He was only trying to protect me. I know that now, but he looked like a stranger to me that day.

I never liked the beard he wore the last years. We're a clean featured family. But Josephina says he had his reasons and even when we went to bury Louis, she said Louis wasn't going to have it taken off.

"How can I touch his sweet cheek, you leave that on?" I asked her. But Josephina can be hard. She was the same about the suit she buried Maurice in. She and Darrell and Louis all decided they wanted him in the white suit—even though Maurice would have been ready to dance, we'd put him in the blue one. "You want that blue suit for Pryor?" I asked her.

"What we don't put on him, we'll burn." She never even turned to look at me.

"You'll burn your brother's property?" I still didn't understand. Maurice, he went so quick, none of us was prepared.

How can you prepare for something like that? my counselor asks me.

You never saw Maurice when he was on the stage, I tell him. He was like magic. My baby was like magic. "Where you think I got it," Maurice used to tease me. "You're my spell, Mama."

It's true I dance better than most anyone I know. Not ballet—you have to go to school for that, like my baby did.

"What you been doing with yourself?" Josephina asked me, checking the garbage, then the shelves in the kitchen, still in her uniform. Like I was a criminal.

"It's all right," I told her. I got nothing to hide. My counselor told me I needed some relief. I told her about my plans to move and she just stood there in that ugly blue uniform, the big black belt around her waist holding her gun and her nightstick. You wouldn't believe how slim she was, slim as her brothers, when she was a girl. Even when she had Pryor, she didn't begin to thicken. Not till she sent Juju's father off and took the police exam. I tried to talk her out of it—but she said it was no worse than living here. "I'd as soon be shot for a reason," she told me. "Not just because I'm crossing the street." And she looked at me as if there were something I could do about it.

She never was comfortable under my roof. My boys, they kept coming back to me, but not Josephina. She didn't move far off, but she keeps her children, Pryor and Juju, real close to her. Rell, sometimes he calls me Mama, but you never hear Pryor and Juju making that mistake. It's like she wants to protect them from me.

"I don't know," she tells me when I call and ask her to send one of them over. I never call without no reason. Maybe the grief's got me by the throat, maybe I've heard a gunshot over to the next block. I never call without no reason. "I don't know," she tells me. "Let me see what work they got to finish. Maybe I'll be over instead."

Like I would be a weight to them, I tell my counselor. And he laughs. He laughs loud as the trains passing overhead and tells me I have too much life in me to be sitting here crying for my boys for the rest of my life. When he talks that way, my counselor sounds just like my baby. He has that hoarseness to his voice, like the sounds are coming out against a force. My Maurice, he always tried so hard. Anyone who tries to tell you different, my counselor tells me, you just pay them no mind. Envy is a terrible thing.

I seen it in Josephina, how she walked past the pile of clothes I brought back from Maurice's apartment, not even looking. Anything you want, I told her. All you have to do is ask. She didn't say a word. And when my back was turned, she went and burned her brother's property.

When Louis died, she did the same thing. Sold most everything he had. Sold the house. I never seen none of that money—but Darrell tells me Louis made his own arrangements. He gave most of it to his daughter. Even though her mama wouldn't let her come to the funeral. What happened to the rest is a mystery. "Don't you worry about it," Darrell tells me. "Last thing Louis wanted was to worry you."

They love me, my children, but they holds things back. Even Rell. I asked him tonight about his father, and he just put his hand to his throat, touching that ring of Maurice's and didn't say nothing for a second.

"What you know?" he asked me at last. "What do you know that I don't, Grandma?" There was something in his voice clear as a bell—that sound small children have.

"Oh baby," I said to him. I opened my arms. "Come over to your grandma. Ain't nothing to worry about. You is safe with me."

But he just stood there, his hand to his neck. "I got to study," he said. "I'll be in Maurice's room. Pryor or Juju come, they'll take my place." Darrell and Rell moved out seven months ago now, just before Maurice passed on. I thought they'd move back after the funeral, but they didn't. Said it was because of their lease, but I think their hearts is all froze up. Rell only comes when I call. He says he's studying. Since Maurice died, Pryor and Rell both got serious about their schooling.

"It don't seem healthy to me," I tell their parents. "They should go out and dance a little." But Darrell and Josephina look at each other, and it's like they put me in a glass box. I can open my mouth wide as I like. Nothing's going to escape.

Maurice and Louis were serious. Darrell and Josephina too.

You raised them right, my counselor tells me. You raised them to love you and one another. You raised them to have price.

Why? I ask my counselor. Why is it not one of my boys is going to live to be thirty-five? If I had knowed this—

What? my counselor asks. What would you have done, Marvella?

And I remember then the fun we used to have, Maurice and Josephina dancing in line to the Supremes, Louis and Darrell playing in the school band, the parties we had come Christmas. I think of Maurice fixing my hair every week. How he would fuss over me. My hair. My clothes. "You're a beautiful woman, Mama," he'd tell me. "You got to show it. Look at me." He turned in the mirror so you could see his physique. "You think I'm going to hide this? You think I'm going to hide all my hard work?"

The world didn't understand my baby, didn't understand there was no harm to him. When the police came, I told them. I told them I didn't mean to call them, but they went upstairs and they beat on him, they beat on my baby till there was blood all over his face. "You can't take him to the jail," I said, it coming over me what might happen to him in there. But they took him off anyway. He was covered with blood, but he was still talking. My Maurice had a mouth on him. He still held his head back the way they'd showed him in the dance school. It didn't matter there was a policeman hanging on to each of his arms.

I called Josephina, but she said once I picked up the phone and called the police it was out of her hands. "It was Dad, wasn't it?" she asked me. "Isn't that what set Maurice off. You let him come back."

"We was having us a talk," I said. "What's wrong with that?"

You're a beautiful woman, my counselor tells me. You need comfort the same as anyone. Nothing wrong in that.

"You have me, Mama," Maurice said. "You have Darrell and Louis. What truck you have with that mean old man?"

Thirty years old and no more understanding about this man and woman thing than he had when he was ten.

Josephina be the same way. Sometimes I think she's older than me.

There's pleasures, I try to remind her.

"Pleasures don't put a roof over our head. Pleasures don't put groceries on the table." She talks to me like I was one of her children.

Last month, when I looked at Louis in his coffin, I thought, what pleasures has my boy had? What's he had in his life that's going to teach him about the one to come?

And what about you, Marvella? my counselor asks me. What's going to teach you?

My children, I tell him without taking a breath. All my children. And I think of Louis, how uncomfortable he always seemed in his skin, like there was another man entirely waiting quietly inside there, just waiting to be revealed.

I think of how they looked together, Darrell and Louis, at the end. Louis just leaning his head a little on the pillow and his twin bending down. Almost like they didn't have to talk in words. Then Darrell began to laugh aloud and Louis began to shake, it's the only way laughter could take him, he didn't have the strength to let it loose into the room. I smiled too. I understood, I'm not a foolish woman, they was laughing at me—but I knew it was worth it.

Louis, he understood me too. He lifted his head and Darrell stood up and brought me over to sit in the chair. I had to lean down so I could hear Louis.

"Don't you worry, Mama," he told me. "I've settled things with Darrell and Josephina. You got nothing to worry about."

"You prepared?"

"Prepared for what?" he asked me, the smile still quivering on his lips. Louis almost never smiled, not with me. He took his job as oldest too serious—that's what my sister Rose said.

"Your promotion," I told him. "Up there, you're going to be top management, that's for sure."

He began to shake, the way he had with Darrell. Then he took my hand. His strength hadn't left his hands although the rest of him was just a tent of skin over his bones.

"Whatever I said to you, I never meant no harm."

"You don't have to tell me that," I said, and then that sound just rose up out of me like a tidal wave out of the sea. The same sound as when I sat down beside Maurice.

Josephina, she took me by the shoulders and shook me. "Take a hold on yourself," she said. "For one time in your life, think of them, why won't you."

She doesn't know, my counselor tells me. She doesn't know. It's the grief's got her confused. It's your job, Marvella, to let it go.

Why, I ask him, if I'm to be left with only one, why should it be Josephina? It's not I don't love them all. But my boys loved me back with the same power. It was like electricity sometimes, the way the feeling would crack in the house. Maurice, he'd look at me in the mirror when he'd done my hair and say, "*There.* What do you have to say to that, Marvella?" Or I'd go see him dance. I'd wear my fur coat. My hair perfect the way he'd made it and I would go to the theater and watch him on the stage and it was like a bridge of light between us. When he was dying, Maurice was waving his hands. He was dancing out onto the bridge of light.

He was seeing you all safely to the other side, my counselor tells me. Once you know the way, you can move back and forth whenever you like.

And Louis, he had a power to him. Louis, he was my staff. And Maurice, he was my light.

"Your problem," I tell Josephina when she comes in dressed in those ugly blue pants, her face set down harder than her father's, "is you don't have no one to open your heart to." I tell her about my counselor, but she tells me she isn't interested.

"Your problem," I tell her, "is you don't have no pity in you."

"Pity?" She throws the word right back at me. "What business do we have, any one of us, with that?"

And then she goes down on her knee, digging through my trash like she was the police or something.

"This is my home," I tell her. "You got no business prying in my trash."

"Rell has to go back to his house. Pryor is coming over to check on you in an hour. I'll be by again after my shift."

She don't even look me in the face, just washes her hands off in my sink and dries them careful as a surgeon, finger by finger, before she takes her keys up off the counter.

"Don't you care for nobody?" I ask her as she walks out the door. "Who raised you to be so cold?"

You just got to hold on, my counselor tells me. It's never so bad as it seems.

After Rell leaves and Pryor comes, I'm still down in the living room watching the tv when my son Darrell calls me.

"What's this you been feeding Rell?" he asks. "There's nothing wrong with me, Mama. Look at me next time you see me. Don't I look healthy? No need to go scaring Rell that way. He's lost his two uncles this year. He don't need to think about losing his father."

"What was Josephina scaring me that way for? She told me Rell had enough to do worrying about you."

"I got troubles with my job, that's all."

Job troubles, I repeat to my counselor after I hang up. There was a time when job troubles was all we had. How I scolded them—Maurice for never holding on to a job, Louis for letting go of his without no reason as far as I could see. "Where you going to get to in this world," I asked them, "you go on behaving like this? Where you think you're going to get to in this world?"

Now I understand why Louis looked at me so queer, why Maurice began yelling at me saying, "You want me to be famous, Mama, it's not going to happen taking orders on a telephone."

"Look at me," Darrell said on the phone tonight. "Next time you see me, tell me what you see."

But what is looking going to tell me? Maurice, when he died, he looked the picture of health. He died so quick, it was like he had been in an accident. Nobody had time to prepare. Me least. It was afterwards, they started talking about this disease. Telling me it was the same thing Louis had been sick with these two years past.

"Three," Rose said to me. "I don't know how you can stand up to it."

So I got to call her back and tell her that the Lord has showed mercy, that I'm not going to lose my last like this.

Before Pryor leaves, I send him to the store for me. "I needs to celebrate," I tell him. "I thought there was something wrong with your uncle, but there's something wrong with me."

"You got the money to pay for this?" His voice is as rough as Josephina's.

I set out four glasses.

"Company?" Pryor asks me when he sets the bottle, still in its brown paper sack, on the table.

"Company is a state of mind," I tell him.

You'll never be alone, Marvella, my counselor tells me. You'll always have me. And me, Maurice says. His voice has that fierceness to it that it always has when he's jealous. And me, Louis says, and you can hear the tiredness beginning to lift from him, like he's able now to share some of the burden.

I pour a little out for each of them.

And then Josephina comes hammering at my screen door. Somehow I know it is her before I ever get there. When I open the door, for a minute I confuse her with her baby brother, the way Maurice looked after the police came. She doesn't even speak to me. She just goes up the stairs to the bathroom, the same one where they had Maurice down on the floor. "He was jealous and he was drunk," I told the policeman. "That's no reason to treat him like some criminal."

"You have a cloth?" one of the policemen asked, and he wiped Maurice's blood off onto my best bath towel.

"Josephina, you don't go using any of those new towels, you hear me?" I yell up the stairs.

But she's in the shower and she can't hear nothing.

What's she done, I wonder. Kill someone? Should have seen it coming. Carry a gun, one of these days you going to use it. No water on earth going to wash her clean.

"Josephina," I yell up at her as soon as I hear the water turn off. But she doesn't answer me. So I calls again. Ever so many times. And then I climb the stairs. At my age, my daughter demands that of me.

Marvella, my counselor says, wouldn't you expect the same of your own mama? I can see he has a point there, so when I go to the door, I'm peaceful in my mind, not aggravated as I was when I started up. And I hear this sound, just a thin sound, like a dog that's gotten whipped.

I try the handle of the door and when it doesn't give, I hit the door. "Josephina," I say in my strongest voice, "you open up for me. You open up for your mama." And to my surprise, she does.

She is sitting on the floor beside the tub, covered over with a big white towel. The washcloth in the tub is pink. She is shaking.

I sit down on the edge of the tub and I put my hand on her shoulder and she puts her head in my lap. She's still shaking and this thin little sound is coming from her, like she was a child again and the worst that could happen was someone stole her candy on the playground.

"Tell me about it," I say to her. "I'm strong. There's nothing I can't hear."

And she just shakes harder. My poor daughter. Then she pulls herself together.

"Look at me." Her teeth is chattering. "Will you look at me, Mama. I need to see if I've got me any cuts anywhere. I've got to see if my own skin's broken."

It don't make no sense to me, but sometimes it's answering the question makes all the difference, not the sense the question had in the first place. My counselor taught me that.

So I pulls my glasses from my pocket and I begin to look at my daughter. I look at her face, that wide forehead just like her papa's, those wide eyes, just like my own. I look at the high cheekbones she and Maurice shared. The square line of her jaw, just like Louis'. The long neck, Darrell's.

"I don't see nothing," I tell her. "I don't see even a scratch."

Maurice's blood on the policeman's white hand, it stood out so you couldn't ever forget it. My daughter's skin is the color of forgetting. So I got to look closer. I look at the back of her neck, her shoulders. It's like I've got the eyes of a lover, I'm looking at her that careful.

I take her hands in mine, one by one, and look first at their backs and then turn them over. I was beautiful, I think. Once I was just as beautiful as she is.

"Nothing," I tell her. I can't see nothing. Not the tiniest scratch.

"Now you going to tell me what this is about, Josephina?"

My voice has that sure ring to it I hear only in my mind when my counselor is talking to me.

"Are you going to tell me?" I ask her again.

But Josephina doesn't speak to me. She rises to her knees and turns to me and I hold her, I hold her, saying the same thing over and over the way I did when she was a little girl.

"Ain't nothing to be afraid of," I keep telling her. "We are not alone."

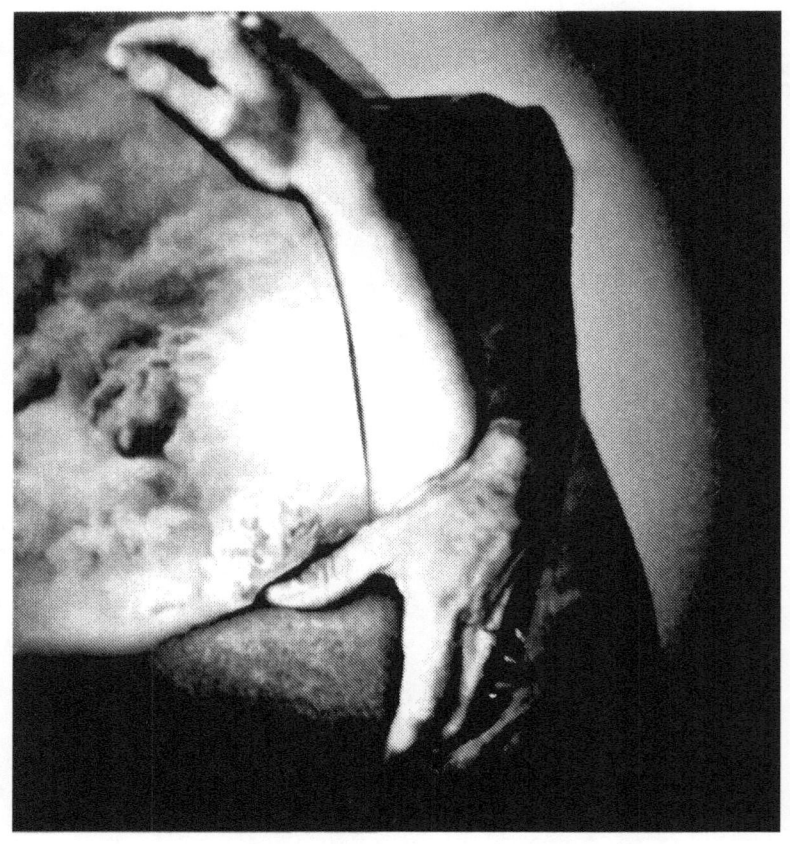

PIERCINGS

Ternura was the word his latest sex interest used to describe what was missing in their relationship.

Andy, of course, flinched at the word relationship. He was all set to correct Worth, when he began to wonder if he had his name right. The young man had been baptized to the two-last-name variety of Southern privilege, ubiquitous in the college, but affected by Andy himself only in even years. His Truman Capotes, Reynolds Prices, Randall Jarrells, Leland Spencers and Lamar Alexanders. But was he Worth Tyler, this young man with the requisite white shirt, striped tie and blue blazer? Or was he Tyler Worth? Once the question arose, it was impossible to set it to rest.

"*Ternura,*" the young man said again, rolling the word around on his tongue with obvious relish. His eyes were the only unexpected thing about him, a blue with the texture of scoured bottle glass. However much you looked into them, you never felt you had focused, taken them in.

He was in his second semester of required Spanish, but was developing a taste for it that Andy was beginning to realize might be distinguished from Andy, his Spanish professor. This, too, gave Andy a little pause. He was used to sending his students, laid or unlaid, on. He wasn't into entanglements. But he found something about Worth Tyler's openness to those foreign words and worlds, his unconflicted relish in them, disturbing.

The young man's tongue touched the back of his upper teeth. His lips stretched and pursed. "*Ternura,*" he said again. "It holds all these interesting trace elements to our ears. You know. Turn. Yearn. It's a trick of the ear, but it still appeals to me. Subliminal effect."

Worth Tyler (or Tyler Worth—the more Andy thought about it, the more he felt he should slip back over to his office and open the grade book tucked in the upper right drawer before he attempted direct address)—this young man with the scoured blue eyes and the two last names—wanted to be a writer. He saw it as part of his cultural pedigree, he told Andy in their first student-teacher conference last spring. No irony, Andy had noticed, and his interest had quickened. Who could survive in the hot house atmosphere of this isolated college campus without irony? But the young man had none— and didn't even have that mildly disoriented look that showed that he could sense, however vaguely, that something necessary was missing.

Andy had let the comment ride, as he had the interest, until the fall, the young man's last required class. His senior year. Andy had his standards. The minority or working class students he chose to ally himself with in odd years, he selected on the basis of something close to this word Worth Tyler was rolling around on his tongue like Demosthenes' marbles. He liked to take up with them earlier in their college careers. Mentor them through the intricacies of coming out of the closet and climbing up the class ladder simultaneously. These others, the blonde, blue-eyed sons of the sons of the sons of privilege, who he engaged with only in even years—he liked to take them on as late in their student lives as possible, to shake them up and then send them out into a world that was now, and he hoped forever, hopelessly bifurcated and entwined, so that they couldn't say us or them with any more assurance than he could say Tyler Worth or Worth Tyler.

But Worth wasn't shaken. He claimed this dimension of his sexuality was a surprise to him, but he took to it as if it were some slight variant of black bottom pie and all that concerned him was getting another slice. "Nice," is what he said to Andy the last time. "Very nice, sir."

"No sir," he said now. "I have to say this even if it gets your dander up. I have my limits."

He wasn't going to go down on Andy until Andy removed his latest Prince Albert ring through the urethra. The young man hadn't noticed the ear stud. Navel stud, he'd accepted without a qualm. The nipple rings had made him hesitate. But they were all done deals. Like the gray at Andy's temples. However, Andy had indulged in this new piercing since the last time they'd made it together, during fall break to be exact, when Andy had flown to New

York to visit with his oldest, homologous friend. Worth felt they should have discussed it.

"It's a matter of respect," he said.

"*Self*-respect," he said when Andy rolled his eyes. "This isn't about me, sir. It's about you."

Andy smiled. He liked the guy. They way he stood at some gentle version of attention he'd picked up at military school or in the boy scouts.

Andy was beginning to wonder now who had signaled availability first. Andy wasn't into seduction—it took too much time and usually had a backlash to it. But he was observant, adept at attuning to the small flickers of interest that occurred when he announced, in his first or second class, his orientation. He did notice now, as he approached fifty, there were no flickers of disappointment among the women. And fewer, he knew there was no way around this, flickers of interest even among those who were openly gay. It was the closeted he appealed to—or the dangerously unrehearsed. Like Worth.

What did the kid know about respect, Andy thought. It was nothing he ever had to work for, had to wrest from unwilling hands. It was like familiar names on grassy gravestones, the rumble of his new SUV, parked, even now, right outside Andy's house. As if everything between them was on the up and up. A piece of cake. Spare change. Low hanging fruit.

"But, you see, these *are* a form of self-respect." Andy avoided direct address, but let a smile play around his lips, one that his friend Keith, in New York still fell for. "I had the first one done when I received tenure. The second when my first book was accepted for publication. The third when I went on my first sabbatical."

"And this one, sir? Where does it fit in your curriculum vitae?" The boy's smile was as engaging, and fleet, as his own.

"Take it or leave it," Andy said with a shrug.

"I'm not rejecting you." The young man ran his hand across the blonde bristle, cut short for swimming team rather than as any social statement. He specialized in the butterfly.

"Thank you," Andy said. He was surprised to realize that he meant it—and that the kid could tell. He was tempted to remove the damn ring— just for the relief. Urine splattered everywhere now. And the piercing didn't seem to be healing up like the others. He wished Worth hadn't made an issue of it. Now it was a matter of self-respect to hold to his position, however quixotic.

"Do you always respond in such an uninflected way?" the young man asked. He took a seat on the sofa, leaning forward attentively, his hands, palm pressed to palm, tucked neatly between his knees.

"Uninflected?"

"I thought the grammatical metaphor would appeal to you. What I mean is without nuance, just black or white. Go or stay. Take it or leave it."

Andy was going to take lessons in ambiguity from someone who was twenty?

"Let's get clear about this," Andy said. He stared at the young man, so much more poised than Andy had ever even fantasized about being at his age. "This is not leading anywhere. Wasn't meant to. Isn't meant to. What you see is what you get. I'm not changing for you. I don't expect you to change for me. I don't expect one fuck to lead to another, if you know what I mean."

"I like what I see," Worth said. "I like what I get. Just without the last piercing, sir."

"Why don't you get one too?"

The young man shook his head, wrinkling his nose in disgust.

"What's the objection?"

"The obvious one, sir. Pain. It looks painful. Whether they are or aren't for you, someone looks at you and thinks of pain. That is part of their intended effect. My younger sister just got her tongue pierced, and every time I look at her, the tip of my own tongue burns. When I start to talk, I feel it's going to catch on my own teeth. I flinch when she rubs it back and forth against the roof of her mouth or the edge of her teeth. It's gotten so I find it difficult to stay in the same room with her. And she's hurt when I tell her. Just as you are. She thinks I've missed the point. She did it to fit in at her college. But I haven't missed the point. It *is* painful. You are, both of you, asking me to enter into some relation to pain that I'm just not willing to. I'm not willing to get it confused with pleasure, sir. I'm just not willing to go that far."

What did this kid know about pain?, Andy wondered, as he pulled his front door graciously aside and waved him out. Or pleasure?

The way Worth understood it, his mother had drowned from the inside out. Fluid seeping from her lungs, filling the heart cavity, the heart itself slowly coming to a standstill under the pressure. It felt, in his imaginings, luxurious towards the end, like sliding deeper and deeper into a bath so hot it became difficult to move. That was why he had climbed into the bed beside her and drew her up close to him at the very end, his hand stroking her dark brown hair quietly.

"There's no fight left in me, Worth," she said. She closed her eyes and a look of pleasure spread across her face at the steady rhythm of his hand, the luxury of subsiding into this last warmth.

"Don't bother them," she said. She meant his sister and his father.

"Are you sure?" he asked. The rhythm of his breath matched the rhythm of his hand. He had the sensation of something equally warm enclosing him. He knew calling out for his father and his sister would destroy the sweet cohesiveness of the moment, but it was his mother's choice, not his. She wanted, this was clear as she rested back against his chest, what he, and he alone, could give.

After her breath slowed, stopped, Worth sat there for a long time staring out into the evening sky so deep and blue, as full as he was of the mystery of night fall. He didn't want to release the weight of his mother's tired, gentle body. He didn't want to rise again to full consciousness. He wanted to stay inside the warmth that still emanated from his mother's body and also seemed to press in on him from the outside, like the weight of water. Then he understood, in a way he knew no one around him would ever share, that he never needed to leave or be left, never needed to wake. This is what she had left him—and him alone—this enveloping warmth that lifted him from the inside and held him close.

His father didn't come into the room until close to midnight. He had been watching the football game. Waiting up for Worth's younger sister, Joy, out on her first date. His father had hesitated at the door, adjusting to the darkness.

"Goodnight," he said and turned to leave.

"It's over," Worth said.

His father shook his head, trying to locate the source of the voice. He made no move to turn the light on.

"What are you doing in here at this hour bothering your mother?"

He switched on the light then and stood there, hands fisted at his sides, blinking furiously.

"It's over," Worth repeated as softly as he could. He knew, how could you miss it, how his father had longed for months now for exactly this outcome. Knew how deep his father's guilt and anger would be if he knew how transparent his desires were to his son.

"What have you done, Worth?" he asked, his voice thick with fear. "What were you doing in here alone?"

"Stroking her hair. Making her comfortable." Worth tried to keep any hint of accusation out of his voice. Both his father and sister Joy had begun to avoid visiting his mother. They couldn't stand how withdrawn she'd become. They couldn't stand the absence of what they'd always taken for granted—that intense but silky attention of hers.

Why was Worth, who had received all his life an unjust share of his mother's love, the one most willing to give her up?

Joy had night terrors for six months after her mother's death. His father, five years later, still hit the bottle too regularly and too hard for it ever to be called social.

Over fall break, both Joy and his father stumbled over their words. Joy's words caught on the tongue stud that so enraged his father, while his father's tongue was so whiskey thick, his thoughts, or what was left of them, came out in a churlish mutter. "Yer mudda—yer mudda."

"Let it go," Worth had advised him. "The less notice you take of it, the sooner she'll get tired of it. At least it isn't a tattoo. Those are the dickens to remove." Joy's new boyfriend Terry had tattoos over the length of both arms and all over his chest, back and ass according to Joy's account. He hadn't, yet, added her name to the roster that decorated his hip bones. Joy didn't like to get too close. A virgin, she only let non-allergenic metal alloys penetrate her tongue.

"If your mudda lived, this would never—"

"Joy would be Joy. The only difference is she might have chosen an eyebrow rather than her tongue," Worth told him briskly. His father had smiled, absolved by his son's presence.

And Joy, too, had come up to him more than once to tell him that when he graduated she wasn't coming home again without him. "But I'll come to see you," he assured her. When she looked mutinous, he added, "Just look at me as a reincarnation of Minnipeepeepoopoo." That was Joy's dog, who died a year after her mother and for whom her mourning had been more vociferous, more inconsolable.

"I've got to get away," she said. "From both of you. You don't look anything like her, Worth—but there isn't a gesture of yours that doesn't bring her back. And he's useless without her. You can't deny that."

"Why would I try to put you, of all people, on?" Keith ran his tanned hand across his short gray beard. "The last three tests came back positive. It's the real thing."

"After all these years," Andy said. The rage he felt astonished him. He'd had his share of friends die, especially at the beginning of the epidemic. But not now. Not now.

"It isn't like it was before," Keith said. "I've got years left. I'm not making any excuses for myself. Maybe I just got tired of being so careful, Andy. You ever thought about that? That life can get so precious it gets put on a shelf to gather dust."

"Fucking idiot," Andy said quietly. He picked up one of Keith's beautiful and macabre crucifixes bought on one of their trips to Guatemala years ago. Nearly three feet high, with cross, the figure was crude but the expression on the face delicate. It was one of Keith's favorite pieces.

"Put him back," Keith said equally quietly. " I don't think he'll break, but you might rip his lace loincloth."

Andy smoothed out the dingy lace with his fingertips and set the figure back in his place of honor in the recessed bookcase. Keith, like Andy, was an academic. An art historian who specialized in baroque art of the nether America, as he said. For his own delectation, he preferred the cruder, more expressive pieces made by native craftsmen that he found tucked away in various mercados. But they never gathered dust on his shelves. That wasn't Keith's way.

"Even if you don't believe in anything, you can feel how much devotion each of them has received," he used to say of the figures in his collection as he ran a feather duster or flannel cloth over them. Later that night, when Andy came back to the living room and found him staring at the statue, Keith mentioned it again. "Sometimes I can't even come in here at night, the air is so filled with prayers. It has nothing to do with beauty, the power he has."

Of course Keith was wrong. The figure had everything to do with beauty. There was nothing in Keith's apartment that wasn't reflective of his uncompromising eye. Including Keith, or Keith of ten, twenty, thirty years ago. The two of them went back to the beginning of Andy's real life, when he left home, came into his own at college. And all their lives, they'd never coupled. The last taboo, Keith had called it. Their pristine place. That space between them which allowed everything in them to pour out and mingle. Men didn't usually have confiding relationships—certainly not with other men. Gay men were no different. There was always some measure of self-presentation that needed to be preserved. But he and Keith had never had any reason to hide anything from each other. Their visits together over the years had been the freest space Andy had ever known. Not that they said all that much. Just that it was an option. He had always known it was an option. And he had assumed, all these thirty years, that the same held true for Keith.

"You had yourself tested three times and never let on?"

"You know how it is, Andy. No one looks forward to the news. And look at you now. You're not exactly a shoulder to lean on—if that was what I had any intention of doing. I have enough self-anger for the two of us. Believe me."

Keith pressed his long fingers against his temples. Sweat was beading on his forehead, making his fingers gleam. "I won't need to be on drugs for several years now."

"What do you expect me to do?" Andy asked.

"I'm making you executor, of course. And I'll want you to keep my lace Christ, if you will. It goes way back—just like the two of us. I'll want you to come visit just as often as before. Especially when I'm in hospice. Maybe we should do another south of the border excursion one of these days. Long before hospice, of course."

"Why?" Andy asked him.

Keith didn't pretend not to understand. "I was tired. That's all. I like my work. I'm good at it. My students go on to graduate school more often than not. I've gotten the grants, written the books that are in me. I don't need anything more."

"What about me?"

Keith stared at him, his fingers still rubbing gently at his temples. He had fine lines around his eyes and mouth. The depressions under his eyes were the color of faded indigo. He had never looked better to Andy.

"What *about* you, Andy? What keeps *you* here?" Keith closed his eyes and kept them closed. His breath was so light and slow, Andy could almost imagine him preparing for the final viewing.

"How can you, of all people, ask that?" Andy pushed forcefully away from the table, letting the coffee slosh in its cup, the chair rock on its back legs.

Keith smiled, but at what Andy couldn't begin to imagine. He didn't trouble himself to open his eyes. "How could you, of all people, *not* ask that of yourself?" he said.

It was then that Keith's fatigue, his life-sickness entered Andy as a physical weight. Whatever Andy said or did, he couldn't get rid of it. There was nothing he could do automatically anymore. Work. Make a phone call. Make yet another caustic comment on yet another earnest, pedestrian paper. Say the names, in whatever order, of this young man who had the presumption to assume that his presence mattered to Andy after only six quick fucks and a semester and a half of public lectures.

"No one knows," Worth told him the next time they met. He had shown up, without warning, during Andy's open office hours. "I know how small the community here is. Whatever we decide on, you can count on me to preserve your reputation, sir."

"I can't tell you what a relief it is to me to know my reputation is safe with you," Andy said. "Since it isn't with anyone else around here."

He didn't, honestly, understand why his behavior was tolerated—except that it had such a pedigree. Who, after all, generation after generation—had chosen to live out here in the middle of nowhere teaching beautiful young men except those who had a true penchant for them? The introduction of young women on campus hadn't changed the predatory ethos, just enlarged its scope. Andy was, by no stretch of the imagination, a predator. But even if he were, what could the provost, recently married to a new hire, or his chair, married to one of his former students and avidly conducting an affair with a current one, possibly say?

"People are kinder than you think," Worth said. "And clearer-sighted than you may imagine." He ran his hands across his stubbled scalp as if the rasping calmed him. He leaned forward and spoke in a very low voice.

Relationship, Andy thought wearily. He wants to talk about our relationship.

"I wish I weren't the one to have to bring this up, sir, especially now. But you need to know there is a rumor going around that you may be a carrier, and that you have infected two students. There is talk of going to the provost." Worth stood up, walked over and closed the door and stood with his back to it, his hands clasped behind him, like an MP.

Andy closed his eyes. All he could see was that dirty lace loincloth, his own fingers straightening it so gently, so goddamn gently, before setting the crucifix back inside the recessed alcove, under the perfectly pitched miniature spotlight, in Keith's immaculate living room.

"Who is spreading the rumors?"

"I've been trying to find out. I don't think you're going to like the answer."

"Who?"

"Maurice. Maurice White and Desmond Miles. I've talked with them, sir."

"That's how you're saving my reputation?"

"Reputations are about perceptions. Norms and perceptions. The truth doesn't have to enter into it at all. They're afraid, sir. They're trying to protect the people they love."

"What's the real story?"

"You tell me," Worth said. "You tell me and I will do everything I can to get it out. They say they both had a relationship with you."

The two young men had been his last two odd years. Maurice, in particular, had not liked moving on. Wouldn't come out. Wouldn't stop calling Andy at all hours of the night.

"If they say I fucked them—or they fucked me—they're right. But it was all consensual. No promises were made—so none were broken."

"But did you knowingly infect them, sir?"

"Me? Knowingly? Even unknowingly? No."

"They're going to use your piercings against you, you know. Use them to show how indifferent you are to suffering—yours or anyone else's."

"I'll go talk with them," Andy said. He knew his status, had ever since they developed the tests. He made it a ritual. Every six months.

"I wouldn't go see them if I were you," Worth said. "They're very upset. People will notice if you meet here in your office. Or at your house. Or in their rooms. Or even in the coffee shop. It will just fan the flames."

"I couldn't do something like that," Andy said. He always used condoms, taught this to each of them as carefully as he did the proper uses of the subjunctive.

"I never implied you would, sir. But they're very scared. Maurice just got his results back. Desmond is waiting for his. They don't dare tell their folks. They think if they can pin the infection to you, there might be some kind of pay out. Not for them. For their families. For what they're going to have to go through. Because you're a teacher."

Maurice and Desmond. His two best students in the last ten years. He'd just finished writing Desmond's graduate school recommendations. He had one mentally prepared for Maurice when the time came. The depth of the betrayal was like a needle stuck through his ribs and stilling the heart muscle.

"Did you?" Worth asked.

"Did I what? Bring them along? Let them enjoy their sexuality in safety and privacy—even here in this god-forsaken, privilege-infested ghetto? Encourage their ambitions?"

"Did you infect them?" He just stood there, his legs planted out on either side, his hands closed over the doorknob. Waiting. He had the eeriest, kindest look on his face. Andy found himself answering without defensiveness.

"I pierce myself to stay awake, to stay alive. Why would I foster death? Why would I do that to those young men I hold in such respect? Who have struggled against such odds to get here?"

"I suggest you get a test taken as soon as possible then, to prove you're negative. And maybe something can be done about setting up a fund. There are other people involved. Girls too, I think. There is going to be a big scandal when this comes out—and it could prove costly. Along with disappointing their families, that's their fear too."

"Whose side are you on?" Andy asked.

"My own," Worth said. "If this works out the way I want it to, you remove your piercings, they get more help than they would otherwise, and I begin my career as a writer with a very new slant on a very old school."

"You don't care about any of us, do you?"

"Of course I do. But whether I do or don't doesn't make a bit of difference. None of you would believe it. It's not your nature."

"I have never, Andy, seen the least respect in your eyes. You've had that baleful look from the time you were a small child," his mother said.

Her name, ironically, was Happy. She was mad as a hatter and had that genius of the mad to name in a way that could never be unsaid.

"You are still my mother," Andy answered, his face flushed with remorse. "However baleful, vindictive, ineffectual, or otherwise like my father I am, I am the best you've got because I am all that you've got—so shut up, will you. Just shut up."

But Happy wouldn't. Why would she change the pattern of a lifetime—that crazy, cracked drone that began at dawn and continued, like the creakings of a settling house, deep into the night: *It's just not right. It's just not right.*

The referent was constantly changing. Andy's taciturnity. His grades. His SAT scores. His choice of college. His decision to marry. Her job evaluations. Their precarious financial situation. Her loneliness expanded each day like macular degeneration, blocking out any clear focus, any distinct object.

This time she was talking about the timing of Andy's coming out—three weeks before his wedding. She didn't know the half of it, of course. Didn't know the convulsions he was sending through his fiancée Helen's family. He had told her first, not Professor Spencer, her father, his thesis advisor—and his lover of the past three years. His rickety next rung on the academic ladder—everything was threatening to pull apart and send him into endless plummet.

But Keith, who had already been admitted to graduate school, had stepped in and offered Andy a place to stay to get away from Happy's obsessive recriminations. Away from Helen's hysterical calls asking why he had led her along.

"I never slept with you," he said. It's all he could cling to. He hadn't gone too far to turn back. "Didn't you ever wonder?"

"I thought it was about respect, Andy. About shyness too, maybe. I didn't know it was about disgust."

"Oh honey," he said. And meant it. Disgust was the last thing he felt for Helen. Sick with regret and self-loathing, yes. But disgust at her. Never.

"Tell her," Keith urged him. "Tell her the whole story. Whatever happens, it is better to have it out in the open." He meant Andy should tell her about her father.

But Andy couldn't. He could just take the dead of night phone calls from Helen. The early morning ones from her father, Leland. Happy's evening tirades.

"I thought we had an understanding," Leland had said once he learned. He thought he was talking to Andy. He had called Keith's apartment ready to play the aggrieved father, but Keith, answering the phone, had cut the ground out from under him immediately.

"What understanding, Leland? What shit are you trying to pull?" Keith asked. Keith spoke with such a degree of anger and familiarity that Andy suddenly knew that Keith had been there too. With Leland. He'd just known when to get out. But it wasn't Leland who got to Andy. It wasn't Keith. It was Helen—that anguish in her voice that pierced him so sharply he couldn't draw breath.

"You are going to get a graduate school recommendation out of this," Keith insisted to Andy. "He set you up. You're taking the fall for him." But Andy wasn't. He was fully responsible for what he'd done. He was on his own now. Just as he had been when he had showed up at the prosperous private college, one degree of separation from Ivy, that had awarded him, a townie, a full scholarship.

When a few years later Andy began to apply to graduate schools, Leland had to call and beg to be included in his list of references. So people wouldn't talk. Andy had been a star student, graduating summa cum laude. It would stand out if his thesis advisor weren't included among his recommendations. At first, Andy had been moved by Leland's request—and then he saw Keith's unscrupulous but steady hand moving them all like shadow puppets. There had been another student. The threat of exposure. Helen, after Andy, was wise to all the rumors and was bringing them home to her mother. Leland was using him as a cover again.

"You *still* can't see what he did to you, can you?" Keith asked.

This was years later, when they were both contributing papers to a festschrift for Leland.

"Don't be naive," Andy said. "Romantic."

"Get it sorted out before you start teaching," was all Keith said.

And Andy did. He was out front, in graduate school and after, about his orientation. Never pretended to respect the student-professor boundaries outside the classroom, but made it clear nothing came ahead of his students' success. He didn't cling. Andy didn't cling. He never used anyone for cover, or refuge.

"But that's what we all want," Worth said. "Someone we can count on. No wonder you're mad."

His sister Joy just wouldn't stop screaming, "It's *my* fault. It's *my* fault."

She had surprised her boyfriend, Terry, in his dorm room with a young man, equally tattooed. They'd just been checking out the designs and, hey, one thing led to another. They were a little stoned, all right.

"He can't even be straight about it," Joy yelled. "Says it was a mistake. It won't happen again. And what am I going to do without him, Worth? I can't bear the idea of a life alone."

"You have your girlfriends," Worth said. "You have me, sweetie. You're not alone."

"You don't have any idea what you're saying because you have no idea, no idea at all, what I'm feeling. She didn't reject you. She didn't leave you without a word of goodbye. And even if she did, I don't think you would have cared. Nothing gets to you, Worth. No one."

"I'm not your problem, Joy. Terry is."

"Dad insists you had something to do with Mom's death, Worth. Is that true?"

"You've gone too far, Joy." Worth's voice was low, almost caressing.

"Have I?" she asked in an equally low voice, hollow where his was rich and resonant. "Or have I finally gone far enough?"

Worth slowly set the receiver down, turned off the answering machine, and left his dorm room.

He waved at Maurice and Desmond. Desmond lay stretched out on his bed with his arm over his eyes. There was such defeat in his posture, Worth almost stopped to say something, but as he paused Maurice looked up from his desk. His expression was so vengeful, Worth looked away. He made his wave slow, natural, but the hairs on the back of his neck stood up. Too close.

Just like Joy.

Just like his father when Worth came to him, the day after his mother's funeral, with the medicines he'd found hidden in her closet.

"Whose choice was it to stop using these?" Worth asked him.

He had believed, all through, that his mother had done nothing to speed her departure, just hadn't delayed it. Until, going into his father's closet to borrow a white shirt and tie for the funeral, he'd found the large shoe box of medicines, right there on the floor. No attempt to hide them.

"She didn't hide them from you—but maybe you hid them from her, Dad. Is that true?"

Worth saw his mother's face lighting up from within as he pushed open the door after school, the hand, which could barely lift itself from the bedspread, flattening the quilt with just the slightest pressure. An invitation for him to approach. She'd held his eyes all the time she spoke.

"This is my choice, and mine alone," she had told him. "I don't want to waste the time I have left paying attention to the wrong things."

"Like what?" Worth asked her. He had never felt so sick, but he made his voice low, calm.

"Like hunting for a new heart, when the one I have is so filled with love. For all of you. It's enough, Worth. It has to be enough."

"It is," he said, taking her hand, so heavy in its exhaustion, in both of his and holding on for dear life. "It is."

But, of course, it hadn't been. Just look at Joy now with her unpierced virginity, her violated tongue. And his father's lust for his Jack Daniel's.

"Your mother and I never hid anything from one another, Worth. Whatever you would like to think, we were partners up until the end."

"That's why you let her sit up there in her room alone so many nights while you watched television downstairs?"

"She wasn't alone, Worth. She had you. It was what she wanted most in the world. To spend as much time as possible with you and Joy. It was the least she could do."

"I don't believe you, Dad. If she wasn't going to extend her life artificially, I don't think she would cut it short artificially either. And I don't believe she wouldn't have told me if that was what she was doing. We had no secrets from each other."

"Who are you to know that, Worth? What secrets were being kept, what promises were being broken?"

"If I ever learn for sure you hurried her death, I know it was against her wishes. I know there's a name for it."

"Then use it. You think I murdered your mother."

"I think you didn't care enough to keep her alive, to keep her fighting."

"Against what? For what?" His father came over to him and took the shoe box. "We're talking four weeks here. No more than that."

"Which you took away from her."

"She made the decision when she decided against the transplant. There was no reason to keep teasing it out."

"She said that?"

"She didn't have to. What were four more weeks to any of us? I wanted her forever, you self-righteous little prick. I wanted your mother here with me forever."

"And I didn't?" Worth screamed out into the forest, the autumn leaves rustling around him like fire. "And *I* didn't?"

He closed his eyes to listen to the echo of his voice battering all around him like a trapped bird. So much fire everywhere it turned. In his mind's eye he could see all these piercings—tongue with its gold stud, eyebrow with three silver rings, a ring in one nostril or the septum, a small diamond glittering in a navel, or several glittering from an ear. He saw those awful rings stabbed through nipples, the foreskin of a penis, the stud through the labia. He could see a needle long as his hand going in between the ribs, the plunger rising again as the vial filled with a clear liquid stained red.

She drowned in that, Worth thought. It wasn't her choice. If he had known, he would have stabbed that needle in daily, taken whatever he could draw out and never give it back.

"They're right," he whispered into the air that glittered with sun struck fragments of leaves drying on the stem. "It wasn't enough, Mom. Whatever you said—or hoped for—it wasn't enough."

And suddenly he understood that he was going to let Joy believe whatever their father told her, just as he was going to believe what his mother had told him. Just as he understood that Andy was not going to get himself tested, was going to let Maurice and Desmond play this out their own way. Just as he knew he was going to do anything he could to stop them. Because Andy, whether he knew it or not, still had everything to lose.

"Tell me the truth," he had whispered to his father. "Just tell me the truth."

"There isn't one," his father had said.

But he, Worth, had felt his mother's hair begin to gleam under his hand in the twilight. He had felt that warmth inside him and outside him. He could choose. Just like all of them, he could still chose where he gave himself and how deeply.

He saw a piece of green glass in the leaves and reached down and picked it up. He ran his finger over the surface, hoping it was sharp enough to break the skin. He took it to his wrist and sawed at the skin until finally a thin scratch opened up. He knelt down and scraped away the leaves, exposing the thick mulch from the last year. He pressed his wrist to the dirt as if he were making it his blood brother.

"There isn't a day that goes by, I don't miss you," he whispered. "There isn't a single, goddamned day that goes by I don't miss you."

"Why don't you try being true, sir?"

"Say what?" Andy asked.

"Why don't you try being true to who you really are," Worth said.

"And who is that?" Andy asked.

Worth had come over to his house on a late Sunday afternoon. He'd been out hiking in the area and decided to drop in. He must have fallen because his hands and wrists were stained with dirt. Andy had shown him straight to the bathroom.

When he came out of the bathroom, Worth stood with his hands behind him in his standard pose of admonitory attention. This could be tiring, Andy thought. All this oversight. All this good faith.

"Someone who wants to wake up, sir. Someone who wants to stand up and be counted when it really matters."

"And in these circumstances, what does that mean?"

"Taking responsibility for your good intentions."

Andy shook his head. He went into the kitchen and opened two beers and came out with them. The light through the trees was a wild, unrepentant red.

"Come again," he said.

Worth reached out his hand for the beer.

"I'd like that," he said. "And you know I'll stand by you whether you decide to fight them or not."

Andy felt a fierce contraction, as if a heavy weight were pressing down on him and his body was instinctively rebelling.

"I'm not asking anything of you," he said harshly.

"But I am," the young man said. He put his hand out and turned Andy's face so Andy had to look directly into those scoured blue eyes that allowed no true purchase. "I just want to be sure you hear me. *I* am asking. You don't need to answer me. I just need to know you hear the question."

Andy turned the young man's hand over, seeing the fine line, a cut, on the wrist. "What are you doing to yourself?"

"Beginning to make my mark in the world?" The young man laughed. "Doing what comes naturally? You tell me. I'm just like everyone else, sir. I want to wake and have someone, something true to wake to. And you're right. That need is a pain and a pleasure. It can be cultivated and it can be perverted. It can be given and rescinded. It can sing its own praises and not have a word to say in its own defense. And it can be recognized. That's all I *do*, know really. It can be recognized."

Andy stared into those strange, scoured eyes in which, hard as he tried, he could not recognize himself.

He spoke as kindly as he knew how. "This is my battle—if it is a battle. I don't want any help."

His fingers kept running across that fine line on Worth's wrist. One he knew he couldn't, in good conscience, cross.

The young man cocked his head to one side, as if listening studiously. He nodded. Smiled.

"*Tender*, sir. I think that word would describe your voice too. But I prefer that Spanish one, the one that holds for us, however improbably, the echo of choice."

"Rather than a cash transaction?"

"Exactly." Andy's thumb kept trying to erase that line on the young man's wrist that wasn't of his own making. Worth watched him, listening, with his eyes closed, to what rose, receded, until the pressures inside and out were equilibrated, tolerable, then drew his own hand free.

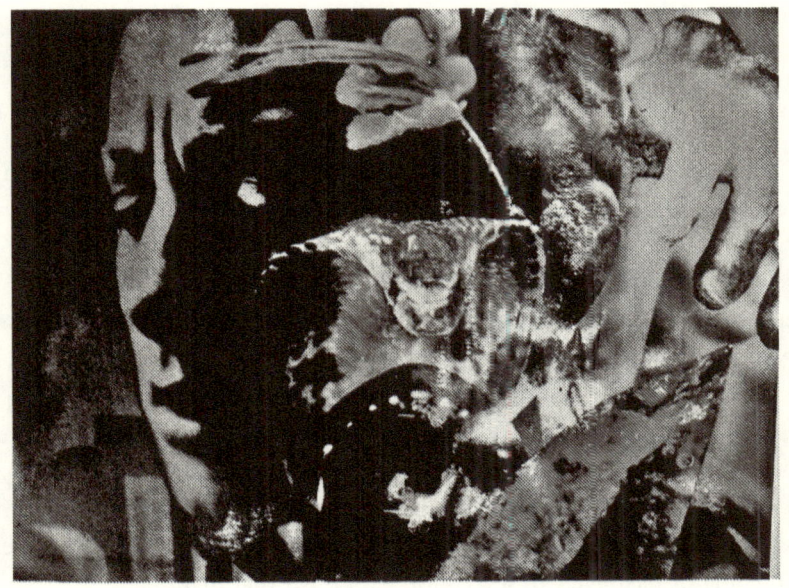

MY KUNDALINI EXPERIENCE

There wasn't one.

Everything was prepared for it. I took time off from work, I was so sure it was coming. I talked to Solár, my bodywork guru, about what I should do when it happened. Not if, when.

"Wow," she said. "Go with the flow!" Solár is street smart, body smart, but doesn't have a large verbal range. I'm a numbers person in general, so we get along well. She's a great masseuse. I keep my eyes closed when she performs the more arcane of her massage techniques, like dusting off my astral body. But this kundalini thing, it resonated, the moment I heard about it, in ways I still can't explain. It's not the theory that interests me, just the phenomenon. The moment I heard about it, I knew, I just knew, it was possible. I don't feel the same way about telepathy or astral travel or channeling or past lives. Resurrection either, for that matter.

Since I'm a scientist and believe in research, I attended a meeting on kundalini experiences held in San Francisco. (I arranged to make a site visit to one of the Superfund sites in San Francisco at the same time, which allowed the Centers for Disease Control, where I work, to foot most of the travel costs. Not for the conference, of course, which I attended secretly on my own time and dime.) Researchers came from all over the world, but mainly from California and Colorado, where, I suppose, more people have kundalini experiences, as well as about every other kind of altered consciousness imaginable. Perhaps alternative states are fostered by the Rockies, the desert, the smog, the New Age zeitgeist. Maybe the forests of central Georgia are an impediment. Location, location, location, as they say.

I didn't fit in, of course. When you look at me, you think dork. I wear fitted suits chosen for their blandness. In a bureaucracy, I think of it as protective coloration; at Solár's, as idiosyncrasy; but there at the kundalini conference, it was just awkward. I should have been wearing a flowing kimono jacket or an Indian dress. I eagerly learned all the signs of a genuine experience, the colored lights, the spastic movements—which they called automatic asanas and mudras, the convulsive rising of energy from the base of your spine through all your energy centers right out the crown of your head and, depending, back over to your third eye. I learned about all the neurological correlates to the chakras, and about the holistic benefit of such an experience. You were never the same, everyone agreed—researchers, therapists, yogis, and your all-purpose New Age yearner after purpose and thrills. Obviously, I didn't fit any of the categories, but I did think, *This sounds right. This really sounds right.*

Five days later, I bought a two-week supply of frozen dinners more nutritious and dependable than anything I ever prepare myself and left them for my daughter and husband and went off to a cabin on the Gulf coast I'd borrowed secretly from my friend Loli. Where I am now. Waiting. Still waiting.

"I'll call in every day," I told Kevin and Melanie as I left. "I just need to be able to control access." I wouldn't tell them the address either, just said I'd be sure to call and, if there were a real emergency, they could always call my friend Loli. I did leave her phone numbers—both work and home. Of course, I had forgotten that Loli was attending a conference in Brussels, but even if they call and somehow hook up with her, I don't think they will succeed in worming my whereabouts out of her. At least not under normal circumstances—like ear ache, flu, or first menstrual period. Probably not even mono. Or stage fright.

Loli has no children—or husband—and is big into self-care and hearing the Goddess out whenever, and in whatever form, she appears. We go to the same bodyworker and work in the same public health agency, where we never let on about our favored extracurricular activities. Actually, we rarely see each other at work since she does sex practices and behavior change over in HIV and I do toxic waste. At the bodywork salon, we discuss auras and chakras, chitta, prana, tantra, and, yes, kundalini. Loli is, I think, a true believer. I'm not sure I know what I believe in, but I know I like the atmosphere there. It is so touchy-feely. So ingenuous. So intellectually undemanding. So not me. I experience that mindlessness like a release of saliva, a shift from my sympathetic to parasympathetic nervous systems. *Cool,* I think with a deep sigh of relief each time I stretch out on Solár's massage table and inhale the aromatic oil of the day. *Cool.* Why would the life of the mind feel over-heated to me, a scientist to my marrow?

When I asked to borrow her cabin, I told Loli I was working on my first chakra issues. Again. "Get *down*, sister," she said with that rich laugh of hers. She told me I'm ripe for a kundalini. Like it's an orgasm and can be experienced thousands of times without recall. Not like it is The Change. But maybe that is because she's fifteen years younger than me and menopause isn't part of her emotional vocabulary.

It sure is part of mine.

But I am not having a mid-life crisis, rather, any time now, I will be having my kundalini experience. Unlike Loli, I feel they are a once in a lifetime event. Like the eviction of the last egg from your ovaries. Whatever I'm going through, I don't want to think of it happening again and again. I guess that is just part of my nature. I'm singular. I've only wanted the one husband I selected for myself when I was twenty-four. It took me six years to get him to see the rightness of our relationship, but I never questioned it. Still don't. He *is* the man for me, even if he sometimes questions whether I need any man at all. I'm not frigid or anything, just reserved and self-sufficient. Even though he was the one who held back originally, Kevin is the connector in our marriage.

He's the one, for example, who felt the need for us to have a child. I felt we were quite complete in ourselves. After we'd been married six years, he asked me to put away my diaphragm, which, somewhat reluctantly, I did. Two years later, we went to a fertility expert who ascribed our problems to Kevin's low sperm count as well as my intermittent ovulation and irritable uterus.

"Do you have anything against adoption?" the doctor asked. He was young but rotund, with hands that bulged like inflated latex gloves. "We can go through all sorts of desperately expensive procedures, from sperm packing to implanting embryos, but there are a lot of kids out there already who could use a home."

I expected Kevin to say yes, he did want his own child, *our* own child—but he surprised me by saying that it really didn't matter to him whether the baby even shared the color of our skins.

"We just need someone to care for, Paula."

"We care for each other."

"We need more than that," he said.

He didn't care about genes, but he nixed the idea of foster children. "I want to make a permanent home for them," he said. "I want us to be at the center of their world."

I didn't mind the idea of fostering, since that felt to me the essential nature of childhood, and parenthood, anyway. On the other hand, I had never been close to my parents—so maybe I didn't know what I was talking about. Generalizing, as we say in my work, from a sample of one.

Kevin came from a big family. Catholic. And his brothers and sisters kept right on reproducing. I always feel that I've entered a hurricane when I'm with them. However, in the midst of so many siblings, so many nieces and nephews, not to mention cousins, uncles, aunts, and godparents and godchildren and just your run of the mill neighbor who knew you in diapers—I've never once located the still eye, although I seek it every time I visit.

I'm an only child—of elderly parents, now dead. Both were college professors. My mother taught art history, and my father taught the other kind of history—"the unaesthetic, the downright savage kind," he always said. He was a very civilized man, never raised his voice, affected a slight British accent, so the comment was always comic. His specialty was revolutions, primarily European, but, as he always said, the topic was universal. Wasn't a country in the world that hadn't experienced one. My mother, who specialized in modernism, would protest that art too had its cataclysmic and destructive side. They would sip their wine and smile at each other. I would find refuge in some formula I was memorizing for chemistry, some equation from calculus, since those looks they exchanged always made me feel excluded. You could say all the energy in our family was cerebral, but that wasn't true. My father and mother's arguments were foreplay. There wasn't room for a third party. When they looked at me, I always had the feeling that all they saw was the act—exclusively theirs—that created me.

In reaction, I developed a contrary streak, always trying to drive a wedge between them, get the intention directed, however negatively, back at me. But the more I tried, the more intermeshed their *we* became.

"Do you agree with mother on this?" I would ask my father—whether it was about Andy Warhol, Egon Schiele, wearing iridescent blue eye shadow in seventh grade, or using contraceptives in ninth.

"Of course we've talked about it, your mother and I, and we're in accord."

"And you?" I would ask my mother. "You agree with Dad on this?" This: my choice of college, the causes of the French Revolution, how many friends I could have over on New Year's Eve and if I could serve alcohol to minors inside their home. Never mine—theirs alone.

I see Melanie try the same thing with Kevin and me. I almost always defer to Kevin, since he is the one who does the majority of the child care. I guess from the outside it appears like the same situation I faced as a child. It's not exactly. I don't feel Melanie wants to divide Kevin and me, more like she wants to engage me. They both do.

"What do you think of Melanie going away to camp next summer?" Kevin asked me just before I left. "You and I could go on a vacation. We haven't done that for twelve years."

"Fourteen," I said. "But who's counting." I didn't mean this as a put-down. I just wanted to point out that we hadn't done it before Melanie was born either. I was very excited about my work fourteen years ago. I had just gotten the position I still hold now, and I was busy learning everything I needed to about toxic exposures, a topic not heavily addressed in my epidemiology program. Kevin had just gone into business for himself, so when he wasn't photographing, he was busy drumming up business. With our fertility obsession, our time together had become a little heavy-handed, cumbersome. We were being kind to each other, keeping the feeling contained in the small doses of time we allotted each other.

Strange that at fifty-two I'm off to meetings about kundalini, isn't it? I don't want compartments or moderation. I want excess, fusion, fizz. Maybe it's because I find my energy waning, my focus diffusing, and I think this might reverse the process. I know there's something missing, you see. I've always known there was something missing.

But I have never, and I pride myself on this, asked someone else to provide it for me. That's what bothers Kevin, and now Melanie, so much. They feel I wall them out. But if something's missing in your life, it's up to you to provide it. Can't go asking someone else to be filling in the gaps. That is why I always felt Kevin was right for me. I always knew he couldn't fill those gaps. That's what made it feel safe to be around him. I knew I'd never get confused. I'd always know whose lungs the breath was coming from. *I would not end up like my parents.*

It would never have occurred to me, obviously, to have a child because I had a need to give. Just because I have a need to give doesn't mean that I feel entitled to go and create someone to *receive.* But maybe that also is why I married Kevin. I have never confused his ways with my own—or thought our life should reflect only mine. I'm fully responsible for my decision to go along with Kevin on this adoption thing.

I was free to say that I didn't think Melanie was the child for us—and I didn't think so. I wasn't sure we were up to a multiracial child, however beautiful. I wasn't sure I was up to a girl. But I didn't speak up. That was my choice. I don't know quite where Kevin scared Melanie up, and I've chosen not to explore this too closely either. The papers are in order. That's all that matters. Some days, she'll turn her head and I'll see Kevin so clearly in her profile. Maybe he has come to resemble her the way masters come to resemble their pets, although Kevin would be quick to point out that he is decidedly in Melanie's thrall, not the other way around, so who's the master and who's the pet is remains a little squiffy. But the resemblance does not. Everyone remarks on it, until they learn she is adopted. Her gold skin just makes her look heavily tanned. Her hair, like his, is a gold streaked brown. She remains strikingly beautiful, just as she was as a child. She has a sense of style, even at this age, and would never, like her mother, be mistaken for a dork.

I am as much in Melanie's thrall as Kevin—now that she's older and has a mind of her own that can put things together independently. Kevin misses the little girl she was. Her dependency. Honestly, I didn't find her very interesting as an infant or a small child. I did my fair share of the feeding and care, but I was quite bored. How long can you watch a baby sucking its toes, a little girl playing with her teddy bear or beanie babies or, in Melanie's case, since she is a tomboy, race cars and trains? Now, I look forward to hearing her daily riff—on why her seventh grade art teacher, Mrs. Rosenthal, keeps the ashes of her first husband on the mantelpiece of her home with her second husband, Mr. Rosenthal; why women can't lift as much as men but boys can't lift as much as girls; why every woman who has ever held the highest political office in a democracy—an admittedly minuscule sample—has proved right wing and personally tyrannical. I wonder what sense she's making of my leaving to have my kundalini experience.

I wonder what sense *I* am, since it doesn't seem to be taking place. I was so sure it was coming. I didn't feel the slightest sense of apology making space for it—not at home or at work. It felt like an urge, a necessity. Like defecating. I'm only half joking. Maybe it sounds better to say that it's like the urge to deliver—but that's an experience I never had.

Now, at fifty-two, I wish it had been possible. I miss not ever having been completely possessed by an experience. Knowing what you want and getting it is not the same as being possessed. It's a difference between containing and being contained. That is one of the big differences between Kevin and me. He sees himself as a river, a fountain, a flood. I secretly dream of being absorbed. So when I imagine delivery, it's not expulsion I imagine, but being taken over by something larger than me, something that reorganizes my whole place in the world. Odd that my fantasy would be this absorbing energy when I don't much care for being touched in my real life. Maybe I'm tired of being so self-sufficient. I don't want to be walled off. I want to be embraced. I want to resonate. With the cosmos. With the snake at the base of my spine.

But here I am in Loli's house, the blue waters of the Gulf just sitting inertly out there, me sitting inertly inside. No resonance. No lift. No possession.

I'm not saying I'm sorry I came. I'm saying this state has some sad similarities to the way I was feeling before I heard of kundalini—and I was hoping for something so different. Maybe that original state is what I should be concerned about. It's like my nerves are going dead. Maybe I have MS or another progressive neuromuscular disease. Messages are no longer moving from here to there with any regularity. In particular, they're not moving from my brain to my pelvis or back. It's like I've atrophied below the waist.

Phantom limb, that's what I thought the last time Kevin and I made love. I didn't like the thought. Still don't. But there's something in me that goes completely passive with it too, like it's completely beyond my control. Like growing up in the family I was born into. Like living in the one I have now.

There, it's out. I can't really feel any difference between the two—except in the second one, my self-sufficiency is a choice rather than a necessity. But if it wasn't a choice, it might very well be a necessity—Kevin and Melanie have always been so close. I wanted that for them, wanted it for Kevin to begin with, wanted it for her later on. Just as I wanted, I'm sure I'm not deluded about this, the distance for myself.

At home, I feel like fathers in the 1950s (any father, that is, except my own uxorious one)—coming home from their law firms and factories and universities and hospitals and insurance companies. Strangers in the homes they financed but never really inhabited. The mother and children were the real unit—and then there was this provider who intruded on occasion, lying in a lounger with his eyes closed, the television blaring, like a forgotten corpse. I suppose Mr. White and Mr. Weatherby were ripe for kundalini experiences too.

I'm not implying that there is a complete role reversal in our marriage. Kevin provides. So do I. But he's a freelance photographer and works out of our home—so it really is much more his than it is mine. I visit. He thrives. This is *his* home, *his* wife, *his* daughter, *his* life.

Melanie's interest in the house, the neighborhood, her father, me, in us as a family, is just as proprietary and unreflective as Kevin's. I'm the only one mute with the mystery of how the three of us came to find ourselves under the same roof, or, even more deeply, puzzling how any one of us came into existence in the first place. It doesn't pay to inspect the whys of our lives too closely, the answers are so fleeting, so contradictory, so inconsequential, finally.

"You really believe this yoga stuff?" Kevin asked me after I'd told him I was going off on this kundalini retreat. "You've never practiced yoga or gone to a class, Paula. All you've done is visit that strange little massage salon. Do you have any idea what you're getting into?" I could see he was skeptical but willing to give it a go. He liked the surprise. I also knew I didn't want company.

"I just know something is happening inside me. I know it isn't a mind thing, although of course I have my thoughts about it. I would have to be crazy not to. But something's changing at a material level. Maybe the balance of my neurotransmitters is shifting, maybe my estrogen levels are rising to the hole in the ozone layer and plummeting back to the earth's core on an irregular schedule. I just know I'll go crazy if I don't go off by myself and hear this out. I'm tired of running scared."

"Maybe we're just getting old," Kevin said with a disbelieving smile. He ran his fingers through his thick white hair. He's eight years older than me and would be eligible for retirement if he were a civil servant. He tells me if you work for yourself and love what you do, the idea of retirement is nonsensical. I count the years, months and days to retirement myself. I feel numb as I do it, and that saddens me. There's nothing luring me on, nothing holding me back. It is just a fact, like so many others. Age. Marital status. Profession. Name.

When Kevin talks about living the life of his dreams, I know I am, as I have always been, the one less than perfectly opportune element in it. I like this. It assures me that I exist as something more than a plot element in his life drama. At the height of an argument, I've been know to tell him this.

"And me? Melanie? What are we to you, Paula?" he yells back.

I honestly don't understand what he is asking. I don't see my own life as a drama. "Amazing, irreducible facts of nature," I tell him. "That's what you both are to me."

"I suppose it's inevitable that someone with a mild to severe attachment disorder would be attracted to a religion that defined attachment as the source of all evil," Kevin said once as I headed off to a massage with Solár. This was after I told him about my plans to go to San Francisco to the kundalini conference and he did a little browsing on the web, just enough to get it in his head that this was about sex.

"Suffering," I corrected him. "Attachment is the source of all suffering."

"But why is an interest in non-attachment associated with so much touch—that's the strange thing. *Reiki. Shiatsu. Acupressure. Rebirthing with water wings*," he read from the brochure for Auracular.

"You want me to make an appointment for you?" I asked. "Solár is great."

He just looked at me, then reached out and took my left hand in his right and studied it like a palm reader. He traced my life line with the index finger of his left hand. It is an unattractive finger, the nail distorted by a blow to the nail bed with a hammer years ago. Unattractive but unapologetic. Kevin's shadow self, perhaps. He leaned down and kissed the heart of my palm, running the tip of his tongue along the creases.

"It's *your* hands I'm missing, Paula. *Your* touch."

That was the night, making up to him, I understood that something was truly going dead in me. The night I understood that I needed, one way or another, to come to terms with this. Phantom limb. *How can you mourn what you never treasured?*

That's what's getting to me about The Change. I never made much use of my being a woman anyway, so why am I so sad to see it oozing away, cell layer by cell layer, lubricious secretion by lubricious secretion, egg by egg? Estrogen replacement therapy, my colleague Colette, an ob-gyn epidemiologist advises me. She's missing the point. I need to understand what this process is that I'm reversing.

"Your Mom's gotta do what she's gotta do," Kevin told Melanie when she started to object to my plans.

"You missed the last play I was in too," Melanie pouted.

"But you were a raving success anyway, weren't you?"

"That's not what she wants to hear, you know." Kevin chided me as we undressed for bed. "She wants you to say you're sorry. To promise to be there the next time."

"I'll try." When Kevin looked at me with a weird expression, I added, "I'll try to reassure her without lying. Without making promises I can't keep. Who *knows*, Kevin. I mean, who knows what's going to happen tomorrow, let alone six months from now."

Kevin shook his head, his eyes narrowed as if he were trying to see something too near for his far-sighted eyes to bring into focus.

"You call it a lie, and I call it an essential promise. Why do we bring children into the world if we can't promise them continuity? We don't tell them we can change the world, just that we'll be there for them."

"God willing," I said.

"Look at our lives," Kevin exploded. "Just look at our lives, Paula. We've lived together for twenty-two years, known each other for nearly thirty. You've worked in the same government agency for all that time. What change are you talking about?"

"That's just my point," I said. "It's gone on forever and at the same time I feel it's never really begun."

"You'll be saying that on your death bed," Kevin said. "And it will make you feel fresh, I suppose. Adventurous."

"Anguished," I said firmly. "It will make me feel then just as it does now—anguished. That's why I need to go off. I need to find a different way."

"Kundalini?" Kevin asked. He closed his eyes. "Just tell her you're sorry, Paula. Tell her you'll watch the video. You'll do everything you can to be at the next opening."

"You talk like she's a child star."

"They all are, Paula. All children are stars. It's their nature. It's our job to see them steadily, sparkling out there in that vast waste of impermanence."

Shiva to our Shakti, just as we are to them.

Except here I am, unchanged and dubious, looking at the unmoved waters of the Gulf, meditating restless hour upon hour, feeling my whole body shutting down cell by cell, nerve end by nerve end, and then extinguish in a little pointless blitz of irritation and restlessness.

Stop resisting. I'm not sure it's a voice I hear. It's an understanding, sharp as the crack of a stick underfoot. The unexpectedness, the realness of the sound make me hopeful. The impatience is reminiscent of Kevin's—and the truth is I miss him more than I've ever missed him in our long lives together. It bothers me, this missing, which is not intellectual, not even emotional, just a hunger in the pads of my fingers for the particular temperature of his skin.

He's a good man.

Did I ever question that? But this was meant to be about me. These thoughts of him, these sensations of him, are a deflection from the real thing.

These unexpected thoughts about him—they're where you're most alive, aren't they? They're where you're most in touch.

What about me? I ask miserably. When am I going to get in touch with me?

The form of science, epidemiology, that I've practiced all my professional life is often accused of being a method without a theory. Popular writers describe it as if it were a thrilling detective story—the search for this malicious organism or that one—HIV, Hanta virus, Nile fever. In truth, it's remarkably boring, mathematical, detached. The afflictions of the body, that's where the excitement is. The relief we feel at being able to protect ourselves from what is not ourselves. Inserting a gene. Blocking one chemical with another. That's medicine. That's not what I do. I look at the distribution of diseases and their determinants in populations. I look for dependable associations, meaning by dependable how an association varies from pure randomness. And no matter what we find, we can never say anything certain about a me or a you in the future. We can talk about the risks of groups but not the destinies of individuals. We can find all sorts of nonsensical but dependable associations, so we don't even use our method, finally. We select results on the basis of plausibility, what we already know of the workings of our bodies in health and disease. On the basis of whatever theory is current, hot.

"Why kundalini?" Kevin asked me.

Why not? Is it, truly, any less plausible a description of my current state than perimenopause may be?

The Chinese ideogram for danger is also the ideogram for opportunity. Or is it the ideogram for death or chance? Whatever, it is the two door theory so popular with every human resources course I've ever taken—from lay-offs to anger management. I could believe that my whole generative system is shutting off—or I could leave myself open to the idea that the energies in my life are just shifting focus, feeding out into the infinite rather than to my uterus.

Why is it that I love this image of a woman, wild, white-haired, immensely sexual, weaving like a cobra up around my spine? I don't know where her image came from. Certainly not the books and articles I've read. But she is indivisible from the kundalini experience for me. Oh, really, I like everything about her. Her heavy warm sensitive breasts, her full belly. She is not nubile, this force. She's thickened with child-bearing, worldly wise but not world weary. She's wonderfully in touch with herself. Her skin and her flesh fit her perfectly. She fills out her body, her psyche. She is alluringly, unapologetically, unbelievably present in her body—but it is a sweet sensuality. Sweet and deep and dangerously self-sufficient. It doesn't come and go with the look in a man's eyes. It has a wonderful confidence and permanence to it—and an element of surprise. It has, this is what I'm so taken with, an inextinguishable pleasure in its own existence. *It takes up space.* It is anything, anything but numb below the waist.

Maybe it's the woman herself that intrigues me, the idea of all this latent, densely physical power that intrigues me. Not its union with the immaterial, the Shiva consciousness. Oh no, I want this Shakti energy to reach up and pull Shiva right down into her. I want her to devour that austere, aloof intelligence. I want Shiva consciousness to lick the coals in her belly into flames, to have the truth of their union be something heavy, abiding, and hot, hot, hot. I want this union to unite them both with the ground beneath them, not with some evanescent aura or energy body spinning out from the crown of my head.

This is what I want, what I sit out on the deck of Loli's cabin inviting, some sense of aliveness down there where it really matters.

Who cares? That voice that is not a voice asks me again. *Who cares where that union takes place?*

Me, I say. I've never been clearer about anything in my life. It matters to me.

Our membranes thin, our secretions lessen, it's not the end of the world.

Something has always been missing, I insist. I want to fill that gap.

Maybe you can't. The voice that is not a voice sounds like an airplane flying some distance off.

But I'm not deterred.

I know different. That's part of The Change. I can *feel* possibility now where I never did before. I will not let that go.

Can't force love. Can't force awakenings. Can't force lust.

I'm talking about energy here. Pure energy and sensation.

You are talking about a meaning for living.

But I have the drill down pat. Life is what it is, I say. I just want it to be a bigger end-in-itself, I insist.

But I am met, again, with dead silence from my solar plexus, my vagina, my mulabandha, my anal sphincter. Maybe I do have MS.

On my third day at the beach, I jettison sitting as the route to enlightenment. I start stalking the long scimitar of white sand. East to west. West to east. Whenever a thought comes to me about cutting my visit short, I rigidly suppress it. Perhaps I should just check into a spa and be massaged with hot rocks and wrapped in sea weeds. At least I'll come back looking as if something meaningful and transforming has happened.

I walk in the morning and again after lunch and nod at the same few people staying in the local motel. I begin to make up stories to tell Kevin and Loli. About the lights in my head, the energy coursing up my left leg, which I must redirect through my spine so that it can run straight out my crown chakra. I describe tinglings throughout my body, just like the sensations my father described after his first stroke when he still retained his capacity for speech. I describe this energy that is like the most delicate dance of motes inside a sunbeam, a bliss nearly past bearing. I describe how, doing a handstand, my feet become one with the sky and my head becomes one with the ground, how my thoughts twine with those of others and we're all one root bed of love and wisdom.

"You didn't call us yesterday," Melanie screams at me when I call late in the afternoon. "You promised."

"But you're all right, aren't you?"

"How would *you* know? Telepathy? Is that part of kundalini too? Did you hear them Mom? When you were tuning in, did you hear them—all those people in the planes, all the people in the stairwells when the buildings fell. You tuned in there, Mom?"

"What are you talking about? Where is your father?"

"Right here," Kevin says. "Give us your phone number, Paula. Enough with the games, already. You can hear how it's upsetting Melanie."

I am not ready to give up. Not yet. I feel, this is part of the singularity of my nature, that I have only this one chance to get it right. Four more days, I think, and I'll concede. But not yet.

"I'm sorry I didn't call in yesterday," I say again. "But it isn't the end of the world. Surely you can get her to see that, Kevin."

"She's not upset about you. You're just icing on the cake. Turn on the television, Paula. Get a clue. They've attacked the World Trade Center and the Pentagon."

Even after all these years, I always fall for Kevin's practical jokes. My skepticism makes me vulnerable, he always tells me. I'm completely dependent on external cues. I don't have any internal shit detector to keep me grounded.

"This isn't the time for jokes," I tell him. "Tell Melanie I'm sorry for the oversight and I hope she breaks a leg tonight—"

"It was yesterday, Paula."

"I'll call in tomorrow."

"Don't bother."

"I feel I owe it to both of you. You've been such good sports."

"As if we had a choice."

"Give me another few days, Kevin."

"You're crazy, Paula. I don't know why I never saw it before. You have you head shoved up your ass and you don't even know it."

"Maybe that's why I need this time. Maybe kundalini will straighten me out." I laugh lightly, but I feel sick. His voice is truly venomous. My Kevin. It's like the world has turned over.

Even now, the conversation makes me sick to recall. I keep hearing it replay as I watch the people throwing themselves off the burning tower, as I see the plane plow into the spine of the building. Kundalini. You want your kundalini? Let's play it again from the beginning.

Once I know, once I understand, I try to call them back immediately. I feel like a monster. I want to apologize. But there is only a busy signal. At first I think Melanie is talking with her friends, but as it goes on hour after hour, I don't know what to think.

I sit on a stool in the kitchen in Loli's beach house watching her little television screen. All the people with their cell phones calling down from the skies. *I love you. I love you. Let's roll. I don't think we'll get out. It's all over.* And the huge balls of smoke and flame as the backbone of the city crumbles, catastrophic story by catastrophic story.

And then as I keep watching the same scenes play hour after hour, the same tower, the same plane, the same tumult of molten steel and ash, the same agonized or stunned faces, the dust, the incredible dust, as I keep hearing the bzz bzz bzz of the busy signal on the phone, stabbing the numbers from my home phone in as regularly as I breathe, something happens to me.

At first I feel as if I am slipping out of my body and entering into the television, entering into the telephone, that I am becoming the static in both of these receivers. And then I realize that I am just slipping inside my body, which is bigger than the world behind the images in the television, noisier than the rasping, briiiinging sound of the telephone. So much space, so much shame, so much emptiness. And no one there to take it in. My body is no more distinct than the air where those towers of Babel and bullion stood only hours ago.

"You tuned in there yet, Mom?" Melanie asked me. She should never have asked me.

What can you hear in a furnace, an inferno, an incinerator, the world as we know it tomorrow?

And all the time that I am listening, my hands keep dialing and dialing home—and the same angry, buzzing sound meets me. I can hear the venom in Kevin's voice. The hysteria in Melanie's.

I didn't know. *I didn't know.*

The venom in Kevin's voice is like the impact of the airplane and Melanie's hysteria, the flames melting the framework of the building.

This is not about you. Get a clue.

I want to say something, I want to feel something, I want to make something clear. But there is always this busy signal. Every time I dial. There's always been this busy signal. My fingers are numb with dialing.

I have never been as gullible as Kevin thinks. I've never been as cold. I've kept my distance from Melanie because if I looked too closely into her face, I would see the truth and I thought, foolish me, that I would never stop falling, that truth was so deep and so cold and so whole. And at the same time, whenever he took her from my hands as an infant, I felt the ground tremble under me. She was my one security.

Who is to say how hot my heart is? Who is to say how loyal my soul?

If I were in that tower or on that plane and I had one phone call, what would I say?

What does the wave know of the ocean?

I know, I would say. I've always known. I'm sorry I let it stand between us for so long. For so goddamn long. You're the one, Kevin. You've always been the one for me. That's all you need to know.

And to Melanie, this stranger I've reared since she was three days old, what would I say to her?

I wanted more time for us, my love. I wanted more than you'll ever know to be your mother. I wanted to see myself in your face and your gestures. *I wanted to be part of something bigger.*

But there isn't for us a last phone call. There's tomorrow. And tomorrow. And there are all those small choices, finite as eggs, that create us.

So my fingers keep dialing and dialing all night long. I can hear the gentle slur of the Gulf waters, feel the wind winding in through the open sliding door.

I know, and it fills me with a desolate clarity, that when Kevin answers I'm going to say, "I know. I've always known, Kevin. And I can't let go of it. I can't move on. And I can't bear what that's doing to me and to you and to

Melanie. I don't want to be dead from the waist down or the waist up either. I don't want to feel like a stranger in my own home. I don't want to feel like a traitor, an intruder."

"I'm leaving," that's what I'm going to tell him. "I'm long gone."

And then it's dawn and I leave Loli's beautifully furnished house with its angel statues and its mandalas and its incense holders and its candles and its white wicker furniture with chintz cushions and that wonderful cleanliness that is possible only if you are a world unto yourself. I walk in the pale sand toward the rising sun and I feel myself dissolving into it, becoming one with its fire. I feel a rage so deep I think there will be nothing left of me, nothing at all. A rage at all that stupid holding back, all those compartments, all that moderation.

It is a terrible thing to believe that we are not enough. It is terrible to create that belief in another. I am the sum of those two terms and they are nothing, absolutely nothing in comparison to all those people leaping to their deaths, all those children left without parents, all those husbands and wives who lie stunned in their empty beds.

My Kevin. *My* Melanie. My *me*. It is as if I have the sun burning inside me and I am growing larger and larger with its heat and completeness. I am angry. Angrier than I have ever let myself feel. And I am filled with mourning for every hour of every day I did not take that child into my heart, my mind, my body. And I am filled with the deepest joy, I am light with it, heavy with it, whole. I close my eyes and I feel the reality of my condition expand and expand and I am large enough, complete enough, porous enough, just like the wave, to know the full force of the ocean.

Then I hear someone calling and I turn—and I would know her anywhere, the way she tosses her head back when she runs, the slight unevenness in her gait, and I know I am not big enough, I will never be big enough to contain the joy her existence gives me and I let it flow right through me, this joy, knowing it doesn't belong to either of us, anymore than it does to Kevin, who walks behind her.

I lift my head from where I have buried it in my daughter's hair. The scent of her hair blends with the smell of the sea. I hold her even closer.

I reach out to him with my right hand and he sets it to his cheek and I pull our daughter closer and I meet his eyes completely, hiding nothing, and I can see he knows, he's always known. Where I was. Why.

"Enough already." Melanie, spluttering, pushes away from me. "I don't want to suffocate. We just wanted to make sure with our own eyes you were safe."

"And we're staying, just in case you're wondering," Kevin said. "That's what families are for— to rub you wrong, get in your hair, grate on our nerves, and keep your feet planted firmly on the ground."

"Lovers," he whispers into my ear as we follow Melanie down the beach, "may have other uses." His breath is so hot and so close I can't distinguish it from the waves. His hand snakes slowly, ever so slowly, up my spine. The sun pours down on our heads. My feet are hot with the friction of the sand. I have never felt so powerful and so empty. So bound and so free. So received.

"Keep talking," I tell him. "And for God's sake, don't stop what you're doing. Something is coming clear." I breathe deeply and take another step forward, trusting him to match my pace as we follow our dancing daughter into the water flushed red with sunrise.

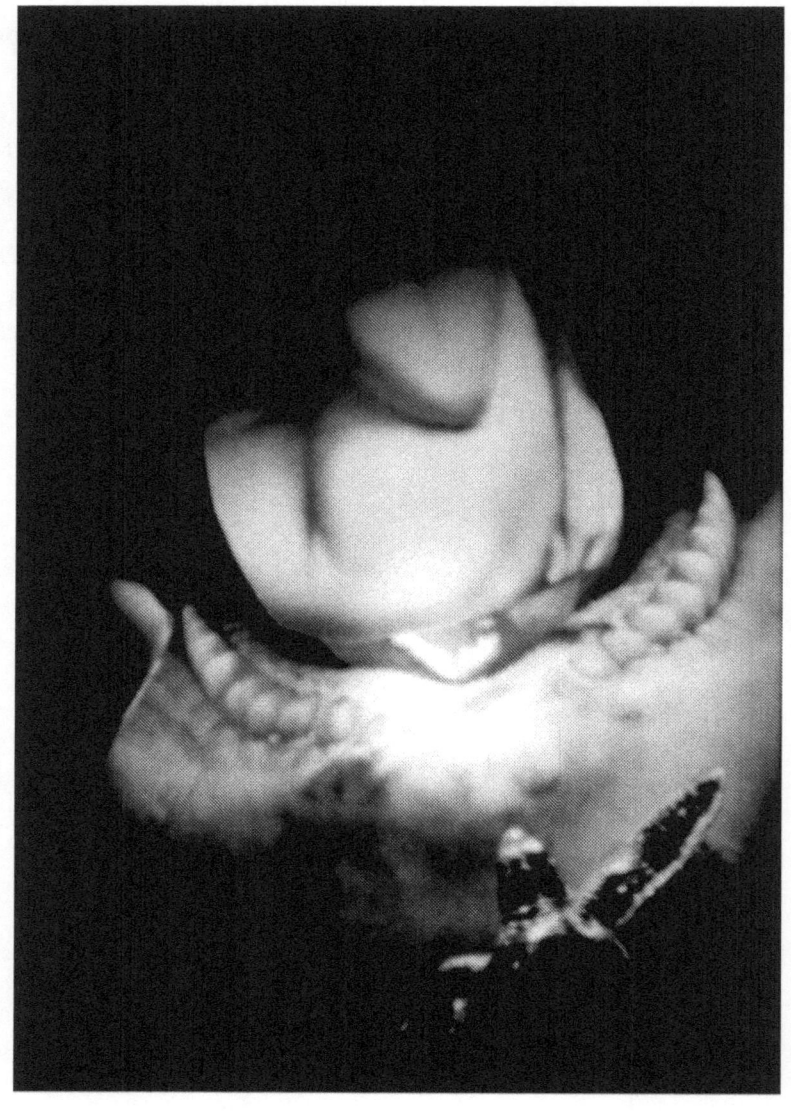

THE CEREMONY

It doesn't matter what I'm doing, that day is sacrosanct. From wherever I am, I get myself on a plane and go and visit my mother's grave with clippers and flowers.

"Like an old biddy," my mother scoffs.

"At your bidding," I tell her as I neatly lay out the gardening tools—trowel, fertilizer, grass trimmer, whisk broom. This time I've brought bulbs, even though it isn't their proper planting season. I suppose I'm trying to buy myself some time. I can imagine missing a year if there are amaryllis and paper whites and crocuses and purple tulips holding my place. I've even brought some canna and day lily bulbs to extend the flowering season.

"I knew it wouldn't last," my mother sighs. "Whatever you said, I knew you couldn't hold out."

As usual, what I do counts for nothing. I'm twenty-six. I've been doing this for seven years.

"Why?" therapists—and my new lover, Lyle—have all asked me. "It's not like you feel she appreciates it."

It's impossible to explain. My mother was always of two minds—pulling me close with one hand, shoving me back with the other. Death doesn't change that.

"It's important to me to hold fast," I tell them. "She was my mother after all."

After all, she was my all for years.

"And do I hear a thank you hidden in there?" my mother asks bitterly.

"One of these years, I'd like to go with you," Lyle said from the bed as he watched me pack this morning.

He's a sweet man. Ten years older than me. He wants to teach me about basic trust.

"Good luck!" my mother says. Her laughter is as clear as wind chimes.

This year I don't join her.

I turned to him, holding my folded sweater close to my chest, my eyes stinging. "Some day I would like that."

He held my eyes and shared with me that lazy, irresistible smile he has when he knows he's found an opening. I have a feeling that Lyle, mild-mannered as he is, is also very stubborn. Stubborn in his affections.

"All you have to do is ask," he said, and turned over and pulled the pillow over his head.

I didn't blame him. It was five-thirty in the morning. After all these years, I've shaved the preparation time down to the minimum, packing just before the taxi comes. Returning the same day.

"Short-changing me," my mother says.

I pull back on my heels and smile. I miss Trudy, that's the truth.

"You never called her Mom or Mommy?" my first, male, therapist asked.

"We were too close in age for that. She preferred to have strangers think she was my devoted aunt. Guys found it a turn on—where if they had known I was her own spare body part, her sex appeal would have been snuffed," I snapped my fingers, "just like that."

"Is that how your mother sounded?" the therapist asked.

"What do you mean?"

"It's like another person was talking."

"You think I'm a multiple?"

"I think she really got to you, Laurel." He was a small man, Dr. Arthur Fink. Still a resident, actually, so his rates were lower. He wasn't much over thirty, but he had a little paunch and a genius for the obvious.

"Yes," I said to him. "I expect she did."

I never could explain to him why I went out of his office and immediately located another therapist—a woman named Marge, a social worker, who made up in pragmatism for what she lacked in tact.

"I'm sure there are times, whatever hardships have followed, that you're relieved she's dead," Marge said.

"Are you going to let her get away with that?" Trudy asked, her voice shrill and smelling like booze, even from the other world.

"Yes," I said, not blinking. "Yes I am."

And then I had to go into the hospital for a couple of weeks because the nightmares got so bad and Trudy just wouldn't stop harping on my betrayal. I stayed on Zoloft for six months, until after my annual trip home to Trudy's grave. Then I quit it secretly, cold turkey.

That was four years ago. I've been my own person ever since, but that doesn't keep me from coming back here every Ides of March.

"You're saying something between the lines again," Trudy says. She sounds suspicious and suspiciously tired. "Why can't you be direct for once?"

"A trowel is a trowel is a trowel," I say, picking mine up and digging into the dirt along the side of the grave.

I thought of having Trudy cremated, but then I thought of her ashes scattered all over the earth and I felt asthmatic. I like the idea of a discrete box, a tattered satin lining, Trudy's bones neatly aligned in there. I like knowing she's all accounted for.

Except the voice.

I suppose I keep coming back here because I have hopes that, in time, just as the coffin contains her earthly remains, this ceremony may contain our conversations.

"I knew you couldn't stay the course," she says again. "You were my last hope, Laurel. I hope you know what you're doing."

All I ever wanted was for us to have a normal relationship, like the ones I saw my friends in high school and college having with their moms. They'd talk to them at the kitchen table or on the phone, tell them things about their lives—but then they'd grab their bags and head off to the mall or to their classes, and that would be the end of it. They didn't carry their mothers' voices around in their heads, blaring constantly like a walkman with no volume control, interfering with all their other interactions.

During the time Trudy was sick, I went to the mall once with Sally, my best friend from high school. I remember going into the changing room to try on a sexy black number I thought might be just right for my second year at college. The minute I pulled the louvered door shut and began to unbutton my blouse, it was as if Trudy was sitting on the chair in the changing room, even though I knew she was in her hospital bed back at the house, busy, most likely, chiding the home health aide about the tightness of the sheets. But it didn't keep her from being right there with me.

"I don't know about that neckline. Your neck is just a little short for turtlenecks," Trudy said. "And you've got great breasts. Why don't you go for a scoop neck, sweetheart. And the hem may be a little on the short side. You have nice legs, but that derriere of yours is just a little bit too pronounced, it makes the hem hike in the back, doesn't it?"

Sally knocked on the door and asked me to come out and look at the formal she was thinking of buying to go to homecoming at her boyfriend's college. A same-sex college was definitely an aphrodisiac. All either of them seemed to think about was how to get it on with each other. I was glad I'd decided on going to the state university where half the students lived at home. People didn't have the time to find themselves—or each other. They were too busy racking up hours on the freeway driving to their classes and to their jobs. And, in my case, organizing the nurses and health aides to take care of Trudy in end-stage breast cancer made worse by cirrhosis.

Sally impatiently pushed the door to my changing room open. I was sitting on the chair, my elbows on my knees, hands over my ears.

"What do you think?" she asked, staring critically at herself in the changing room mirror. She was a dashing redhead, and the dress she'd chosen was a slinky violet affair that clung desperately to every inch of her perfect figure.

"Do they make a gauntlet of sabers for you to walk through?" I meant it to come out purely curious, but Sally looked at me a little put off. It's true, I did sound like Trudy.

"Rodney's family has been military for four generations. They're real proud of it."

"And he'll be real proud of you in that dress," I said sincerely. "I wish I could carry something like that off."

Immediately, Sally lost her defensiveness. At that time, she wanted to become a nurse and loved tending to people who were at an obvious disadvantage.

"Stand up and let me see what we have here," she said.

So I did, stretching my thick squat neck, tugging on the back hem.

"You don't look quite yourself in that," she said.

I looked in the mirror and saw my long straight brown hair falling to my breasts, my long legs. "It does make me look a little assembly-line," I agreed. "Generic sophomore arts major."

Which I wasn't. I was pre-med with a minor in poli-sci. Which is why I now work for a small non-profit that lobbies against the drug companies. Sally is divorced and recently re-engaged. She is a high school health and phys ed teacher, but is pursuing a massage therapy credential on the side. She thinks it may allow her to travel on cruise ships at a discount, something her new beau and she would like. "After Rodney," she tells me, "I vowed never to play things so close to the chest again. Security is one thing. Claustrophobia another. Those three years with him, I gave up everything. My friends, my studies. For what? He said he wanted a stay at home wife—and then he went and slept with that hulk Marjo who was in his squadron. Taught me a thing or two."

Like how to lift weights, file for a divorce, insist on a pre-nuptial agreement.

"And dress like a whore," Trudy says.

"Who are you to talk?" At first I think it is the new Sally speaking up for herself and then realize it is me.

"Really, Trudy, I don't mean to offend—but you liked to flaunt yourself."

My mother had a thing for semi-sheers—so when she walked down the street with the sun shining through her clothes, all the construction workers would hoot, but she could look as if she were completely unaware. The expression was so convincing, I'd have believed her if I hadn't walked by her bedroom and seen her holding her dresses up to the light with one hand behind them, checking to see how little detail was left to the imagination.

"You have no sense of play," Trudy says. "That's always been your problem.

"What I love about Lyle," I tell her, "is that he makes me feel light-hearted."

"It wasn't my fault you were dreary, dear," she snaps back at me. "I certainly never wanted that. Imagine how it made me feel to greet that glum little face of yours every morning."

I keep wondering what in the world I could ever say to Trudy that she wouldn't be able to turn back to herself somehow. This was her true gift. It required imagination, perseverance, and powerful insouciance to be so self-absorbed.

"I still don't get why you didn't get away from her as soon as you were able," Lyle has said more than once.

"There was nowhere to run," I said. "Still isn't."

It wasn't just the changing room, but all my classes, everywhere. Trudy's voice never left me when she was alive, why should I expect death to make much difference?

I drop in my third iris bulb and tamp it in with the rich dirt of the cemetery. I feel the sun on the back of my neck and my spread hands, hear the bird songs, the distant thrum of traffic. I remember those last days before Trudy's death when the world became so clear and so still. All we'd have was the sound of infrequent traffic on our residential street, those shallow breaths, the pump gurgling in the fish tank in my own bedroom across the hall, the scratch of my pen, the rasp of paper as I turned the pages in my textbooks, trying not to fall behind in my classes. Those last two weeks of her life were the only time Trudy's voice has ever stopped. Soon as she died, it picked up again. And she talked herself right into that last coma, filling me with instructions about her funeral, my career choices, the furniture I should never dispose of, the man I should go out and get for myself.

I loved those last quiet days where I sat by the window watching the bright unobstructed sunlight wash over my mother's increasingly vacant face, her wasting body, and felt perfectly free to see her as she now was, to love her as she now was. At that point, I still felt there was a clear separation between life and death and that the two of us were engaged in a complex operation where our brains and hearts needed to be delicately extricated one from the other so that she might go on to a better life—and I might at last get one of my own.

"Well, have you gone on to a better life?" Trudy asks. "You're so into blaming me, Laurel. But you're the one who didn't go to law school or medical school, who has brushed off all the guys who showed any interest. You'll probably do the same with this one if you insist on wearing that unflattering black dress every chance you get.

"Lyle likes it." (Trudy, of course, doesn't because I bought it over her objections that day I went to the mall with Sally, and went on to wear it at her funeral and, since then, on each of my yearly visits to her grave.)

"So now you dress for him, Ms. Independence?"

"I don't need to. Unbelievable as it may sound, he takes me as I am, Trudy."

"You're saying I don't?"

"Didn't. I'm saying you didn't."

"All I ever did was accept. Seventeen years old and this weight in my belly that made it impossible to walk. I accepted that for nine months. And then this little girl with her glum face and disturbing eyes—everywhere I went, your eyes went there first and put a hex on things."

"Trudy, did I ever call you mean?" I lean back on my heels and close my eyes. I am debating planting those cannas and day lilies. To hell with extending the flowering season.

"I knew what you were thinking. It made me take up drinking, that look in your eyes."

"Did it make you choose gin over vodka? I mean, how specific was it—this responsibility of mine?"

"Go on. Get it out of your system. You can't hurt me anymore. God and I have a special understanding now, one we should have come to a long time ago. I feel one of those little slings of outrageous fortune and I turn to Him and He just takes away the ache with one look of His tender blue eyes. Oh, that you might enjoy just a tenth of what I have now, Laurel."

"Has it ever occurred to you that even now, at twenty-six, you might be ten times what your mother ever was?" Lyle asked me the other night when I tried to explain a little about my trips, the ceremony. "When do you get to stop apologizing for your gifts, your strengths?"

"Don't you think, without you, I'd have made ten times more of myself than you have?" Trudy says, reading my thoughts. "I sure wouldn't work for pittance. I'd have an MBA from Harvard and be raking in those over the wall executive salaries."

I don't understand, actually, where this wealth fetish of Trudy's comes from. It seems to have increased with death, so maybe there really are streets paved with gold up there, enormous investment portfolios St. Peter hands you when you make it through that narrow gate.

"I always thought you were my destiny," Trudy muses. "I never tried to escape it. Didn't I take you everywhere with me? No matter what a cramp it put on things. Didn't I do that for you, Laurel?"

"Do you want me to say thank you? Is that what this is all about?" I feel an eagerness inside, as if finally I am seeing a clearing in the thicket, a way out. "If that's the case, I'm truly sorry. I do thank you for everything. All those years. The burden of my existence. Truly I do, Trudy."

"She had energy," I tried to explain to Lyle. "She had all these expectations life couldn't meet—but she didn't give up on them, just clung to them more fiercely as the reality of her life got further and further out of sync. There she was, a bookkeeper, with her dour daughter, her supply of gin, her fading looks. But she was made to be special, favored. She never questioned that. That's why she was so angry most of the time. She knew something was being maliciously, unjustly withheld. In some crazy way, as much as she resented me, she also, because she couldn't make much distinction between us, wanted me to have that privilege too. There's something grand about giving life that much power to make or break you."

"And taking it back with the other hand."

"That's my Trudy," I said fondly. "She was wily. There was, finally, nothing she held herself accountable for except not letting go of those dreams."

"And you," Lyle asked me. "What *don't* you hold yourself accountable for, Laurel?"

These returns. They're not chosen, and that feels so unfair to both of us.

"I know you don't believe it, Laurel, but I *was* good enough," Trudy says with dangerous gentleness.

Good enough for what? Is that why I keep coming back? I don't have any of Trudy's clarity about what life owes me—or what I owe it. I don't know where to put my disappointments or my pleasures. She did. I envy her that. You have to have a little awe for someone who can reduce Hiroshima and Auschwitz to similes in her own life story.

"You're saying I was selfish?" Trudy asks. "Why can't you say anything directly, Laurel?"

"I am," I say. I am working furiously hard now, tearing open all my bags of bulbs and mixing them up together and then just grabbing at them blindly as I dig and bury, dig and bury.

"I'm saying I miss you, mother. I'm saying I miss organizing my life around you and I don't know how to replace that. It was such an essential push-pull, I don't know myself without it."

"Did it ever occur to you that you do to me what she did to you?" Lyle whispered to me the other night as I sobbed out, coming, "No. Please God. No." Pushing away from his chest with one hand, pulling his buttocks close with the other.

He held my face in both his hands and made me look at him. "It hurts," he said. "Did you know that, Laurel. For the person who loves you, all that pushing and pulling hurts."

I am crying now. I can't get the bulbs in the ground fast enough. I can't get that look of his out of my mind or my heart. I can't stop the sick lurch of my stomach as I think about losing him too. And then I realize that this is all I can hear, the sound of my hands fumbling in the dirt, a family talking quietly together as they look for a grave, the sound of a distant lawn mower, the trowel clanging against a large stone. I know then that I will not be returning here again, with or without Lyle. I know what I need to do when I get back. I know I can trust what Trudy has said to me today. I know I'm not going to push my luck and see if she will ever repeat it.

"I'm happy for you, Mom," I tell her. "Really I am. I like imagining you finally claiming your rightful place inside His eyes."

And I do. It feels so much safer for her. She's right, my eyes were disturbing.

I can see her when I was ten years old. I was standing by the door to the living room. She was on the couch, drunk, staring down into her glass, the tears plinking against the gin. Her hair the color of our dead lawn.

"Nothing I do ever matches up, does it, to that perfect picture you have of how your Daddy might have been, does it? Is that what you call him inside your head, *Daddy*? His name was Fred, you know. And he was a cold son of a bitch. Whatever you may think, you are better off with me."

"Of course," I said. (And, actually, in this case, she was right. He wasn't cold, just completely indifferent, when I looked him up a few years after Trudy's death. Indifferent is not a word I'd ever use to describe Trudy, then or now.)

But what I remember is how far away she seemed that afternoon when I was ten and so woefully inadequate. It was as if she was at the far end of a very long tunnel and the light behind her was so bright she looked like a stick figure. Soon, I knew, if I didn't do something, she was going to disappear completely.

She looked up at me and said, "You're just like him, you know. You don't need to worry about losing him. He's in your genes, your eyes, your heart."

That was when I let her inside my mind, you see. It was the only way I could keep her from slipping completely away. If he was part of me, like she said, I needed her to be part of me too, didn't I?

But now she has someone who can hold her more steadily in their attention than I ever could. Inside me, she racketed around just as wildly as she did in life. There wasn't enough of me there yet to hold her safely in place.

I gather all the brown paper sacks and flatten them and fold them up. I put the trowel and fertilizer and clippers and whisk broom back in my knapsack. After I stand up, I lean over and dust the dirt from the knees of my tights. I straighten the hem of my black dress.

"It hurt, Trudy. All that pushing and pulling hurt like crazy."

"You're saying I don't have a right to my feelings?" she asks. I am so relieved to hear her again, I begin to cry. "Really Laurel, I'm tired of all this. Where I am now, I can't be bothered with your petty resentments."

I don't know why, I just start to laugh. Because at this moment I feel—this is the crazy thing I'll take with me to my own grave—completely loved.

"You're sure you don't want any help with this?" Lyle asks me when he looks at the two large spades and the garbage can I have brought over.

"Just your hillside," I said. "And no questions. This may take some time."

I'm not sure exactly where the image came from—images of those huge Buddhas the Taliban exploded, ensconced so neatly inside little alcoves in the mountains, or a Diego Rivera mural with women sprouting in the earth. I don't know why I need to act on it, not just see it in my mind's eye. But I do. I don't know what I am hoping for, and, for the two months it takes me to hollow out a cave in the hillside above Lyle's house, I don't need to ask. I just need to drive the shovels into the dirt, fill the garbage can and drag the dirt down to the garden below the house, loosen and relace roots.

Lyle never gives me the impression he is in any hurry—which is comforting. Maybe he thinks my constant visits are in themselves an answer to his proposal. If he does, he's sadly mistaken. I really don't know anything right now except that I have to keep digging, finding safe places for the dirt I displace, dreaming of this little cave or shrine getting deeper, readier for me. I feel I can do all this without self-consciousness.

Lyle lives quite a distance from the city in which we both work. His house is halfway up a steep slope. There are no visible neighbors because of the forest looming on either side of his property. Above the house, the land has gone back to brush. That is where I'm working, screened from the world by this scrabble of bare branches that come to my shoulders.

As I drag my garbage cans of dirt along the slope, I can look down on the roof of his house. I can see him out on his deck with his coffee and his papers. He is careful always to look off at the horizon, never back at me. I know he is acutely aware of my presence, but he's enjoying the tacit rules here. I am very alive to his curiosity and restraint. I think he knows this and it pleases him. He feels, by doing nothing, he is winning me over just as if I were an aborigine.

Lyle is a professor, an anthropologist, which means he believes in what he calls thick description. It's not his job to judge, he says, just let his heart and mind go out and engage with all that delectable strangeness. Perhaps he thinks of me these days as a little Yanomamo, or would, if I were stripped naked.

But I'm not. I'm dressed in coveralls and a turtleneck. Spring is later here than it is at Trudy's grave. I'd give anything for some new leaves, a few tulips and day lilies. But the forsythia flowers have only just sprung free of their casings. The dirt, when I pull it out with my hands is very clammy and cold. Heavy too. My back aches at the end of the day when I come back down and find Lyle in the kitchen making some exotic Caribbean stew out of dried cod and limes and avocado. It isn't, he assures me, authentic—just what one could do with the limited island inventory if one had some imagination. Which Lyle does. I do not, I think.

I can't see what it is I'm doing now. I can just enact it. So, if I have imagination, it's somewhere my mind can't touch, something only my body knows.

Some nights, when Lyle and I are lying quietly together, looking at the stars through the skylight, I wonder what it might feel like to describe what I'm doing—the mental blankness and the deep, free physical urge of it. But most of what happens up on the hill doesn't have much to do with words. Some days, I'll start digging and the shape of the tiny roots I uncover will look so beautiful to me, so frail, I'll drop the shovel and just take a handful of dirt in my hand and start blowing at it until the pattern of the most delicate roots appears, like some primordial lace antimacassar. And I'll weep at the discipline it takes not to destroy anything. And other days, I'll be so impatient, I'll take the spade and hold it over my head and just jam it into the roof of the cave. I'll feel like a fierce and fearless warrior stabbing a spear into the flank of an animal. I let the dirt rain down on my face like lifeblood. Or I'll throw myself at the back of the cave clawing furiously with my hands. All I'll be thinking is *soon, now, no more time.* And just giving myself up to the crazy, greedy, frenetic impulse organizes it somehow, so I can begin playing with the speed of it, enjoying the anger that turns my fingers into claws, sends such strength through my back and down my arms.

Some days, like today, I'll seat myself exactly as I imagined I would when I had my vision at Trudy's grave. My legs are folded, my hands are in my lap, my gaze is fixed a foot or so beyond my crossed legs. I am, for a split second, the embodiment of enlightenment—until the need to move sweeps me again. *I need more room.*

Roots are clogging everything—but when I go to cut them with the large clippers and handsaw I bought, I find I can't. Just the thought of cutting through the tough skin makes me want to throw up. The hardest thing to describe is how intense the feelings I am having are. I don't feel aversion, but intense, body-convulsing revulsion. When I feel pleasure, it rushes straight to my sex and heats the soles of my feet. When, for a second, I experience peace, my forehead relaxes as if there is some space now between my skull and my brain, my eyes glow with colors that have nothing to do with this world, a faint sea sibilance fills my ears.

What I'm making bears little or no resemblance to my original vision. I thought I was making a space for myself, but what I'm doing now is more like excavating a gravesite, the way those forensic anthropologists brush the dirt away from the bones with tiny paint brushes, showing the small bullet hole in the skull, the machete blow that severed the cervical spine. Except there's nothing horrible here. Just this dense network of roots, the space that I've made by weaving some of the roots together so there is room for a person to slip in behind them. It's nothing like Rivera's mural of women sprouting like bulbs, where there seem to be no impediments to their growth, no snarl of roots, no stones. When I slip in, all I can see are the roots caging off the cave mouth. I don't know if I feel safe or constrained. Some days I feel one, some days the other.

I've actually cut off some of the roots when they interfered too much with what I'm sensing is needed here. The back of the cave is dirt and stone. I've brought all the roots to the mouth of the cave, like a screen.

I dug out the cave high enough so I can stand with my legs spread, my hands outstretched. Late this afternoon, I went to the hardware store and bought gold paint. I am so excited now, I find it difficult to hide it from Lyle. I love the idea of the paint brush coating the roots with gold paint. I love the image of a human body, mine, naked, barely visible behind them.

I love that in this cave there is no room for two—it has been made exactly to my own specifications. I like that I'm straining my environment, that with a heavy rain or two, Lyle may lose some bushes and trees because of what I'm doing. I love that what I've done won't last. That's what makes me feel I can't get in there fast enough.

Which is why I am up at dawn this morning, throwing on my still grimy coveralls and turtleneck.

I can feel Lyle's eyes on me, even though I've moved very quietly.

"So," he murmurs, "today is the day?"

I look at him startled. He's right, but I don't understand how he knew it before I did. I wonder if I *would* have known it if he hadn't said.

"Some day," he says, "I'd like to see you in your own environment."

For a minute I freeze, closing my hands over each other and bringing them to my chest. I realize that all these months I've never felt as if he were judging me, just watching me with a curiosity that was as detached as my own but far more appreciative.

I come closer to the bed, trying to make out his expression in the dim light.

"I'm not prying. I'm just saying, when the time is right, I'd like to be part of it."

His voice is both cool and warm in the dark room. It is like moving through a deep stream, always being a little surprised by the sudden shifts in temperature. I feel I want to bathe in his voice, in the feel of his eyes holding me in my grimy, half-dressed stasis.

"Trust yourself," he says.

"I don't think I have any choice," I say. "It's the only thing that keeps me from being defined as mad."

That and the secrecy with which I carry out these overwhelming impulses.

"You think you are so clever," Trudy says, her first words since I left her grave side, but her voice is slurred, slow—like the gin is, at last, putting the malice to sleep. I feel tears burning the inside of my eyelids.

"Defined by who?" Lyle asks as I leave the room. His voice is deep but has an openness in it that is fresh as the morning air I walk out into carrying my paint can and brushes.

And then I am in the thick of the thicket, where there are no voices, just the motion of my body as I open the can and slip in the brush and stir the paint. I hear the birds calling out to each other, a squirrel scrabbling in old leaves, sounding like something far more massive. The gold paint gleams in the gray light as I coat the screen of roots. Paint splatters onto the dirt, to be stubbed out by my old boots as I slip inside to paint the roots from within my sweet, crazy, friable sanctuary.

I leave the paint to dry and go back down to the house. Lyle is drinking his morning coffee out on the deck. I wave to him as I go off to shower the dirt from my hair and my skin. I take my time with this, rubbing a cloth carefully over every inch of my body, bringing my skin to a keen, aching wakefulness.

I know I'm not finished yet. I drive into town to buy candles. Tiny votive lights. I buy fifty of them. I take them back up to the shrine and start hollowing out little holding places for them. I've bought long matches for when the time comes to light them.

And then I take all my clothes off and leave them in a pile at the opening to my safe place. I slip inside. I spread my legs and reach my hands up and place my palms flat on the roof of the cave. The air on my skin is exactly as cool as the dirt under my hands and the soles of my feet. I close my eyes and breathe in the rich damp aroma of the earth. I am filled with a desire that has no urgency to it, a desire to feel the air between my legs, against the lips of my sex, my nipples, my eyelids, my lips. A desire to push against the roof of my safe place with the same building pressure my feet exert against its floor. A desire to be perfectly still and part of something more solid, larger. I have a desire to hear my own blood coursing safely through my arteries and veins, loyal to the force of my own heart. A desire to be in a place where there is no push and no pull, just this awareness of the four points where I connect with the earth, of the air that embraces all the rest of me.

I have a desire to hear God speak clearly to me and to feel truly free to listen. I know this begins with my skin. The simplicity of feeling exactly where I am in time and space. I know I can't do this without some external pressure that is made exactly to my measure.

Standing there with my eyes closed, I can feel the presence of all the unlit candles nestled in the walls, the wild whorls of glowing roots that shatter and recombine the view of sky and ground and bare trees like an extravagant abstract stained glass window. I can feel the air thicken around me and a sound like a powerful surf surging everywhere. I can feel Trudy's voice pour out of me into the earth above me, the earth below, like a gift, an exorcism, a blessing. I can feel something quieter pressing against the intact skin of my hands and feet, asking permission to enter. I can feel how, when I refuse, it simply begins to run across my skin like water, wonderfully purifying, enlivening. I can feel my own heart filling up all the available space inside me, how that sound has a rhythm quicker than the rumble of the surf, but reminiscent and, at the same time, unique and sweetly responsive to every shift in my balance or state of exertion. I feel as if I have all the time in the world. I feel a hunger without bounds that I have no need to fill.

And then it is over. I drop my hands, slip out from the cave, wriggle like a dog to shake the dirt off. I brush the dirt lightly from my hair. I slip my clothes back on and return to the house.

I can feel Lyle watching me as I make coffee. In my mind's eye, I can see how I am going to take a hacksaw to the top and bottom of my screen of roots, so they will open out, hinged like a door. I can see how I will light all the candles in the sanctuary and sit before it, feeling as I do so a figure forming in the flickering of the lights and shadows, fitting into the hand and footprints left there. I can feel that figure made of light and shadow slipping back into my own body, informing it so when I leave the hillside I will feel the same strength, the same stillness wherever I am. I know that I will keep needing to do this—never entering the cave again—but returning to it, feeling the solidity of the experience.

I turn and hold Lyle's watchful eyes, smiling. I like feeling seen, met, as he would say, in my delectable strangeness. He wants for me to come out to him, which I do. I look out from the deck over the long valley, smoky with mist. The world feels so clean and so big. I can feel the soles of my feet meeting the floor of the deck, I can feel my hands stretching out, pressing gently against all that space, feeling the weight of it.

"It feels like today is the day," he says. He has a small crease in his forehead that belies the calm tone of his voice. I want to reach out and smooth it with the heel of my hand. He clears his throat. "And the answer is—"

"Yes.

So we sit there silently, looking first at each other and then out at the valley and surrounding mountains, the bare trees that are just feeling the first slow surges of sap.

"I am so glad," he says at last. "I wouldn't have asked again."

"I know. That push-pull hurts like hell. No reason to repeat it."

Then, changing the subject, or not, I say, "I have something to show you, but not until sunset."

I spend the late afternoon with my hacksaw creating a real, freely opening door, and when the time comes, I bring Lyle up there and he helps me light all the candles and then we sit there, shoulder to shoulder, watching them flicker and flare with the wind, no more questions asked, no more answers given, but some deep sweet certainty taking root in us nonetheless.

"To Trudy," I say, tipping the champagne bottle up and draining the dregs.

"May she rest in peace."

"Good enough," I agree.

In the morning, our sheets carry the traces of everything we have just passed through, dirt and gold paint, semen, dry leaves, wax, and roots finer than my mother's hair.

KEEPSAKES

So much has changed with these cocktails. My friends may seem like the mechanical figures in Bavarian clocks, their alarms going off every hour and the ubiquitous pillbox pulled from their briefcase or bag, their heads bobbing as they select and swallow. But it's nothing like those years where I seemed to keep constant vigil at one deathbed after another. And the quilts. In May of 1993, I had six friends die within two weeks of each other. For the next few months, I felt like we were in an illegal sweatshop, working nights and weekends trying to get the quilts ready for the last complete showing of the whole quilt in Washington. My fingertips were covered with so many small pinpricks it looked as if I was sweating blood.

The fights we had trying to fit everything into those small rectangles. Whole lives squished into a space smaller than a coffin lid. We didn't want anything left out—bathhouses and one night stands, long-time companions, his secret high school crush, favorite food, the face of his mother, the address of his estranged father.

"Jim would have wanted," Paul would say, laying claim. And Steve, Jim's lover for ten years but not for the last year and a half, would lash back: "Don't tell me who Jim was." Don't tell me, Steve meant, who *he* was. Or was not. We were all trying to order our own lives, salvage some meaning from all the debris. Dead people leave so much debris: papers and books, the odd, chipped yellow dish, new black leather sofa, geometric patterned sheets, briefs. As you clean out attics, closets, bureaus, the dust clings to your sweating skin like ash, but you can't bring them back.

And that's what each of us wanted—the one memory, the one memento that brought them back, one by one, bitchy or breezy, demented or sane, uniquely and for all time: Jim, Curt, Jody, Greg, Alan, Ricardo, Jésus, Mario, Luis. We wanted to stitch into those quilts the contradictions that made them complete. The way Alan couldn't walk through a room without leaving a chaotic wake—papers on the floor, books over-turned, sugar on the table, but his clothes always looked as if he had just slipped them out of a dry cleaning bag. Or Luis' penchant for multi-colored condoms and plain white briefs. We wanted people looking at our quilts to know exactly who we'd lost, just as, when our own time came, we wanted our friends to bicker and boss us back into existence: "I have a lock of his hair from—" "I have a cryptic love note from—" "I have the label from his favorite bottle of wine. We drank it just last month. A Pier 19 discount Chilean, but who's complaining?" Given all this, it felt no end weird to receive the letter from my sister Karen suggesting that the seven of us collaborate on making a quilt for our parents 55th wedding anniversary. She provided us with the dimensions for each panel and asked that we all try to contribute more than one. Laura and she would commit to sewing three each, to make up for any time pressures the rest of us might have. Each panel was to be one foot square, with a 5/8 inch hem-width border. All on permanent press cotton for easy maintenance. No constraints on color. But they wanted us all to concentrate on significant moments in our parents lives. Nothing conflictual, they added.

I put the letter down, laughing, and Miguel looked at me puzzled. Unlike him, I almost never communicate with my parents or the majority of my siblings. I visit my parents for one token weekend every year. My youngest sister, Chris, visits me every couple of years, as does the sister closest to me in age, Maggie. The whole quilt project would never have been suggested if my parents' off-spring didn't list slightly in favor of the female persuasion. But the emphasis on nice is a gender-free family trait. In all my fifty years, my homosexuality has never been spoken of directly by anyone in my family except, once or twice, by my sister Chris. They have never met Miguel, my companion of twenty-five years. They have never mentioned any of my six novels with their obviously homosexual protagonists. When asked what I do, they all volunteer the name of the university where I have an adjunct teaching position but are vague about my discipline, leaving the impression it is something utilitarian and stultifying that begins with an *a* or *b*—accounting, business management.

When I tell Miguel about the quilt, he looks at me seriously, pushing his long black hair behind his ear. "But of course you will do this, Roberto. It is good for you. You are fifty this year. It is time to make your peace."

I look down at my hands, suddenly able to recall all the pinpricks from those other quilts. "I'm not handy or hypocritical enough."

"I will help you then," Miguel says with a laugh. He flexes his paint stained fingers eagerly. Miguel is a painter, very handy, and his Latin background means he has a highly developed tolerance for ambiguity. I keep trying to explain to him how this differs from the frank repression and denial of my midwestern childhood.

"My mother, she never talk about us either, Roberto. She just say she have two sons she love with all her heart."

I think of the first five years of our relationship when, fired by all the liberation movements, we thought there was some chance they might accept us. How Miguel would come with me to Columbus and we'd stay on the outskirts of town in a Holiday Inn way beyond our means as starving artists, and I'd go over to the house and see if there was an opening to bring up Miguel, who languished in the hotel watching X-rated movies to improve his English. There never was. Everyone made sure of that. Frank, Karen, and Laura were married by then, with a baby each. Maggie was engaged. Dan was looking for work. Mother seems to be slipping a little, they would whisper to me in the kitchen. Dad's business is on a down-turn. It's better not to say anything that might upset them. By the fifth year, I was as amused as I was pissed by the performance. To while away his time, Miguel began to explore the gay bars in Columbus thoroughly—since his English was now more than sufficient for all his basic needs. After that, Miguel began to make excuses—an exhibition he couldn't miss, a friend's birthday—which I accepted gratefully.

But we've made a point of going together to see his family in Vera Cruz every year. I sometimes think the visits are more important to me than they are to him. They say Latinos have no tolerance for homosexuality. But, like so many intellectual positions in Latin America, that applies only in the abstract. Faced with a competing value, like family for example, *maricón* dissolves into *hermano mío*, *hijo mío*. Americans remain the worst idealists around human relations, and midwesterners, the most American in this way. "Our son, the bachelor," my parents both say.

I can't figure what Miguel is up to with the quilt, but I'm curious. So I write my sisters back and let them know they can count on us for three. I like using us and I don't make any promises about content. Is there any story you know worthy reading, any painting worth returning to that doesn't have, as its lure and its consolation, the equipoise of tensions, that doesn't suggest that every storm has a quiet eye, every full heart an unquenchable emptiness? Besides, to remember my parents' marriage at all, at least for those first twenty years which formed me, is to recall conflict. It amuses me to see how my siblings will resolve this tension, how they will manage to hit each critical stage in my parents' marriage sanctimoniously aslant.

It would be like telling the story of my life leaving Miguel out of it.

Lavage

There are many things I dislike about my father, but his relationship with my mother isn't one of them. I'm not speaking for her, mind you, rather for myself. When I think of my father during some of the worst times, my mother in the hospital or beginning the slow slide that would result in another stay, what I remember is his baffled constancy. My father, comprehending or not, stays the course. This may not make him the most flexible person on earth, but it makes him one of the more dependable.

And it has paid off, that is the remarkable thing. I have such a clear image of this from my last visit to see them., almost biblical in its simplicity— except, like any good story, its power comes from all the expectations it subverts. It is just something I glimpsed walking through the living room with my bag. The intimacy still startles me. My mother is leaning down to rinse and massage my father's feet. They have been out at the mall all day. My father's circulation is going, due to hypertension and late-life diabetes. My mother, seated in a chair opposite him, leans down over the red plastic basin, pulling one swollen foot out of the water. As she massages in some liniment, they talk quietly. It isn't, like the woman washing Christ's feet with her hair, an image of self-abjection, rather of simple companionship. At another time in my life, at other times in my mother's life, the scene would have read quite differently. Just one more unconscious demand from the old man, another furious submission from my mother. But the tables have turned now. They both know she will outlive him. They both know he will be deeply missed. The contented expression on my father's face comes from this shared knowledge. His deepest wish has been met. This is all he's ever wanted, a little gratitude, a little acceptance.

What is most startling about this image is the quietness. What they're talking about has no interest to anyone but themselves. How many revolutions of the mall they made, the price of photo developing at Walgreens or Revco; what movies are showing; which friends of theirs are moving, at their children's insistence, into homes. They will need to move too. Everyone knows this. But no one is willing to take the first step. My father is buying time for my mother, since she is younger and more vigorous. She is buying time for him by quietly assuming some of the duties of a daily health aide— the foot massages, the supervision of his numerous medicines. It isn't a task but a benediction, this prolonging—just one day, one year more—of what they have finally come to appreciate.

In this, of course, they resemble my own friends. It is so strange, though, to see mortality quietly accepted, like a dutiful servant cleaning the crumbs off the table, settling chairs, returning dishes to the cabinet shelves, leaving a thin film of light on the linoleum. Even today, I can't remember the loss of a single friend without experiencing an intense wave of rage at the senseless waste.

And this image too, for me, triggers both quietness and rage. I don't understand how they have arrived at this place of understanding between them, which is not just an acceptance of mortality but also of what has happened between them in their long life together. Nothing in their early years together prepared any of us for it. But I am pleased for them. And I am enraged that, even at this age, they would deny me the same.

Twenty-five years, I want to tell my father, I have loved this one man with all my heart. I have stayed the course. So often, I felt as if you were inside me, just behind my eyes, looking out at the world from here, helping me regard Miguel with the same baffled loyalty that you felt toward my mother.

"And what makes you so more holy than me?" Miguel would explode when he saw the expression on my face. For where I felt my father standing, steadfast, behind my eyes, he only saw the unforgiving eyes of his own father.

I'm not sure what my mother saw when she looked at my father in his moments of greatest forbearance, but her response was similar to Miguel's. The only difference is we called it madness—and perhaps it was, and is, madness to take the world's assumptions on directly and unequivocally. "You can't," she said, sounding like a petulant child, "You can't make me be quiet. Don't even try." She had, obviously, her own form of steadfastness— although some, my father among them, might call it intractability, instability, or, at its worst, a psychotic slough.

She didn't want her life to be a clack-clack-clack one track train ride from the marriage altar to the funeral bier with frequent intermittent stops at delivery rooms. She wanted some excursions on the side. She wanted a wild ride.

"Love is not about having an easy time," Miguel says to me maybe once a day. It stretches the envelope of time, it turns solid land into quick sand, it is a constant assault on our private sensibilities. It is all the small mementos we insist on embroidering into quilts, those tiny irritants that death makes lustrous. I miss you because you drove me crazy with your hyena laugh. I miss the way you changed your cologne when you were seeing someone on the side. I miss you because you never cracked a smile at a single joke I told you, you always made me pay for movies I didn't want to see, never cleaned the bathtub or said a kind word to my mother.

"Ah yes," Miguel says, misunderstanding me completely, when I share the image for the quilt panel with him. "She is to be like Magdalene, no?"

"You've got it all wrong," I tell him. "This is about partnership." He shrugs. He prefers the other image. He is, even now, a little sexist. And then there is all that religious overlay—the power of pietàs and all that. Besides, little in our lives has prepared us for images of quiet accommodation.

Neither Miguel nor I are HIV positive. It is proof, if one ever needed it, that life is unjust. And it means we sit across the table from each other these days looking a little startled—two middle-aged men with a long history behind us and an equally long history to follow. We have always lived as if there were no tomorrow, not because we were nihilists but because we were, and are, realists. Now it would be equally foolish not to do the opposite, but when we bring home information on Keogh plans and IRAs, we look at each other amazed. Who would ever have dreamed it would turn out this way?

"And my mama, we will invite her to live with us?" Miguel asks when he can't stand the dazed self-congratulation in my eyes.

"And why not your sisters and their children, your cousins and their cousins? A *tía* here, a *tío* there."

"You know, *mi amor*, I would like to end my days there," Miguel says, quietly putting his hand over mine.

"I'd find it rather nice to be nursed by your great-nephews and nieces. I'm certainly not going to end my days in Ohio."

"If I can forgive them, Roberto, why can't you? Truly, you must go to this fiesta with your quilt panels. You must do as your sisters suggest and choose images that cause no harm."

I look carefully at this man who I cannot begin to fathom. The one who has violent fights, even to this day, with his mother over the character of her husband. "And why," he yells at her, "do you not divorce that *cabrón*? How dare you give that *pendejo* a cent from even one of the dollars I send you." Who has spent his life shaking up everyone he comes in touch with. Returning to Mexico with his long hair and earring and his lilting gait and his body-builder's shoulders, everything in him saying, *I dare you.*

"They're old," he tells me. "Your anger isn't going to keep them alive, you know."

"We're not prepared," I tell him. "We're not prepared to live until we're old."

"Preparation, *mi amor*, *vale nada*, it's useless. Life is more like lust than thinking. Just let it carry you." He smiles his fatalistic smile. "Something in us always rises in response."

I think of my father leaning back in his chair, letting this new sensation of peace fill him—so linked with, but larger than, the steady pulsing of my mother's fingers on his swollen ankles.

With Miguel's help, I prick out on a deep blue cotton square this image of puzzled but grateful partnership that is my parents' old age. As I work, I feel as if I am setting a small floating lantern alight and pushing it off into a jostling stream of other lanterns all making their luminous way seaward on an erratic current. And as I do this, I grieve for my own steadfastness, what it feels like to see and not be seen.

Between us, Miguel and I create two old people, man and woman, in wingback chairs. She leans slightly forward, he leans back. She has his lame right foot in her hands. The finishing touch is the water falling like small teardrops from her hand, which cups his heel, into the red basin. Miguel suggests them, but insists I stitch them in myself with silver thread. At my insistence, we both sign and date the panel.

Frottage

My mother never could accept the hand life dealt her and, defying all cries of poor sportsmanship, kept trying to hand it back.

The fourth child in five years, I was the first to inspire a visit to the psychiatric ward. It gave me dubious, but dramatic, positioning in the family—at least until the births of Dan and Chris occasioned the same responses when I was three and five. Why Maggie, born only a year after me, didn't drive my mother over the brink again is a mystery to the two of us since she is, by far, the hardier character. My older siblings, Frank, Karen and Laura, simply use my birth as the dividing line that defines the caste system in siblings. Those who knew mother before she knew breakdowns and those who don't.

It is true that my concept of my mother includes in an inextricable way her capacity to chitchat with shades and to sing arias in tongues. It— madness, imagination, possession, post-partum depression, true soul or sexual oppression—was part of what made her Mom to me, not something dangerous, unexpected and intrusive, like cancer or amoebas or HIV. My experience of my mother was that she returned from her excursions to the mental hospital more relaxed, more deeply rooted in her true self. A healthy part of that self was a woman in her late twenties in powerful rebellion against all those small, helpless gaping mouths that threatened to devour every dream she had ever had of romance or independence. And she had no one but herself to blame. Anyone could look at my father, so numb and loyal, and know anger couldn't flow that way. All they had to do was look at all our small tow heads and know it couldn't flow in our direction either. So, no wonder my mother began trilling to heaven until someone was called in to give her a break.

I can afford, of course, to be sanguine about this because I had a wonderful wet nurse in my mother's distant cousin Janeen, a large, good-hearted woman in her mid-forties, childless herself but who had raised a large slew of step-children. I ascribe some of the strange tensions in my own character, the sense of being both chosen and exiled, to those primordial experiences: the steady unconditional warmth of this stranger who took to me immediately as her own—replaced before I was old enough to tell the difference by this other woman, already fat with her next child, who tended to me with the cool thoroughness of hired help but who was said to be my real mother. Sometimes, in my brother Dan and my sister Chris, I can see a substrate of sadness, some essential fear that the promise of life is hollow, which may have been their response to our mother's early absence in their lives. They remain especially close to her to this day—as if she could still make up for those few months she took off early in their earthly stay.

But, for me, I can't imagine a healthier beginning actually—the dark, faceless acceptance of Janeen like a tactile memory I can retrieve whenever I touch human skin, and the detached acceptance of my mother, curious to see who this creature was whom she had birthed but never nursed.

I suppose, because I always saw my mother's breakdowns as rebellions, as ways of being true to herself in impossible circumstances, it helped me when the time came, to see my own sexual nature as something similar, both a miracle and a natural disaster. I suppose I've stayed as loyal to Miguel as I have because he replays both these early experiences. His warmth, his priapism, all this magnificent skin, bring back that early, ineradicable yes. Then we pull away and there is an equally ineradicable foreignness to him as well. Nothing in him has ever, praise God, reminded me of Ohio. Just as nothing in me reminds him of Vera Cruz.

There was a time, of course, when we couldn't accept how other we were to each other, any more than earlier we could accept the otherness of our own sexuality. I remember how, in my first sexual encounters, I felt like my mother must have when she held yet another newborn in her arms and was equally mesmerized by its sameness and its strangeness, equally repelled. My life began to cohere when I met Miguel. All that friction, both psychological and sensual, helped me discover, and love, my own edges because they are where the energy and excitement live. Even today, I look at Miguel's cinnamon skin, I listen to that Mexican lilt to his English, the florid hand gestures when he is among his Spanish-speaking friends; I feel the sweet floral embrace of his *mamacita*; immerse myself in the indecipherable chattering of his nieces and nephews like a warm surf—and I know that love isn't just the spin we put on circumstances, a fudge factor. It is as close as Janeen's first touch. It is as cool and intrigued as my mother's first gaze at me. It is all there in the deep relief and attraction I feel toward Miguel's exoticness. We will never, praise God, be one however close we come.

I suppose that was what my mother was ensuring when, during one of her episodic escapes to the hospital, she saw her wedding ring bounce into the wash basin and, instead of trying to retrieve it, ran the water full blast sending it into the deepest recesses of the Columbus sewer system. To my mind she was saying she didn't want any part of a relationship that asked her to forfeit her reason as part of the natural order of things. (Any more than I want to be part of a world that ignores those capacities that are most central to me—my capacities to love, lust and grab madly for that which is more than myself, even, especially, if he is of the same sex.) Imagine, truly, what you might have done at thirty with seven unintended young ones, a strong sense of duty, and a heart you couldn't quiet that kept whispering, *What about me? What about me?*, insatiable as any of those babies. Where could that anger go in a world that couldn't even feel the anguish she felt, any of us might feel, to be asked to become nothing more than a thoughtless teat. At some level, it must have felt like the most vast and intractable conspiracy—when it wasn't feeling like the abysmal will of God, or the private malice of my father. Be nice. Be nice. She couldn't escape it like a tree frog's monotonous two-tone hum on a summer night. *Be* nice. *Be* nice.

Now, when I think about it, I don't quite understand why my mother didn't take longer and more frequent breaks. I suppose for the same reason she couldn't make herself reach out and catch the ring as it swished once around the basin and slipped into the drain. Or actively shove it down that mildewed opening either. To do so would shift the balances decisively, and that wasn't what she was after. She was striving for equipoise. What she wanted wasn't that different from what my father was after—a little consciousness, a little gratitude. An objective correlative to the pain she was in, not out of cruelty, just so she could see it and take it in.

Now, all these fancy forays into empathetic interpretation are as lost on my mother as they are on my father. They're just my take on things. From my mother's point of view, the loss of her wedding ring in the mental hospital after the birth of her seventh child in ten years was an unfortunate accident. My mother had already turned the water on to rinse her hands (for the eighteenth time that morning) and the ring, loose because of all the weight and water loss associated with birth, just washed away. There wasn't any moment of conscious collusion, no *frisson* of freedom. Those are my contribution.

What the rest of my family remembers is how we all went together to get her another ring just as soon as she returned from the hospital. I must have been five then. At seven and eight, Karen and Laura were at their most directive, telling my father where to park, ushering my mother into the jewelry store. This decision was no longer just between her and my father. Her older daughters wanted to assure her return to normality just as much as he did, perhaps more. *Be* nice. *Be* nice.

I think all my father wanted was to look into her eyes and feel recognized. At that point, he would have let everything else go—thin gold bands, regular trips to the grocery store, car pools. *Niceness.* At that point, a baby in his arms, six young children crowding around them leaving clouds of mist and thumbprints on the jeweler's glass case, he's ready to abandon all of them if he can just have my mother's arms snaking willingly around his waist, feel her tongue tasting the roof of his mouth, hear her laugh. He's imagining the second where she sees the ring in the basin, where she reaches out to turn the faucet on. He's wishing her on.

My sisters are tugging at his arm. "How much money can we spend?"

"Ask your mother," he says. "She's the one with a head for numbers. I've only got a head for one figure."

My mother just looks tired.

I expect she put the ring on, at my sisters' request, as soon as it was purchased, but I like to imagine that they both held out and waited until later that night. I like to imagine my father looking at the ring gleaming in its little cotton nest and thinking about the weight of it. He closes the box up and hands it over to her saying, "I don't know if I can ask you to put this on again."

For the first time since she left the hospital, my mother suddenly sees him in focus, as if a strong wind has picked up and is thinning the mist of Miltown. She finds his diffidence a welcome balm but wants to ease it anyway. "It's not again. I mean, the old one is lost forever. You're asking me to put on a completely new one, aren't you?"

"We all are," he says. "But only when you're ready."

My mother nods and takes up the box and holds it to her chest for a second then places it on the table beside the bed.

"Harold, I feel so much stronger without it. So much surer of what

I'm doing." As she speaks, she hears Chris crying. She imagines how easily she can pick her up, change her, without that ring weighting down her hand so heavily, taking all the initiative away.

"I don't know what to tell you," my father says helplessly, his large hands hanging between his knees. "They feel safer seeing it there. I do too. But all we really want, Jess, is to have you back with us. You know that."

So my mother and father develop a secret ritual. Every evening, just before they go to sleep, he slips the ring off my mother's finger and sets it on her bed stand. Every morning he slips it back on again. The experience, for both of them, is frankly erotic.

I suppose it is the way Miguel and I feel about our own relationship, that there is nothing automatic about it. If anything, it is just the opposite. We amaze our friends with our continuity. Still together? they are always asking. And I suppose, in that small pause before I say yes, I feel as I imagine my mother did when she felt that small, essential friction that let her know, praise God, that however close they came, they would never mistake this for destiny. They would never take her good will out of it.

I sometimes wish I could give my mother my own experience of society's resistance to my own closest relationship. Show her how all that pressure that threatened to dissolve her, to fuse her unwillingly with the will of the world can suddenly turn, prove as powerfully centrifugal as it was, for her, desperately centripetal. Perhaps death has reversed the direction of that force for her, just as it did for me.

I describe my idea for the next panel to Miguel, but this time he looks dubious. I want, in the foreground, two hands of equal size. One hand is a right hand, the other a left. They could be the same person or two different ones. The right hand holds a small band, which it is sliding towards, or away from, the first knuckle of the ring finger of the left hand. Behind these two hands, I want, on either half of the panel, a couple. On the left, a man and woman. They are looking into each other's eyes. Their unringed hands are clasped. On the right side, a matching pair, but they are both men. They too wear suits, like grooms, best men, undertakers. Their clasped hands are ringed. Miguel and I negotiate, harshly, over the altar. Miguel, who to heighten his acute taste for ambiguity remains a practicing Catholic, insists that it would be blasphemous. We compromise more easily over the figures themselves. We decide to embroider them out of transparent thread, so they will be invisible, both sets, unless you know what you're looking for.

If we were blind, this would be unkind, like yelling. But for us, repressed, midwestern, far-sighted, it is just nice. This transparent stitchery is my job. Miguel's job is to embroider those two hands in cinnamon thread. Out of sheer perversity, I make the wedding band blood red.

"Two down," is all Miguel says as he folds it, like the preceding one, in pale blue tissue paper.

Hommage

It's strange that I've spent most of my adult life keeping house with a Hispanic when the language of my dreams is French. *Lavage. Frottage. Hommage.* I don't understand this internal repository of French, actually. I wasn't a particularly good student. My pronunciation was enough to give even Mrs. Hazada, with her heavy Czech accent, fits. But some part of me hungered, even back in seventh grade, perhaps especially back in seventh grade, for an alternative vocabulary.

I love the verbal matching process Miguel and I are constantly engaged in: *amigo*—friend; *amor*—love; *maricón*—stud; *compañero*—companion; *mi vida, salvación, alma, muerte*—my life, salvation, soul, death; *cabrón*—son of a bitch; *que chévere*—great. Between us, we have built a crazy polyglot, selecting for our private use whichever word, English or Spanish, holds for us the most shared allusions. But even so, within each of us, we still seek an alternative language that breaks through the daily din of our interior life, undercuts our assumptions, and lets us be true. It isn't chance that both Miguel and I are artists. It is something we sought and keep seeking in each other.

I love Miguel's paintings, although few of them will find their way into any gallery. Miguel makes no apologies for the objects of his desire *or* his desire. So he sells steadily to our friends, and through them to those who don't mind the lines between aesthetic appreciation and lust heavily blurred. Our apartment is filled with his work. Sometimes I feel I'm in a hardcore porno store, at others that I'm in a church with images that occasion my own devotion.

I've always wondered how Chris and Maggie describe our apartment to their husbands and children. Perhaps, just as no one mentions Miguel, they also strip his handiwork from their descriptions of my living conditions. He has, you know, a bachelor's pad, stark but trendy, they say gesturing vaguely.

(I keep imagining Maggie after one of her rare visits returning home to her large home in Shaker Heights, sitting down to breakfast with her physician husband and 2.3 children saying, "He lives, I kid you not, in a den of love. It's like you set a match to Fire Island. Hot. Hot. Hot."

"Butter?" her husband asks sleepily.

"I just got in last night, Fred." Her tartness startles her, makes her immediately apologetic. "I'll pick some up after I drop the kids off."

And there you have it, my whole reality erased by one word, "Butter?")

It's time, Miguel keeps telling me, that I make my peace. I'm fifty. My father is eighty. Until his cataract surgery last month, he hasn't really been able to see me for the last two years. So why am I so mad? The other forty-eight years, of course, when his eyes worked if anything better than mine.

We've fought so hard, Miguel and I, for our lives together. This crazy disease, immigration, sexual prejudice, and *niceness* more abrasive than the coarsest sand paper. We've lost our mainstays of resistance. Miguel has citizenship; with our subsiding libidos we're likely to remain negative—more at risk now from aberrant cells in our prostate, plaque in our arteries. It gives me vertigo, to be honest, to think that one day we too will celebrate our 55th anniversary. In our case, of course, it will be the anniversary of our first, chance, luridly libidinous encounter—but the principle, ah, the principle isn't very different.

I have the image for the last panel. It came to me this morning with a single word, *hommage*. I see two old people in wing chairs, side by side. It is as if they are holding a royal audience. A figure, gray haired, slightly stooping, approaches with a silver tray on which are six books. Instead of individual titles, one title spans the six spines: *My Life As A Man*. Five words. What adjective should I use to complete the symmetry? Nice? Gay? Old? Angry? Real?

It is the stoop in the shoulders that shocks me. The real deference. The way the books are stacked, like slices of white bread. In the far right corner, looking out toward the viewer, is a tall thin man with long black hair. He is radiant with youth. He is ready to step out of the picture plane. The old man shuffling deeper into the distance with his silver platter is the butler. The even older couple are blind and deaf and dumb. Utterly defenseless except for the deferential ministrations of the butler, who acts as if nothing has happened to them, years haven't passed, senses haven't dulled or shut down completely.

At the feet of the young man, there is a title for the panel: *Time Will Tell*. It is part of the dedication of every book I've written. To Miguel, my beloved partner of one year, five years, ten years, fifteen, twenty, twenty-five—*Time will tell*. . .

Every book I've written has been an expression of my need to claim the life I'm living as a good one, whatever the world might say. They have also been a mad struggle with death. I keep feeling if I can describe what excites me, what makes me feel whole, exactly enough, I can preserve what has given my life meaning so someone, years later, can experience it too with a feeling of relief and recognition. If I can just describe, for example, the light in our kitchen the December morning fifteen years ago when we decided that our brief attempt at a *ménage à trois* wouldn't work for us—how it caught Luis's face, so round but collapsed into itself like an old pumpkin, and caught Miguel's long fingers wrapped around his obscene coffee cup, and tipped with gold the phallus that broke through the surface of the coffee as Miguel brought the cup to his lips. Describe how giddy I felt with rage and victory. Describe, years later, Miguel and I taking turns dabbing a little water on Luis' lips as his breathing slowed, so reluctant, both of us, to let him go.

We struggle with death in many ways. I have sent a copy of every book I've written to my parents. "Why do you keep doing this?" Miguel asks me. "It is like the *clavo*, the nail, in your hand isn't it? You have developed a taste for it?" He laughs as he presses his long dirty fingernail into the center of my palm until the skin turns wax white.

Miguel doesn't understand this compulsion of mine at all. He would never show his paintings to his mother. He is offended at the mere suggestion. But he wouldn't change his life for her either. We go to Vera Cruz every year because it is easier than cleaning out our cluttered loft to make it presentable. When we are there, our relationship is anything his mother says it is. "And why not let her love us in her own way?" he asks me. "There is so much my mother cannot escape."

So many of his Latin friends share the same attitude. How many nights, especially before the cocktails, they gathered to construct the stories they would tell to explain their deaths to their families in Rio, Cartegena, Caracas, or Viña del Mar. Cancer was the most popular, but encephalitis, amoebas, hepatitis, and heart attacks were also common. They would all get together, Luis and Jésus, Guillermo and Mario, drinking rum and tequila and weeping with love for the dusty, poor, intolerant world they had left behind. Miguel would have me research the symptoms of whatever was their disease of the week so they could give the descriptions of their deaths strong verisimilitude. And the families, when the time came, responded by taking in the grieving friends as extended family, no probing questions asked. It was enough to know their sons were loved and mourned in a world so far away it was beyond their imagining. "Why not let them sweeten such an enormous sorrow?" Miguel asked. "Wouldn't you have me do that for you?"

My parents have never opened any of the books I've sent them or, in later years, as my success has increased, had my publisher send them. They have never watched a talk show where I've appeared. Never asked who is the person with the heavy Spanish accent who almost always answers the phone in our apartment.

I would have said I was completely adjusted to this state of affairs. I make jokes about it with Miguel and our friends. Even with my sisters, Maggie and Chris. Every visit, I pull my books out of the cabinet at the bottom of the pine bookcase in the guestroom where my mother has hidden them and return them to the open shelves in the living room. I insist, on those brief visits to their home, in introducing Miguel's name whenever the conversation allows the least opportunity. "Miguel and I will be going to Vera Cruz next month," I may say when we see something on Mexico on the nightly news. I appreciate their equal alacrity in racing to slam each door shut. "It's so nice that you have close friends, dear," my mother says equably. "Without family nearby, that must be reassuring. Did you know that Karen's best friend, Kathleen, just found out her daughter is pregnant?"

But when I sit and think about this quilt, this niceness project, so carefully gutted of conflict, I feel a brutal anger at everyone, including myself. Why in hell is this butler shuffling eternally away from all the promise of life toward this senseless couple who cannot read, hear, think—do anything but swallow and shit and implacably deny. I do not want to know this guy with his silver platter and his loyal shuffle. But I sure want to fuck the glowing young man with the cinnamon skin and be fucked by him in return.

What homage do we owe those who ask us to deny everything that makes us whole, happy, vital? Nothing conflictual, my sisters warn us all. Be nice. Be nice. But what is nice about what they have done, will always do, to me? You would think, at fifty, I wouldn't even have to ask the question. Or know by now that I will never stop—and accept it as I would the ringing in the ears that follows stroke.

Miguel, this morning, is buzzing around like a hungry mosquito taking photographs of my hands and earlobes and feet. He sometimes does this when he's trying to complete the finishing touches on a painting and suddenly finds the basics of anatomy startling. "Ear lobes," he will say at times like this. "Have you ever really studied ear lobes, Roberto?"

For whole bodies, Miguel usually commissions younger men to act as models now. This has been a gradual process. He stopped using me about ten years ago. Two or three years ago, he stopped using himself. He will never stop trying, in his canvases, to bed his dreams—or, when I'm usefully occupied elsewhere, to make it with the models in real life.

As I sip my coffee, I watch all the polaroids Miguel has taken deepening in color. The first liver spot on my hand comes out clearly. Compared to Kaposi's, it's nothing, but it still gives me a charge that is so intense it is almost erotic. Art is about this essential rift, what it feels like to know ourselves from the inside out, the outside in. I touch Miguel's cinnamon skin, thickened now with its forty-seven years of experience, and I am back in that primordial yes that began before language, when touch was truth. Then I open my eyes and see liver spots. Why not?

I could not give it up, this crazy yearning process, this stubborn matching process, any more than I could give up Miguel. To be human is to dream of being known—if only for a second, if only by oneself. In Miguel, graying, painting his ageless young men, I see and love this tension. And he, I suppose, can come as close as anyone to loving that shuffling butler with his platter of unopened books, their dedications forever secret.

"In my world," Miguel once told me, "we respect our parents not because they are intelligent or good or even take sufficient care of us—but just because they gave us life and that is the greatest good. To respect them is to celebrate our own existence."

I try to reconcile that image of Miguel leaning cloyingly over his *mamacita* murmuring sweet nothings, tossing his long graying hair over his shoulder, his diamond stud glittering in the lamplight, and my own ritual annual visits—Saturday morning to Sunday afternoon—with its token family dinner, its walk around their neighborhood, the stubborn absence of any questions about my own life in Jamaica Plains.

"No," Miguel says, collecting the polaroids from the table. "Don't even ask. I have a painting I want to finish. I can't get away."

So I sip more coffee. I listen to Miguel off at the far end of the loft preparing his paints, singing one of his favorite *rancheros*. I begin toying with a short story: Juan Gabriel and Me. I see my panel a little differently now—as if the butler has reversed directions, received the books from the old couple and is carrying them to the young man. I imagine him opening his chest and slipping all those books into his glowing heart and wrapping it shut again with a vine of thorns. A gothic, Catholic flourish I am sure Miguel will relish.

When I go to tell Miguel about the last panel, he is busy preparing a quilt of his own out of polaroid images he's taken of the two of us— my right profile, his left one, his ear, my breastbone, his buttocks, my left thigh, his right foot, my eyes open, his eyes shut, his smile, my grimace, his hands cupped prayerfully over my most private parts, my head held to his. "Mementos *del momento*," he says. "It's time we made our peace with this." His hands sculpt the air around us both. He shrugs, tucking his graying hair behind his ear. "*Viejitos*." Old guys.

I feel absurdly shy when I look at the images, as if we were meeting each other for the first time.

The image for the panel shifts again before I've even described it. Now the two of us are carrying a large portrait of my parents toward them, seated patiently in their wing chairs. We are two tall handsome middle-aged men. We could be mistaken for day laborers because of the vigor of our stance. The title changes too: Gift of Life. The painting we carry is of my parents standing half-submerged in a surf of children. All you can see are seven gold heads of varying heights. My parents look startled, bemused. They are holding their gripped hands a little above the squabbling sea of life. The detail is too fine for a square foot panel. I don't need Miguel to tell me so. But I like, in my mind, entering deeper and deeper into the image. It feels like picking up a book and beginning to read, one's whole body opening in expectation as the narrative voice takes over: And then? And then?

"Nice," Miguel says when I finish describing it. "Very nice. And now, *mi amor*, like the good sons we are, we can begin to mourn what made us."

We stand there staring at each other, a couple of *viejitos, compañeros, amantes*. Our breath quickens inexplicably with lust, that blessed irritant that death makes lustrous. We make the most of it. *Sí cómo no?* Why not?

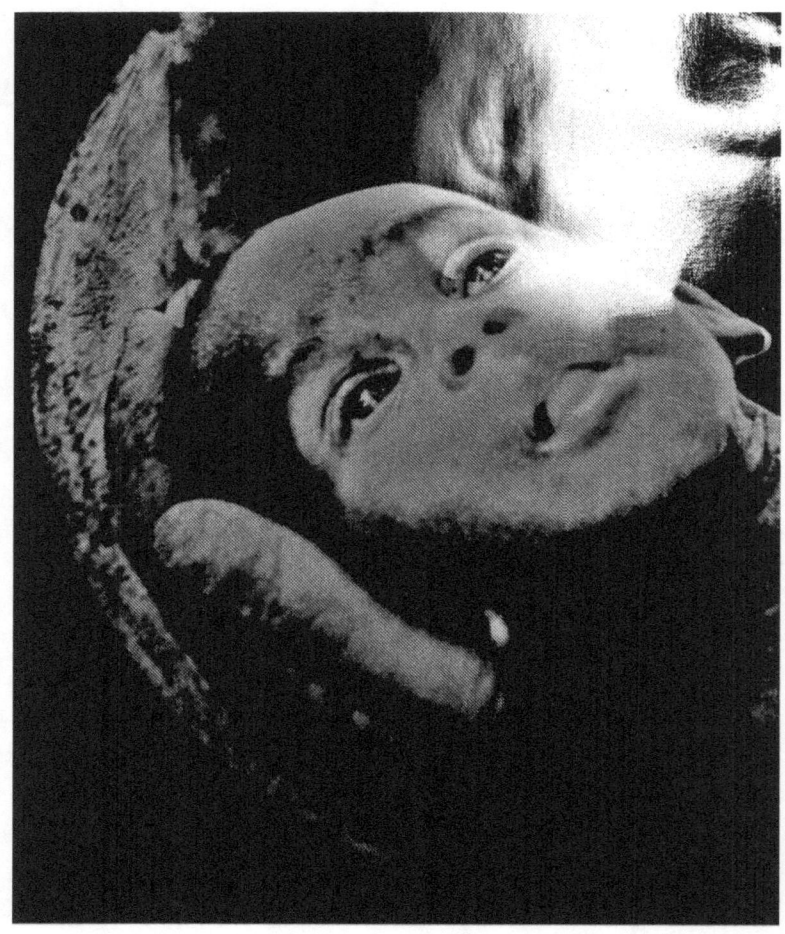

MY POWER IS IN YOU

When I had the vision that changed my life, I was sitting in the driver's seat of a borrowed van waiting as my sister Marisol unloaded her new paintings from the back and carried them into the gallery with the help of my husband, Carlos, and a workman at the gallery.

"Gentle, gentle," Marisol kept muttering as Carlos and the handyman grabbed the large paintings.

I was peering up at the sky wondering if it was going to rain and what the roads would be like on the twelve hour ride to our house on the coast. Since the tragedy last year, we all fear rain that lasts longer than an hour. We know it can bring down mountains in the blink of an eye. I had closed my eyes, savoring the light on my eyelids, delicate as a lover's kiss, and then, suddenly anxious, I looked up again scanning the sky for clouds with dark linings. That was when I saw him.

He was indescribably beautiful, as young men in their twenties can be, filled with a joyous, untested manhood that lights their unmarked skin from within. They have as much strength as they will ever have but a sweetness that connects them to the boy they once were. They have not lost the last traces of the mothering that brought them into being, a kind of trusting stillness. It is what has already begun to disappear from my own son's face.

But it was there, on the Savior's face, that sweet, feeding attention. I understood I was seeing him when he was still a carpenter, before his years of healing began. He was staring into my eyes with this kind but intense interest. I couldn't take my eyes from his. They were deep brown, and his long dark hair gleamed like the ocean lit by a full moon. I felt a wave of the deepest sadness, and I put my forehead on my hands, which were still gripping the steering wheel, and I said, "Forgive me."

I heard his voice then, making my head thrum, as if he were whispering directly into my ear. "There is nothing to forgive. My power is in you. Use it."

Even as I describe this vision, as I have done many times since then to my family, friends, and neighbors, as I did just minutes after it passed to Marisol and Carlos, I can still feel that sweetness pouring through me hot as the sunlight through the windshield. I can still feel the way my heart seemed to grow to twice its size and my body began to hum with an excitement that was almost sexual. I can still feel his deep sweet voice reverberating through me: *My power is in you. Use it.*

"Yes do," Marisol said when she came to the window of the car to find out why I was not moving. "Make my exhibition a success."

At that moment, my jealousy of my sister disappeared completely because I understood that I had been shown my own true gifts. For so many years, I have attended her openings, watched her as she greeted people, and felt as if some essential fire was missing in me. We look very similar, with our curly brown hair and even features, but there has always been an energy, a glow, to Marisol as if everything about her is slightly electrified. When she stands before her vivid, tumultuous paintings, an energy flows continuously between the canvases and her. I know it comes from her because when I am alone with the canvases, they are dramatic in color and scale, but they don't reverberate. While she, even walking down the street, seems to have a field of energy around her that makes people look up as she passes. I'm not sure she even notices because she has always been this way.

"Your sister sends off sparks," Carlos said to me the first time he met her. "But you, my sweet Alicia—"

"Yes?"

But he stopped, looking a little puzzled, a little guilty. I looked at the engagement ring sparkling on my finger. Should I, I wondered, have waited for the wedding band before introducing them.

"Yes?" I asked again.

He took my hands and smiled. "You are like the touch of a soft towel, or cool spring water, like the brief brush of velvet or a feather boa. You make all my senses come alive. There is something in you that makes me want to approach, let go."

He pulled my hand up and placed it on his cheek. "Look at me," he said. But as I did, my eyes filled. I wanted to send out my own energy field, not just excite someone else's.

"What power is it that you have now?" Carlos asked me as we drove along the mountain road that opened here and there to show the many islands scattered along the coast like beads from a broken necklace. "It obviously doesn't affect public opinion." The reviews for Marisol's show had been lukewarm. There was some suggestion that she was repeating herself, that her taste in color camouflaged a shaky sense of composition, a redundancy of theme.

"They sold," Marisol said, tearing up the review and throwing it in the trash. "What more do I ask?"

"I'm thinking that we may not need to stop and buy supplies if you can do fishes and loaves."

"Do not mock what you can't understand," I said and turned my face away from the islands to my left and studied the tropical vegetation growing along the side of the road. It was less various than the vegetation on our mountain. I was eager to return to our small house, even if our cupboards were bare and I had no power to remedy this. I twisted my wedding ring. Even after two years, my hands still try to adjust to its pressure.

"We will live on air and sunlight," I had told Carlos in delight when we first saw the cacao *finca* and decided to buy it.

But we are not children, or young lovers, and a diet of sunlight and air, after a few years, is no different from fasting. We never say anything of this to each other—but sometimes I look at Carlos after he has come back from a day guiding the rare tourist, or he looks at me after another day spent weeding the garden of our tiny rented house in this poor dusty town that time has forgotten, and I can feel how parched our souls are. We never expected this. When we met, I thought, I will never thirst again. I will never hunger. I have found my soulmate.

And perhaps I have. But some days, in our tropical paradise, a shadow passes across the floor and I can see in it two figures crawling exhaustedly over bright desert sands.

But that was all over now, I knew it, as I sat in the car and stared at my hands and heard that deep voice echoing in my head, making my heart grow large, my sex wet, making my fingers tingle with energy: *My power is in you. Use it.*

I did know, Carlos' gentle mockery aside, exactly what I was called to do. I placed my hand gently over his, practicing.

"I love you," he said. "I know this has been hard for you, Alicia. Can you give us one more year?"

I felt the Savior's energy running through me.

"Don't worry," I said. "Be happy."

Carlos looked at me, surprised to hear his own line coming from my lips. He was moved, I could see, by my sincerity. He didn't know that it was God who was speaking through me. I never knew grace had such an erotic charge to it. I was amazed, at fifty-three, what I had left to discover. I couldn't wait.

But I didn't begin to practice my gifts in any serious way until I flew to the States to visit my son, Vicente, some weeks later. Vicente refuses to come visit us. This is his country, but after all his years of living in the States, he does not feel at home here. Indeed, he feels endangered. The last time he came to visit, he was robbed twice, once at the airport and the second time on the bus on his way back from our little house on the coast. "I'm never coming back to this *pinche* country," he said when I talked to him next.

I thought at the time he was just reacting, but he was serious. "Surely, there is no more crime here than in Orlando or Miami," I said to him.

"But in the States, the crime is not directed at me, Mamí. That is the difference. Here in the U.S., I am one of the have nots, there I am one of the haves."

But I think the truth is when Vicente has come to visit us, he has felt robbed by Carlos of the woman I once was. He does not see the beauty of the little house we live in until our dreams come true. He does not see the promise of the *finca* we have yet to cultivate and build on (for air and sunlight do not buy lumber or cement). Does he not remember my sorrow in that boring house in Orlando? Does he not remember the bitter fights his father and I had? Why does he not blame his father for the changes in *his* life? Why does he not feel robbed by his father's new, young, American wife with her bright blonde hair and an accent that makes her sound as if she were sucking on caramels? Why does he not feel robbed by the little half-brothers and half-sisters, no older than his own son?

But as I flew up to see him and my grandson, Eduardo, these bitter questions dissolved as I stared at my hands lying quietly open in my lap. I was filled with a sweet confidence. It was Vicente who would understand my new powers—because they are very near the powers he experienced in me when he was a child.

I have, you see, the power to heal by touch. I knew that when I set my hands on someone else's skin, the Savior's loving energy would pass right through me. I could feel my nerve ends quickening at the very thought. As I looked out the plane window and saw the coral reefs darkening the sharp green waters of the Caribbean, I wondered why I was not sharing my gifts yet with Carlos and my neighbors. It was not as if I had any doubts. It was not as if they didn't need them. I was just growing into my powers, not denying them to the world. That would be too cruel.

The first night I arrived in Orlando, I told Vicente about my powers as we sat drinking tea in his little garden.

"This is amazing, Mamí," he said. "We must try them out immediately. Perhaps tomorrow you will go over and visit Mimi and heal her migraines so she can take Eduardo for the weekend like we planned." He was not mocking me. Mimi is his ex-wife, but they are close friends, bound by their love for the unexpected Eduardo. They trade off caring for Eduardo as equally as they can, but lately Mimi had been having terrible migraines and was having Eduardo stay with Vicente almost every night.

"If she doesn't object," I said. For I wondered whether those migraines might have a name and leave behind them stains on the sheets and a slight smell of fish. But it was not my place to ask.

I did put my hand on Vicente's cheek before I went up to bed. "I am so pleased to see you," I said. And at my touch the softness that was in the Savior's face returned momentarily to my son's.

"Me too," he said. And then his face tightened and he was a completely different species again. "Can you pick up Eduardo at school if Mimi is out of commission again?"

Vicente called Mimi in the morning, and she surprised me by saying yes, she would like to have me try to heal her headaches. Vicente left a note about this, which I saw when I came down to the kitchen. He was busy getting Eduardo ready for school, checking to see if he had his homework, his lunch money. He pulled a transformer doll and a squirt gun out of Eduardo's knapsack. "School is for learning," he said. "You play when you get home. Understood?"

Eduardo, who is a little imp, snapped to attention and saluted his father. He is American, my grandson. No respect for his elders. Vicente's father would have slapped Vicente if he ever behaved this way, but Vicente just laughed and said, "If you're here tonight, we'll go off and play some soccer. See if you have that little grin on your face when you're finished." He touched his son's face as he said this, and Eduardo wriggled with pleasure.

They both came over and gave me big hugs. I am only fifty-three, but standing there with my hair unbrushed, in my worn bathrobe, I felt as old as my own *abuelita*. I smiled brightly and waved them off.

Vicente had left me Mimi's phone number, but I did not call her until ten, just in case her migraine had a name. She answered the phone immediately in her soft, little girl's voice. "Who is it?"

"Alicia, Vicente's mother."

"Do you really think you might help me? I'm desperate. The medicine the doctors gave me doesn't work. The pain is so intense I want to cut my head off, but I think, what would Eduardo do with a mother who cannot see him or laugh at his little jokes." She choked back a sob.

I told her I would be over as soon as I could dress. I told her she did not need to give me directions, I still remembered the way to the apartment she and Vicente shared for the two years they were married.

When I got there and rang the bell, Mimi just called out in a weak voice, "Come in. The door's unlocked." She didn't even wait to hear my name. I looked around me to make sure no one had heard.

"You must be more careful of yourself," I scolded her as I entered her bedroom. "Anyone could come in."

She just closed her eyes. The room was dark, with only a glimmer of the bright Florida light coming through the heavy drapes that Mimi had inherited from her grandmother. It was an old lady's room—not just the heavy pale green drapes, but the dark oak bed and the mirrored armoire. Mimi looked much younger than her twenty-three years.

"You have destroyed your lives," I said to them when I learned about the pregnancy. Mimi, at sixteen, barely had breasts. Vicente, at seventeen, didn't even have a full beard.

"Don't worry, Mamí," Vicente told me. "This is my responsibility. I will do the right thing." His father had moved out eight months earlier. He was the man of the house now. He was proving it by getting married, fathering his own child. I have always regretted what I said that day and feel grateful that Vicente ushered Mimi, her face awash with tears, quickly from the room saying, "She will come around. Trust me."

And I have come round. But that first objection still reverberates somewhere. It is why, I think, they have not asked me for very much help, even when, before I married Carlos and still had my alimony, there was help I could give. That was why I returned to my country soon after their marriage. There was no one who needed me—and I live to be needed. Don't we all?

But this morning, Mimi needed me. She stretched out her hand, and I took it. She was so very white and gold, this young woman. Not like my brown son, whose darkness mildly shocks us all since his father and I look pale as proper Spaniards. But who knows who our ancestors bedded, or what traces we carry of these matings. This doesn't matter in our country, but it matters in the States. There, your destiny is as dark as the pigment in your skin.

Mimi had a golden future—if it weren't for the migraines and her dark son. I rested my tanned hand on her pale forehead and felt the slightly clammy skin.

"My poor child, what can I do for you?

"Make the pain go away," she said, and tried to smile.

Suddenly the energy left my hands and I did not know what I would do. I felt very foolish sitting there beside her. She looked at me so trustingly, and that just made me feel worse, so I busied myself with shifting the bedding around so she could lie with her head toward the foot and I could stand as I tended to her. She winced as she slowly turned herself around.

"I'm so glad you came. It's so lonely without anyone when you're sick. But I send them all away because all motion hurts me. Send them away and then just lie here feeling sorry for myself."

"Let us begin," I said. I raised my hands in blessing as I remembered the priests doing in the masses when I was a child. I never much liked church as a child, and stopped believing, or so I thought, as soon as I left my parent's house and could think for myself without giving pain to anyone. Marisol has always called my discretion hypocrisy, but she is wrong. I have just never felt a need to share my beliefs, until now. *My power is in you. Use it*, the Savior said to me.

I kept my hands raised and did not say anything. I let my doubt pour out, I breathed in the promise I was given. I breathed it in again, and again, letting it flow all through me. I was filled with the deepest love for this young woman with her milk-white skin and her misery. I was filled with love for every object in the room: the heavy, imposing furniture; the light cutting sharply across the pink carpet just under the drapes; the sound of the refrigerator humming in the kitchen; the sound of a nearby door being slammed shut. I was filled with love for this energy that now filled me.

I lowered my hands to her temples, and I just stood there without saying anything, feeling that love flow through my fingers, through the walls of my skin into her.

I will not leave you comfortless. I will come to you.

It was not as if I heard those words in my head, I *was* those words. I was the reality behind them. I let this understanding fill me and I felt so light, so happy. I breathed in Mimi's pain, the throbbing hallucinatory aura of her migraine, her loneliness, her love for my grandson, her exasperation with him too. I breathed in all her unthinkable thoughts—about what it would be like to start life again tangled in these sheets with a beautiful young man, no anchors, no responsibilities, no stretch marks. I breathed in her anguish at the disloyal thoughts, how she must keep cleaning her house, all the weighty, humorless furniture of her grandparents, to erase them. I breathed in the constant hum of conversation, all the ringing of the phones, all the smiling and nodding, that went with her job as a receptionist. I breathed in all the bills that hid, unpaid, in the kitchen drawer. I breathed in her parents' disappointment every time she visited them, the ache in her womb when she saw them look with the same sour look of disapproval at Eduardo, with his dark hair, his olive skin, his father's Latin mannerisms.

I breathed in and released everything I was learning about her. And then I let the love that was in me and around me pour through my hands. I could feel my heart grow so big and hot with all this love. I am a small woman, but at that moment I felt so large and so still and so powerful. I felt a pleasure sweeter than my first nights with Carlos rush through me, and keep rushing, rushing, the pleasure building and building. At first, I felt that I would come right there, but then I understood this pleasure was without beginning and end.

I felt Mimi's skin begin to warm as she opened to this pleasure too. I looked down at her sweet, unmarked face held between my two dry hands and I was filled with love for the two of us, for the trust that was running from her to me to the hot heart of the Savior, which was my own heart, and the trust that was running in the opposite direction, from the Savior through me to her. "Oh yes," I thought. "Oh yes, oh yes."

"Bless this lovely young woman with your healing love," I whispered.

"Ease her pain. Give her peace."

And then I found myself singing a song without words, just pure vowels, like a bird. I looked out across the room and let my song swoop from my mouth, wing into the air.

Slowly, gently, I touched her soft, plump shoulders. I ran my hands down her arms. I saw her body arch a little, her nipples harden under the thin blue nightgown, and knew then she was feeling what I felt.

"Give yourself up to it," I whispered, drawing my hands slowly back up her arms, and laying them quietly on her shoulders again. "Give yourself completely up."

She opened her eyes, and I was transfixed by their clear blueness, by the way her mouth opened slightly, as it must have when she nursed Eduardo in the middle of the night, as it must have when she felt Vicente's first kiss on the nape of her neck.

"You are safe," I told her. "All this pleasure you are feeling belongs to you. Receive it."

And I felt her eyes locking with mine, something opening inside her, and I knew she was trusting me with her perfect nature and I couldn't have enough of it. I did not break our gaze, just let this energy flow back and forth between us.

"More," she said, and her body arched up under my hands. "Dear God, more." And then she slipped back on the bed and was completely still, a sweet smile on her face. I touched her eyelids, her cheek. I tucked her hair behind her ears.

"There, there," I said. "This is yours too. Along with the pain, this is yours too."

My face was wet with tears, but there was no grief. I felt I had been present at a new kind of birth.

"There are no secrets here," I told her. "There is nothing you can't share." Her smile was radiant. I felt as alive in it as I did in the gaze of the Savior.

"Can you stay here until I fall asleep?" she asked.

So I did. And as I waited, I sent my power out into the room and made it safe for my grandson, I made it safe for her, I made it safe for the new young men who would, inevitably, tangle with her in this bed. And it flashed, briefly, across my mind that I wished my ex-husband Ricardo well, with his blonde wife in their American life. I saw myself on the plane returning home, so eager to see Carlos, to open my legs to him, my mouth, my heart. I saw the heads of the people in the airport turning as I passed by, drawn by something that flowed from me now, delicate but irresistible, like an expensive perfume. I saw the people of our village knocking at my door, I saw the sick children, the pregnant women, the old people who could not walk without canes, and I could hear my voice like a gentle stream, my hands like silk, giving them relief. I had never felt so beautiful, so blessed. I had never felt so sure of myself.

When Carlos met me at the airport, I took his face in both my hands and rose on my feet and kissed him fiercely. But for several days I did not tell him what had happened. I savored it in secrecy, like an irresistible infidelity.

"Do you think it might have been just a little too much of a good thing?" Carlos asked me gently, when I finally described my session with Mimi to him. "Do you think you might like to rein that power in just a mite?"

"Why?"

I could see he was excited and a little frightened by what I was telling him. A little possessive too. He ran his hand across my naked hip, slipped it back between my legs and opened my sex and let his fingertips just rest there. Carlos is a magnificent lover, so sensitive and inventive. He has learned well from his other wives, much better than I learned from Ricardo. But what I do is not about giving pleasure, even though pleasure is intimately involved.

"What is it about then?" Carlos asked.

"Holding the world in my heart, just like God does."

Carlos pushed my legs a little wider. He smiled and leaned down and kissed the sides of my mouth. "This evening, will you hold just a small part of me again?"

The excitement we felt as he entered me flowed back and forth between us, so gentle and intense it made us moan with wonder, just like we used to when we first met.

The next weekend, when we drove to the next town to call Vicente, my son was so excited. "You are a miracle worker, Mamí. She has had no headaches since you visited her. All my friends are asking when you will come back again." I could hear that I had gained a little stature in his eyes, and I enjoyed it.

"I need to use my gifts here," I told him.

The next day when Mattea came to the house to clean, I followed her around describing my gifts. "Perhaps you should let the people know," I said.

"Ah, Señora, you are blessed," she said as she knelt down and ran a wet rag under the bed to wash away the ever present layer of dust that billows in from the road, drifts down from our cane roof. She stood up, twisting the rag until the dirty water ran into the pail.

"You are blessed, Señora," she repeated. "But so are many people in this village. Señora Luz is visited by Santa Barbara, and Señora Milagros is visited by Maria Lionza, while the boy Roberto, Jorge's son, is visited by Guaicaipuro and Bolivar and, once or twice, has had the good Doctor Gregorio Hernandez speak from his mouth as well."

"That's different," I said impatiently. "That is black magic and superstition." People here are always going to the *perfumerías* and buying spells to cast over their croupy babies, their malarial teenagers, their unfaithful husbands or wives, their ambitious colleagues or jealous neighbors.

Mattea stopped pushing the wet rag across the floor and looked at me. "How? How is your power different?"

I could see the Savior looking through the window with the same intense kindness he had shown before. He had a small smile flickering on his lips. He winked at me, but he didn't say anything. I put my hands against my lower back and stretched and drew a deep breath.

"Just let the people know. When they come, they will see the difference."

"Do you want them to bring cigars and rum?" Mattea asked. "Of course not. There is no need for bribes," I said. For props, is what I thought. I have not been to any of these possessions, but I have heard about them. They are an excuse for vengeance, release. Just like the heavy drinking that goes on in all the villages around here on the weekends when the men aren't out on the sea. No wonder they do not know what to do with these miraculous gifts of mine that I so freely give—that are not designed to gain someone's peace of mind or happiness by punishing someone else. The common people here do not know what to make of Carlos and me, for we do not drink, I do not appear at the market on Monday with bruises on my cheeks. We are cultured, but are not much richer than the people around us. That makes us, by my son Vicente and my sister Marisol's standards, very poor indeed. But my powers, as the Savior keeps reminding me, are a treasure without measure.

"If you have aspirin to spare, or contraceptives, or medicine for the flu or the liver, the people would be very happy to come to you," Mattea said.

"I have my own oils for the skin. And teas for asthma and colds and troubles with the kidneys."

"We all make our own medicines here, Señora," Mattea said with a shrug. "But I will tell my neighbors that you believe you have been blessed with the gift of touch."

Of course, I was frustrated by her stupidity—which is actually not so usual for Mattea—but I had great confidence in my gifts and knew, just as soon as one or two people experienced them, the news would spread through the village like wildfire and I would wake each morning to a line of devoted followers waiting outside my door. This isn't vanity. In my country, we are always looking for new politicians and new saints. Our capacity for devotion is one of our biggest strengths.

"How *will* you know if this is the real thing?" Carlos asked me that afternoon as we sat on the patio sipping some of my nirvana tea. "Don't you have any doubts, Alicia?"

"Talk to Vicente," I said with a shrug. "He knows."

"I wouldn't dare doubt Vicente," Carlos said with a smile.

I could see a line of worry on his forehead. I know he doesn't want to see me disappointed. This past year, I have spent so many days in our bed under the mosquito net finding the strength to breathe without wheezing from the dust, finding the courage to get up. We hoped for so much, Carlos and I, when we moved here. A new life together, love that spread out from our busy, astonished bodies, our awestruck minds, like heat from a furnace.

"Your touch means everything to me," Carlos said, coming over and kneeling before me, taking the mug of nirvana tea from my hands. "Maybe I'm just jealous. I don't want to share it."

"My love, my love," I said, pressing the creases out of his forehead with my fingertips. "There is more than enough to go around."

"Well, what are you going to do, Alicia," a clear voice woke me from my dreams, "if no one wants your gifts?" I peered around our room trying to see who was speaking. It was a woman's voice, very similar to my own—or

Marisol's.

"I don't know," I said, "but it is a little early to give up, don't you think?"

I closed my eyes and tried to feel that warm breath in my ear, those words humming in my head, to see Mimi's perfectly trusting blue eyes holding mine.

"Not too early, surely, to prepare yourself," the voice said. "You don't want to spend even more time lying like a corpse under your mosquito net."

My fingers tingled, but the energy was confusing, like I had just touched a live wire and everything in me was leaping back from the shock.

All my night fears were forgotten in the morning when I heard the first ring at the gate and went out and found Mattea and her cousin waiting for me. "It can't hurt," Mattea was saying to her cousin, who was clutching a bundle to her chest. "And it's free, so what do you have to lose?"

"Do you think, if it doesn't work, the Señora will give me money for the hospital?"

"They are poorer than we are, *mi amor*. Whatever airs she puts on, she counts out her *bolívares* for arepa meal and sardines, just like the rest of us."

"Why bother?" her cousin said, turning to leave.

"Please," I said, pulling the door open and reaching out my hand. I didn't even bother to pretend that I hadn't been listening. "Let me see if my gifts are of any use to you."

Mattea's cousin, Angelina, shrugged away from my hand but turned around. She handed me the still little bundle, which I cradled in my arms as I led them into my beautiful borrowed house. There is nothing in our house that does not speak of how we choose to live—not only my sister's paintings, but the healing herbs I have grown with my own hands, the birds that sing from their cages in the patio. But Mattea, of course, didn't bother to register its beauty, neither did Angelina.

Carefully, I pulled the edges of the blanket apart. I was a little afraid of what I might see—perhaps a child with a cleft palate or with water on the brain.

"This is Angelina's first grandchild," Mattea said. "But something went wrong with the birth. The baby came out all twisted."

I carried the baby over to the bench by the window and laid it down, then carefully unwrapped the blanket as if I were opening a birthday present. The baby, a boy, was all contracted, his shoulders drawn up around his ears, his head twisted dangerously far over to the left side. His little forehead was all wrinkled and his bare gums were exposed by the grimace that bunched up his cheeks.

"What is his name?" I asked Angelina.

"My daughter, she will not look at him. The labor took two days and she is a little crazy with the pain. She told me to give him a name."

I was sure she had done more than that. She had told Angelina to get him out of her sight and never bring him back. Sentiments that Angelina had then expressed to the drunken father, a boy of eighteen who had spent the past two days celebrating the imminent birth of his first son. "You want him," she yelled at the father, holding out the contorted child, "you take him. Otherwise, you never come here again."

"What's gotten into you?" the boy asked, weaving in his tracks. "Why are you acting like that?"

Angelina's daughter was thirteen, the oldest of Angelina's children. Angelina was pregnant herself. She did not want this little knot of misery any more than her daughter did.

"What can we do?" she asked me now. "*Dios mío*, his heart is strong. I fear he will live for years."

I flattened out the blanket, straightening the infant as much as I could on it. My heart was beating very fast and my hands felt numb. I had this terrible feeling of flatness, emptiness. The way I felt every morning now, lying under the mosquito net, willing myself to get up and pretend to a hope and happiness I no longer felt. The way I felt watching the shadows crawl across our living room floor, like dying people dreaming of water. "I'm sorry," I said. And I could feel my own knuckles on the back of my forehead as I sat in the car in the capital, and then, again, I heard those words: *There is nothing to forgive. My power is in you. Use it.*

I didn't really want to touch this poor, misbegotten child. I understood Angelina and her daughter's responses completely. But then I felt my hands grow warm and move with a sureness that I watched with surprise, as if they belonged to someone else. First they covered the baby's forehead and the back of its head. My hands didn't try to force anything, just stayed there. I could feel how terrifying it must be for the infant to turn and look at us. Would I, if I were he? Oh, I could understand it so clearly, as my hands rested there, how he had turned his head to find some release in the birth channel, how it had stayed fixed that way as if he were holding on to the warm, inviting gaze of the Savior rather than turning to see what was here in this world waiting to greet him—a child-mother crazed by labor, an exhausted grandmother saving her energy for her next baby, a drunk punk whose only real love was focused on the twitchings of his own prick. Surely the Savior's sweet brown eyes were more promising than this.

"Do you have a little formula?" I asked Angelina.

"Señora," Mattea chided me. "Who has the money? The mother's milk hasn't had time to come in. These days are a time of fasting."

"A little honey," I said to Mattea, unwilling to take my eyes from the baby.

When she brought it to me, I took my hand from the baby's forehead and dipped my index finger into the honey, then touched it to my lips, then set my finger against the baby's lips. I took my other hand and rested it on his cheek, relaxing the muscles to allow him to begin to suck, ever so gently. I put my hand then on his neck, giving him the courage to begin moving toward the finger, which I began to edge toward me. I could feel my own face relaxing, just as it does when I love, when hunger and satisfaction become one.

I *wanted* this baby to turn its face to me. I wanted to see there that sweet feeding attention I had seen so clearly on the Savior's face, on Mimi's, on Vicente's when he was a child.

There was something about the intensity of this wanting that conveyed itself to Mattea and Angelina, for they stopped talking to each other, stopped moving entirely. They began, I could feel it, to share in my desire.

I have no idea how long it took for the baby's head to turn toward us. I can still feel how the muscles in its neck, at first as tight as harp strings, loosened. I can remember the small sweet sighs that escaped from each of us when the baby's face finally came into view, his forehead now smooth, his little mouth, pursed like a bud, busily suckling. I can remember taking my finger from his mouth, slipping my hands under him and bringing him close to me with that same fierce love I felt toward Vicente when he came into this world.

I held him up to my cheek. I closed my eyes, letting the tears and longing flow out of me and through his pure pure soul. That channel of love that can flow between us, it is what I live for, what I grieve for inconsolably when it closes off. My love for it, I understood, is where my power comes from. *My power is in you*, the Savior said. What he meant was his hunger, his desire, his need to touch and be touched without impediment, without apology—these are *our* power.

"A miracle," Angelina said, ready to take the baby back, but I told her we were not finished.

I set the baby back on the bench and set my hands on his skewed shoulders, gently pressing them back toward the bench with the lightest pressure my fingers were capable of. I was asking him for another kind of commitment, another kind of trust, and I could feel his small soul resisting, wanting to keep his loyalties divided, so even if he seemed to be feeding at our breast, feeding on our faces, his heart was turned away, facing only God.

Oh, it hurt so much to ask this of him. What guarantees could I give him that he wasn't opening his heart to tragedy, just like the rest of us? *My power is in you. Use it*, I heard the Savior whisper again, and I could feel my own heart grow hot with his love and I knew it was not wrong to increase the pressure on the baby's shoulders ever so slightly, that what he sought was right here before him, in me, in Angelina, in Mattea, in his child-mother and punk father too. And I understood then that I couldn't learn to use my own gifts if I turned away to look for the Savior's gaze, I could only use them if I dared to look deep into the eyes of a stranger, to take the chance, again and again, of seeing God's heart beating inside them, reaching out to feed me too. This healing, I understood, moved both ways. And so I let all my need and desire and crazy fear and hope pour into this little child not one day old. *My power is in you*, I whispered to him. *Use it. Use it.*

And slowly his shoulders began to relax, to rest against the bench. It was as if I could look inside his chest and see his heart burning, so big and bright, could see the thorns circling it. *My power*, I whispered to him again and again, *is in you. Use it.*

I was ready to begin on his hips, but Angelina said she had to leave to make lunch for her children, and Mattea had another house to clean.

"But it must be done soon," I said. "He's so malleable now, but in a few days, our opportunity may be lost."

"God willing," Angelina said. "But thank you for what you have done so far, Señora." She wrapped the baby up tightly, able now to smile at him before she dropped the corner of the blanket lightly over his face to protect him from the dust.

I saw them off with such a mix of emotions. It was as if I had been interrupted just before climax—a feeling of frustration and incompleteness, and also a sweet furtive interest that just wouldn't leave, that came awake again at the slightest brush of my own fingertips, cloth, the petal of one of my hibiscus flowers.

I sat out there in my garden feeling quite exhausted and chastened. I hadn't understood that this healing required as much of me as it did of the one I was reaching out to. I could feel, then, how complex the invitation the Savior had made to me was. As complex as the invitation that Carlos and I, starving on light and air, now make to each other. I sat there feeling the same disappointment and exhaustion I feel lying under the mosquito net each morning, watching the sunlight blaze across the walls, wondering where all the easy freedom has gone to, all that promise. But what I'm learning, what I can feel running all through my body this morning, is what it feels like to understand that these reorganizations come from God, that we can relax into them, feel them shudder through us like the sweet sweet illuminations of physical love. There is no love, human or divine, that doesn't find us here, in our sweating, hungering, passion-baffled bodies, our huge, hot, troubled hearts.

"What makes your gifts different?" Mattea asked me.

This morning I understood these gifts were not different from the ones I had been given at birth and had used already, wisely or unwisely, with Ricardo, Vicente, Marisol, Carlos, myself. My vision, I understood, my new gifts, would only lead me deeper into myself—but with this difference. I would do so sure that there I would find the Savior's power and know it as my own, not as a dream, but as a knowledge heavy as my muscles, quick as my breath. There was, I understood, no escaping—and so those words of the Savior's, echoing in my head like some divinely sent tinnitis, took on yet another meaning.

ORDERING INFORMATION

STUDY GUIDES

We have developed two series of discussion questions to accompany these stories. One series is focused on the concerns of health care providers, physicians, nurses, therapists of many kinds, and home health aides and hospice workers—those who need to talk daily with people who are trying to make faithful sense of their own illnesses. The second series is of more general interest and can be used by people who are in support groups or book clubs. We will provide these electronically free of cost to anyone who has purchased the book.

Wising Up Press
P.O. Box 2122
Decatur, GA 30031-2122

404/276-6046

wisingup@universaltable.org
www.universaltable.org

HEATHER TOSTESON, a writer, visual artist and spiritual director, has received a Nation/Discovery prize for her poetry and fellowships for poetry, fiction, and photography from MacDowell, Yaddo, the Virginia Center for the Arts, and Hambidge Center for the Creative Arts and Sciences. Her poetry, stories, and essays have appeared in numerous literary magazines. She holds a B.A. from Sarah Lawrence College, M.F.A. in Creative Writing from the University of North Carolina at Greensboro, and Ph.D. in English and Creative Writing from Ohio University. She has worked as a science writer, editor, and communications consultant in public health, where she has had a long standing interest in social trust, professional identity, and the intersection of belief systems. She is co-founder and co-director of Universal Table. She lives with her husband in Atlanta, Georgia.

www.ingramcontent.com/pod-product-compliance
Lightning Source LLC
Chambersburg PA
CBHW030330030726
47499CB00003B/708